THE PIPER'S WARNING

M MacKinnon

Published 2019

Printed in the United States of America
Print ISBN: 978-1-951490-08-9

Publisher Information:
DartFrog Books
PO Box 867
Manchester, VT 05254

www.DartFrogBooks.com

This book is dedicated to my father, Jack McKinnon,
who inspired me to read and instilled in me
a love of fantasy and wonder.

CONTENTS

ACKNOWLEDGMENTS

Kathleen Kiel, my lovely assistant and the inspiration for Kate. I couldn't have done it without you.

Carl Dannenberger, my husband, who continues to be impressed by my writing no matter how many times he has to listen to a chapter.

Máiri MacKinnon, my kinswoman in Inverness and invaluable resource for all things Scottish--a Highlander of the first order.

Kenny Tomasso, my deliverer of weapons and mahem. Never lets me down when violence is on order. And it always is!

GLOSSARY
OF SCOTTISH TERMS
(UNDERSTANDING ANGUS AND OLD HARRY)

Auld – old
Aw reit – all right
Aye – yes
Braw – fine, handsome
Dinna, didna – don't, didn't
Fur – for
Gae – go
Gang – go, went
Gie – give
Eejit – idiot, fool
Jumper - sweater
Ken – to know, to understand

Mair – more
Minny - busybody
Nae – no
Nivver - never
Noo – now
Plaid – kilt, tartan
Sassanach – outsider, English
Tae - to
Verra – very
Whingeing – whining
Willna – will not, won't
Ye – you

So it's true, when all is said and done, grief is the price we pay for love.

E.A. Bucchianeri

SCOTLAND 1644

The last mournful note melted away into the Scottish air, and silence descended, deep and heavy in the black of the moonless night. The piper let the blowpipe fall from his lips. It was done. His clan was safe.

It would be his last act on this earth, he knew. Already heavy boot steps could be heard on the stone stairway leading to the turret where he stood staring out into the darkness toward the distant hills, wishing for a last glimpse of his clansmen. They were his not by birth but by adoption—his responsibility nonetheless. He had fulfilled his duty as piper for the clan.

Rough hands grabbed him, wresting the pipes from his shoulder, and he was dragged away. He did not struggle. The four men did not speak as they shoved his unresisting body down the steps and into a tower room he had never seen before.

"No!" a voice screamed, and she pushed past her father's men to kneel at his feet, clutching his plaid in desperation. "No! He is mine! You cannot do this!"

His eyes met hers, and in them he saw the love that had grown between them over the months of his capture, the love that would sustain him as he went into the dark. He pitied her, knowing that it would be harder for her than for him. He was leaving her behind to face the future alone. Perhaps he was the lucky one.

For he knew that her words meant nothing, not anymore. What he had done was unforgiveable. These men did not answer to a lass, no matter how high-placed she might be. Her father had decided, and thus his life was forfeit. He had known it even as his lips had tightened on the pipe and the first note of "Piobaireachd-dhum-Naomhaid" had soared out over the Highland hills. "The Piper's Warning to His Master." Even now his adopted clan was melting away into the hills, making their way to the sea and safety. Because of him, they would live to fight another day.

He had not been sure he could do it. Not after meeting her and falling under the spell of those eyes, bluer than the sky and more radiant than the stars of a Highland night. They had made plans, the two of them. They would leave, become invisible—just two more people in the wild lands of the north. The lady and her piper would disappear, never to be seen in these parts again. They would be free. Even though they knew it was only a dream, they had planned.

His attention returned to the tower room. One of the guards stepped forward and pulled his beloved to her feet, careful not to hurt her. They could not give her the one thing she desired, but they would not be cruel—not to her. Only to him.

She screamed as she was pulled from the room, but

she was no match for their strength. He heard her wails drifting down the hallway until at last they dwindled to nothing. And then he was alone with his captors again. Silence returned to the tower room, and with it an apprehension that cut into his soul.

How would they do it? The swipe of a dagger across his throat? A sword thrust to his heart? No matter, it would be quick. He was ready.

In the next moment, he was shoved into a small alcove in the wall. His arms were bound by ropes to hooks on either side of the small recess, his bagpipes thrown in to lie at his feet. He looked out of his prison at the implacable faces and the pile of grey stones that stood behind them, and the color drained from his face. Not quick. Fear clutched at his throat. They had prepared for this day. He would get his wish after all— he was going to disappear. A small moan escaped his lips, and he sagged in the restraints.

Not a word was uttered as the men went about their task. As the last stone was pushed into place and his world dwindled to an impossible darkness, the piper allowed his thoughts to drift. He had done what was needed; it must be enough. He closed his eyes and waited.

CHAPTER 1

REIGN

"I can't believe that bitch Bianchi got on the task force and I didn't!" The voice was the venomous hiss only a woman wronged can deliver. It reverberated around the tiled restroom walls and bounced off the metal doors.

Kate Bianchi pulled her feet up onto the toilet seat and wrapped her arms around her knees. *This is so embarrassing! Leave, please just leave so I can sneak out of here and save some dignity!*

No such luck.

"I've been on the force two more years than she has, and she gets picked for the most exciting team this place has ever put together!" It was Cassandra Fenelli—Kate recognized the whiny tone.

"Come on, Cass," another voice soothed. "Kate's all right. It's not her fault Mulgrew chose her. Morelli probably told him to."

"I know," Cass's voice sighed, calmer now. "I like Kate, really. It's just that *everything* always seems to go her way. It's like she leads a charmed life. Youngest female to make detective, Rob Morelli for a partner, and the hottest husband in Harrington. Plus, she's gorgeous. Naturally curly hair, tall and slim—stop me, I think I'm going to be sick!" Fake gagging commenced.

A giggle from her friend. "Eddie Bianchi is a hunk, isn't he? But don't go messing with him. They've been together since grammar school. Married four years and they still act like newlyweds."

"Tell me about it!" Cassandra moaned.

Kate buried her face in her arms to keep the laughter from bubbling out. Then her head snapped up and she leaned forward as Cass continued in a lower voice, "Remember the Christmas party last year? Well, I got a little drunk—don't look at me like that, Julie! Anyway, I kind of came on to him, and he told me in no uncertain terms that Kate was and always would be the only woman for him. It was so mortifying. Ugh, I don't want to think about it! Let's go." The voices diminished as the two women exited the restroom, plunging it into silence.

Kate sat for a moment longer, a huge smile on her face. She didn't really care about Cassandra's opinion, but it was nice to hear that her jealousy was because of Eddie. And Cass wasn't wrong. He was indeed a hunk. *Her* hunk, to be precise. The grin remained as she made her way to the squad room and slid into a seat next to Rob Morelli.

The room held an unnatural hush fueled by anticipation. Kate forgot about Cassandra as her heart began to pound. She slanted a look at her partner and wondered if she would ever be able to exude that kind of calm. He had been doing this a hell of a lot longer than she had, of course. He was only five years from retirement, but still—the man seemed impervious to emotion of any kind.

She knew better, though. Morelli's calm, dispassionate demeanor at work concealed a warm, generous nature that was a gift for those he deemed friends. She had seen him at his daughter's graduation from medical school and at his grandson's first baseball game. When it came to his family, Morelli was a different man, and to him Kate was family. He had become like a second father to her, imparting his wisdom with incredible patience, cajoling and sometimes bullying her into becoming the kind of detective who deserved to be chosen for a job like this one. Along the way they had learned to trust each other with their lives, both professional and personal. Next to Eddie, Morelli was the human being Kate trusted most in the world.

Well, maybe after Aubrey and Fitz. Her two best friends were her constant, her conscience, and her solace when the work she had chosen became too sordid. When the darkness threatened to close in and she wanted to quit, they were there to remind her that no matter how many times man proved his capacity for cruelty to his fellow man, life contained hope and joy, and her contribution was essential. The three of them had always been there for each other.

Things were changing, though. Bree was half a world away in Scotland, and Kate knew she'd never be coming back. She had met the man of her dreams in

Inverness and was set to marry him in eight months, and it was all Kate's fault. She had helped to send her friend there, she and Colleen Fitzgerald and that crazy old Scot, Angus. So now she and Fitz were the only ones left here in Harrington, New Jersey. And Eddie, of course.

Her hero, her knight in shining armor, the love of her life. She owed it to him to make this assignment work. He was so proud of her, so sure that she could accomplish anything she set her mind to. His buddies in Rome Construction rolled their eyes and told her that Eddie was a complete bore when he got started on her accomplishments.

"Whipped, he is," they said, shaking their heads in mock sadness. "Poor guy."

This task force was a dream come true, and Kate knew it was the chance of a lifetime for a rookie who had gotten her gold badge less than a year ago. She'd had such lofty dreams when she graduated second in her class at the academy—she was going to stop crime in Harrington single-handedly, put their little police force on the map, and become police chief within five years. Well, that last sounded more like Aubrey, the one with the imagination.

But so far, her rise had been quite satisfactory, if not meteoric. Her male colleagues were starting to take her seriously, and Morelli had given her the chance, asked for her as his partner and made himself her mentor. She swore never to let him down.

The job itself had not evolved with quite as much satisfaction. Life for a cop in a small South Jersey city was nothing like the way it was sold on TV.

Harrington, nestled between Philadelphia and the shore, was not immune to society's ills. The city had a curious mixture of urban and rural issues, none of them mind-bending. Most days her work involved interviews with store owners about the latest rash of shoplifting, or talking Freddie Como's wife out of beating her lazy shit of a husband with one of his own bottles of bourbon. Fun stuff. Robbery and murder? You had to go to Philly for that.

Sure, they had a drug problem in Harrington, despite the local politicians' insistence on denying that such a thing was possible. Most of the time it was relegated to teenagers smoking weed behind the bleachers, although there had been that high school teacher busted for cocaine last month, and heroin was always a problem. The homeless population camped out behind the defunct Broadway department store was not there because of the job opportunities.

But this—this was something new. New drugs were appearing on the street every day as desperate junkies scrambled for new ways to get high. The news out of New York, only two hours up the turnpike, was rife with speculation about a new drug that would "make ecstasy look like a bit too much caffeine," as one of the papers described it. The mother of all recreational drugs, a killer. Nothing like it had ever been seen before.

Kate's face grew pensive as she remembered what her husband had told her last night. Even the men on his crew, he said, guys who on a normal day didn't think much beyond the next beer, were buzzing in the break room about the new designer drug that had hit Harrington.

"Joe Sipchak's cousin's kid ended up in the hospital after getting ahold of some of that stuff," Eddie had told her, waving his fork for emphasis. "Climbed up on their roof and started yelling at his parents that he was in charge and they had to do whatever he wanted, and what he wanted was for them to catch him. Then he just launched himself off the damn roof! Lucky for him, he landed in the bushes, the dumbass. Broke his leg instead of his neck. But the hospital had to keep him overnight, until the drug was out of his system. Idiot won't tell them where he got it. Joe said the kid's parents are beside themselves. But you and Rob are going to figure it out, honey." His warm brown eyes were filled with pride. "Those bastards don't know what's coming with you two on the case."

Kate smiled at the memory of Eddie's words, feeling his love curl around her heart. She hoped he was right. All her life she'd wanted to be a cop. She'd read every *Nancy Drew* book she could get her hands on. Instead of dolls, she asked Santa for a magnifying glass and a chemistry set. And Eddie had supported her every step of the way. Cassandra was right—she'd won the lottery with him.

Her attention jerked back to the room as throats were cleared at the front and Chief Garrison Mulgrew stood up, silencing the conversation in the crowded room.

"Thank you for being so prompt. You all know why I've assembled you here this morning. Before we start, I want you to look around. You are the best and the brightest this city can offer. Your performance records are evidence that you have the strength, the intelligence, and the will to get the job done.

"As you know, we are facing a problem unlike anything the city of Harrington has seen before," he continued. Bodies became still and all eyes went on alert. Chief Mulgrew was not given to fancy or dramatics. Everyone in the room became aware of a new chill of anticipation.

"You have all been selected because of your exemplary work in the field," Mulgrew went on, looking around at the rapt faces before him. "I want you to have no doubt that it is an honor to have been selected for this team." He let the silence lengthen until the atmosphere was almost electric with the waiting.

"I also want you to know that this may be the most important job you are ever asked to do as members of the HPD," he said, dropping his voice so that they had to lean forward to hear.

"We are facing a new enemy here in Harrington. If you've studied your file—he narrowed his eyes and fixed them with a gimlet stare—you know that Reign has made its way from Europe to the US in the last year. It appeared first in New York, then spread to North Jersey and Boston. Now it's in Philadelphia, and that means it's here. All of you have heard the name, of course. For any of you who *haven't* done your homework, I'll give you a bit of the history that brings us all here today. You will find this drug unique in that its base, while augmented with chemicals, seems to derive from a natural substance, one that science has not seen before. Europe has experienced a sharp rise in physical violence connected with extended use of the drug, and panic is rising as authorities have been unable to trace its origin or method of dispersal.

"The drug has been called Reign because it causes the user to think of himself as invincible, all-powerful, like a king. He loses his inhibitions, feels euphoric and empowered. Nothing can go wrong, he thinks."

The chief spread his hands. "The drug's effects last only a few hours, at first. So, the perfect party drug. Where's the harm? I feel happy, I'm not anxious anymore, life is fun. The world has more color, everything is beautiful. Much like the high from ecstasy, but so much better."

Mulgrew paused to collect his thoughts, and when he resumed speaking his words hung in the air as if weighted.

"Repeated use of Reign, however, has been shown to increase the drug's hold and its effects. Users lose perspective, fear nothing, and begin to feel that they have power over those around them. They think that other people should exist to serve them, and that nothing on earth can harm them."

He stared out over the silent room.

"And then it gets worse. Like kings throughout history, the user of Reign finds that other people do not support his self-assurance of power and right. He becomes frustrated by his subjects' lack of obedience and attempts to bend them to his will by force. He puts himself in danger from retaliation by others. Often, he becomes suicidal or homicidal. 'Death by cop' is on the rise."

Mulgrew's face was drawn, his face bleak. "Reign is spreading from Europe as surely as the plague spread in medieval times. The DEA has authorized the formation of task forces like this one all over the state; ours is just the latest to be called up. And from now on, we'll be using the name by which law enforcement in Europe now knows this drug. They call it 'Regicide.' He stopped then, allowing his words to sink in. The room was quieter than Kate had ever heard it. The eerie silence grew until it filled the space, as the gravity of this task force began to make itself known.

At that point Mulgrew called a break. Kate took the opportunity to step into the hallway to call Eddie, but the call went straight to voicemail. She sent him a text instead, and then stood staring at the green wall across the corridor, thinking about everything she had just heard.

This is bad. Like the plague? Jeez.

"Yo, Bianchi." Morelli leaned out of the doorway. "You ready? Break's over." Kate blinked, pushed her unruly dark hair—those curls Cass envied so much— behind her ears and rejoined her team.

"I'm handing out a list of suspected cases of Regicide use in and around Harrington," Captain Mulgrew told them. "You'll be split into teams of four, partners with partners. Any questions before we get moving?"

"Sir?" A hand went up. "Do they have any idea where this stuff originated in Europe?"

"As a matter of fact, Thompson, they do. Oddest thing. Regicide seems to be coming from Scotland. The Highlands, to be precise. Not your normal venue for a dangerous substance such as this, as you might imagine. Police Scotland is on it, working around the clock, but they're stymied."

Kate, who had been pouring over the list, jerked in surprise. Scotland! She'd been to the Scottish Highlands. Mulgrew was right; it was not the kind of place one would expect to find a drug conspiracy. Or many people, for that matter. She hadn't even seen a policeman on the streets the entire two weeks she'd been there. Plenty of violence in its past, with all those claymores and Highland charges, but nowadays the biggest crime in the Scottish Highlands seemed to be the theft of a farmer's sheep or disorderly conduct in the local pub after a tourist had imbibed too much single malt.

Kate and Eddie would be traveling to Scotland in October because she and Fitz were bridesmaids in Aubrey's wedding. Fitz had already put in for a two-week vacation from her nursing job at Nesbitt General Hospital and had been talking of nothing but the trip and the wedding for months.

Kate shuddered. She hoped against hope that she wouldn't have to wear some frou-frou tartany thing. Fitz would love it, of course, but Kate hated bridesmaid's dresses. She trusted Aubrey's taste to a point, but Bree had become so damn *Scottish* since meeting Fionnlagh Cameron.

Then she grinned as she remembered the lovely knives she'd seen in so many of the shop windows. Sgian-dubhs, they were called. If Aubrey would let her wear a sgian-dubh, she'd do anything her friend wanted. She'd wear a kilt and play the bagpipes. She'd do the Highland Fling with a sheep!

"Bianchi?" Chief Mulgrew's voice broke into her thoughts. "Phone call for you, in my office. It's your friend Colleen. She says it's urgent."

CHAPTER 2

CASTLE BY THE SEA

"And have you decided where you're going on your honeymoon, dear?"

Aubrey looked over the rim of her teacup at Gladys Chesher. The Englishwoman's face was tilted to the side, her myopic blue eyes round and innocent. Aubrey was not fooled for a second.

"What do you mean, Gladys?" she asked, narrowing her eyes. Gladys always had an ulterior motive.

"Well, it's just that you seem to have a list of some of the most haunted castles in the empire there." Gladys's wiry white curls bounced as she talked. "They're all lovely, mind you, and I know your lad loves the history and all, but I was just thinking that being haunted might not exactly be what a couple needs when they're starting out on their sojourn of love. It's not always conducive to . . . well, you know." She sipped her tea, never taking her eyes off Aubrey.

Aubrey's cup rattled in the saucer as she fought to control her laughter, but it was no use.

"S-sojourn of love?" she sputtered. "Did you actually just say that?"

"Do not laugh," cautioned Maxine Deyaux, who was sitting beside Gladys in her customary place on the couch. "It is not good to fool about with those who are still lingering on this side of the veil. It is not wise. Who knows why it is that they have not passed on?"

Well, thought Aubrey, *that much is true.* If only Maxine knew. Aubrey had faced just such a restive spirit eight months ago when she'd first come to Scotland. It hadn't been so bad, when all was said and done. A bit frightening at first, of course, but it helped that the ghost had been her ancestor and needed her help. *And,* she thought, her face assuming that silly smile she wore when thinking about "her lad," *that's how I found Finn.*

She looked with affection at the odd assortment of characters gathered in Nessie's sitting room. Gladys and her taciturn son Ronald from the Lake Country in England. Maxine, a still-lithe former dancer from who-knew-where in France. And Old Harry. She glanced at the corner chair where a newspaper sat perched on the lap of her second favorite old Scotsman. Gnarled fingers were all that showed around the edges of the paper, and if it weren't for the occasional Gaelic snort that emitted from behind it, one might have thought that Nessie had placed a wax figure there for effect. But Old Harry missed nothing. None of them ever did.

Aubrey had christened them "the Owls" when she'd first come to Nessie's. She'd been in a bad way, then, despondent over the betrayal by her fiancé Marc back in Harrington, determined never to trust a man again. Angus, the toothless, bandy-legged proprietor of the odd bookshop in Harrington where Aubrey worked, had sent her to Scotland and to his friend Nessie, who ran a boarding house in Inverness. Looking for all the world like a parliament of owls as they stared at her out of unblinking eyes, her housemates had surrounded her with kindness and concern, clawed the story out of her, and whacked a band-aid on her aching heart. She suspected that they were a bit magical themselves, but it didn't matter. She would love them forever.

"But they're wrong about ghosts," she said to Finn later, as they wound their way toward the North Sea over the narrow Highland roads in his ancient grey Audi. "Ghosts can be quite wonderful, can't they?"

His blue eyes crinkled at the corners as he grinned. "Aye, they can. Although we were lucky to meet such a lovely ghost as wee Ailith. I don't think I'd want to tangle with one of the mean ones. And you never really know till you meet them which kind they are, do you?"

Fionnlagh Cameron was a history professor at the University of the Highlands and Islands, and a part time guide for Dougie's Tours, which was how Aubrey had met him. A Scot through and through, he never discounted magic in his view of the world, and recent events had conspired to prove him right. Since their encounter with the ghost of Rait Castle, he had been toying with the thought of researching some of his country's many ghost stories and their place in the history of the Highlands, with the idea of writing a book on them.

Thus, their honeymoon was going to be spent at one of the ubiquitous Highland Castles that dotted the hills to the north of Inverness, "so we can do a little exploring, aye?" What Finn meant was that he was going to pick his host's brain and maybe his archives for any tidbits on the castle's resident spirits that might not be known to the general public. Aubrey wasn't sure how she felt about that, but her imagination had no such qualms. It was fired up, envisioning a partnership of ghost chasers. She would be the Watson to Finn's Holmes, or the Mrs. Peel to his John Steed. Together they would hunt down those tragic spirits who were tethered to their former homes, free them, and send them on their way. They would be famous. Finn's book would be number one on the bestseller list.

She hadn't confided her mind's wanderings to her fiancé. He would have gotten all professor-y and explained that the book was not about *chasing* ghosts, but about researching the clans and castles that claimed them in order to further the cause of Scottish history.

"*History*, Aubrey," he had told her more than once. "Not *fiction*. There's a difference."

Aubrey found it amusing that to Finn, ghosts were not fictional but a part of history. What *was* fictional, he had told her in frustration, was the idea so many of his tour groups had that Scots ran around all day dancing over swords and singing about the bonny heather in tartan underwear like in *Brigadoon*, or painting themselves blue and cavorting in burlap bags as Mel Gibson did in *Braveheart*.

"That movie was so inaccurate. William Wallace wasn't even the real Braveheart, that was Robert the Bruce!" he sighed in exasperation.

When they first met, Finn had taken great delight in mocking Aubrey's attachment to a certain television show which chronicled the exploits of the world's most perfect example of Scottish manhood. He seemed to find it necessary to remind her that the people in her books and period dramas were not real, and therefore her love of them was just silly.

"There were many Highlanders named James Fraser throughout history, Aubrey," he'd told her more than once, "but I doubt very much they looked like that paragon on your favorite television show. They likely looked more like Angus."

Aubrey knew he was right, but fiction was just as good as reality in her opinion, sometimes better. She supposed that there was no point in telling Finn that the girls on his tours who *oohed* and *ahhed* over him were doing so because he bore a striking resemblance to the *fictional* Irish chauffeur on her other favorite TV show, *Downton Abbey*. He probably thought it was the wonderful presentation of his country's history. She'd give him that, and his natural charm that made him one of the most popular guides at Dougie's. There was also a good chance that part of it was the kilt he wore on the job, which if she were completely honest with herself, might not be far off base. There was just something about a man in a kilt.

Aubrey giggled, and Finn slanted a suspicious look at her. She favored him with a brilliant smile and was rewarded with that lopsided grin she loved so much. Another thing she wasn't going to tell him, because he was a man and it would swell his head, was that to her *he* was the perfect Scotsman. Besides being gorgeous, he played the bagpipes, and well, too—his band had won awards. He had introduced her to single malt whisky with great success. Most important—it bore repeating—he looked great in a kilt.

And he loved her. She had never before felt so treasured by another human being. She knew that he was hers, body and soul, that he would never abandon her. It was a new joy in a life that had seen her father leave her when he had a massive heart attack at the kitchen table, and her fiancé dump her via text message to reconnect with his high school sweetheart. Finn had come into her life at a very low point and proved that it didn't have to be that way, that she deserved better.

It wasn't just Finn. She never would have met him in the first place if it hadn't been for Angus, the crusty old Scot who had found her in Harrington, New Jersey and challenged her to come to Scotland and break a centuries-old curse placed by one of her ancestors. *When th' Comyn lass finds 'er Mackintosh, aw th' pipers in Scootlund will begin tae play*, he had said, and somehow convinced her she was that lass.

She had done it, had come to Scotland and broken the curse. Finn, though named Cameron, had in truth been a Mackintosh by birth. The pieces had fallen into place, and on a cool summer's night in the Scottish Highlands, when all the pipers at the European Championships had played in unison, she had known for certain that this man was the one.

"So, what's going on in that head of yours?" Finn glanced over at her as he pulled into a passing place to let an oncoming car pass on the single lane road. "When you get all quiet like that, I know there's something happening in there, and I like to be prepared."

Aubrey laughed. "You know me too well. I was just remembering how we met."

He pulled back out onto the narrow road. "Aye, the Loch Ness tour? I'll never forget it. There was this beautiful American lass sitting in the second seat and I put on my best performance, but she didn't fall for it. I had to chase her down to get a date. It was embarrassing."

"And the Owls loved you at first sight," Aubrey continued the story, "so I should have known right then and there, but your name wasn't Mackintosh, and—"

"And then I touched your hand . . ."

"Yeah, and that was weird. Felt as if I'd been electrocuted for a second. Scared me."

"And then the date sort of just fell apart," he said. They were both quiet, remembering the reason for that. Connor MacConnach, the big Scot who could have given Jamie Fraser from *Outlander* a run for his money. He'd interrupted their dinner and broken the fragile bond that had been forming between them— and he'd done it on purpose.

"And then, on our second date, which wasn't really

even a date, you had to go and talk about your college sweetheart and how broken up you were when she left you!" Aubrey punctuated her words with a light punch to his arm.

"Well how was I to know you'd just been text-dumped by the biggest arse-hole in America?" he demanded. "You hadn't bothered to tell me!" They'd been through this conversation many times, and both knew their lines to perfection at this point.

"And besides," Finn went on, "you were drunk on whisky, and that imagination of yours is not a man's best friend even when it's sober, let me tell you!"

Aubrey was laughing too hard to rebut, and besides, he was right. Her imagination had done its best to convince her that he was the wrong choice for her, but he had persevered, and she'd wised up in the end—with the help of a ghost. Their story was too fictional for television, she thought, yet it was real.

Finn reached out his left hand and she linked her fingers with his as they drove on in companionable silence. This would be the third castle they'd visited in their quest for a honeymoon venue. There were a *lot* of castles in Scotland, and more of them than you'd think were still lived in, most open for tours, and many offering the amenities of a resort. Some sported world-famous golf courses, others the opportunity to try falconry or salmon fishing. Finn didn't golf, and Aubrey couldn't think of anything less appealing than standing waist-deep in cold water trying to catch a fish.

But the one they were checking out today had possibilities. Dunebrae Castle, home of the Munro clan since the early seventeenth century. Once owned by the Campbells, and before that by the MacDonalds, it also had ghosts.

According to the brochures, guests had reported seeing an old woman in clothing from the seventeenth century wandering the halls. Others told of waking to the sound of bagpipes in the middle of the night. Since the castle's current owner was also captain of one of the most famous pipe bands in the country, The House of Munro Highlanders, the sound of bagpipes should not have been uncommon. The stories did increase interest in the castle, however, which attracted ghost chasers as well as bagpipe aficionados from around the world.

The House of Munro had won at the Worlds twice in the last five years. The chance to mingle with some of the world's best pipers, combined with a colorful history and a couple of ghosts, put Dunebrae Castle at the top of Finn's list. Aubrey liked bagpipes at least slightly more than she did salmon-fishing, so she was fine with it as long as the ghosts didn't want anything from her. Once had been quite enough of that.

The smell of the sea filtered into the small car—a primitive odor of salt and seaweed and marsh. So different from the Jersey shore, so *old*, like everything else in Scotland. It brought with it a chill not entirely due to the February weather. And then the castle loomed out of the Highland mist like an apparition. Aubrey's imagination went on alert, all cylinders firing, and her stomach clenched. The place looked like something Count Dracula might hang out in. Suddenly, she wanted to turn around and head back for Inverness—but then she looked at Finn's eager face and reined herself in. It would be fine.

Finn deposited the Audi in the car park and jumped out, extending a hand. "Ready, darling?" His voice was tense with excitement. "Isn't it amazing?"

As Aubrey climbed out of the car, she heard the roar of the sea in the near distance. It sounded mournful and angry. *Sure. Amazing.* Pulling the hood of her parka up and fixing a brilliant smile on her face, she took Finn's hand.

Her phone rang, and she fished it out of her pocket. Glancing at the display, she frowned and stood still. "Finn, it's Kate. I have to take this—she never calls at this time of day. I'll be quick."

He grimaced. "Tell her she's ruining our honeymoon!" He moved away to give Aubrey privacy, shuffling his feet in his eagerness to be off.

"Hi, Kate, what's up? Aren't you supposed to be at work?"

Silence, and then a voice she didn't recognize came over the line. Low, shaking, it carried all the raw pain and agony of a soul lost in time and space. Aubrey's throat closed as she received the worst possible news.

"Bree? H-he's gone. Eddie—he's dead."

CHAPTER 3

PIPELINE

The piper stood waiting, his feet shuffling in the thin ghillie shoes. Lord, this country was cold—he'd never felt anything like it. How did human beings survive in Canada? People made fun of the Scottish weather—hell, the Scots made fun of it themselves. "No one comes here for the weather, ye ken," was heard frequently from tour guides as unprepared tourists stood shivering in their shorts and tank tops.

Their own damn fault, of course. Brash New Yorkers thought that summer was warm everywhere, because they hadn't bothered to do their research before hopping on the plane to Scotland. What the hell did they expect? Scotland was a northern country and an island. It rained in the Highlands, a lot, something about the air brought by cyclones hitting the mountains and cooling to form rain clouds.

But what the tourists didn't know and couldn't appreciate, as they rushed into the stores to buy garish fleece-lined, tartan-printed rain jackets, was that the rain was also the reason for the lovely whisky they all crowded into the pubs to swill. "Today's rain is tomorrow's whisky," was an old Scottish proverb, and it was true. You gave and you got.

The piper stomped his feet, trying to feel his toes. But this place! The chill snaked up his legs and burrowed under his kilt. He was pretty sure the cold was doing some kind of damage to his manhood, and soon he might very well see his balls fall off and roll across the parade ground. Of all the odd places they'd been sent to play, this was the worst yet.

If he hadn't known the true purpose of the trip, he would have thought his boss was crazy to send his award-winning pipe band over to this God-forsaken country in the middle of winter. There was a very good reason pipe band championships were held in late spring and summer. These frigid temperatures couldn't be good for the pipes, let alone the poor men playing them, marching in kilts and bare legs around a parade ground where it was a miracle the spectators could see anything besides their breath.

There was a purpose for this particular venue, though, an ulterior motive. The boss had a hidden agenda known only to a few, and even for those chosen few it was cloaked in mystery. They were sent to play the bagpipes in foreign countries, and they went without question. They did it because the promise of unimaginable wealth at the end of the day made all the wondering, all the shivering worth it, a hundred times over. It was the reason he didn't really mind standing here in the cold.

It had everything to do with his bagpipes, the piper knew that much. Bagpipes were valuable and needed constant care and vigilance to keep them in perfect working order. Normally, they would never be subjected to these conditions. But there was something about these particular bagpipes that made all the difference. All the piper knew was that his was no ordinary set of bagpipes, and that they would not be in his possession much longer.

He had examined them, when he was alone. They looked like any other high-grade instrument: gleaming drones, silver-filigreed tuning slides. The equipment expected of a World Class Pipe band. Nothing unusual. But he'd been assured that they held a secret, the piper's inheritance, a promise of wealth that he never could have dreamed might be his. A treasure beyond reckoning, and the promise of more to come as their message was spread to the Americas. He didn't care what the secret was; he trusted in the process that had brought him to this frigid country of snow and endless cold.

Not all the band members carried the special instruments. This also the piper knew. Some of the poor shivering saps were there only for the purpose stated in the *Piobaireachd Canada* brochure: "One of Scotland's premier pipe bands will perform selections from last year's World Championships. Pipe Band aficionados will not want to miss this once-in-a-lifetime opportunity to experience the best at work!" They were there to spread the joy of piping to new acolytes, regardless of the weather. They were paid very well and didn't ask questions.

A select few like himself, hand-picked by the boss, had been chosen to spread something entirely different. They were the inner circle, those trusted with the knowledge that they carried something special, that they were an important step in a process that would lead to a life of wealth and privilege. None of them knew or cared to know more about the secret they shared. They all knew it was better not to know. They would meet their contacts, exchange their pipes for another set, and board the plane for the trip home to Scotland with a different set of bagpipes and a handsome paycheck tucked into their wallets.

The piper blew on his hands to warm them, but the glow that spread through him at the thought of what awaited him at home could not be touched by cold. The money transfer at the time of exchange was more than a piper would make in six months, but it was a pittance compared with the payday that had been promised. The true reward was still to come. He was being asked to trust in this venture, to take the risk in order to assure a future of untold wealth. The piper was excited to be included, happy to take the risk, proud of his status in the enterprise. This new venture was going to change the world, and he was a part of it.

In the last year, the band had visited New York, Chicago, and Los Angeles, widening the golden net, spreading their influence to more and more places, to people who had never given a single moment's thought to a small country in the North Sea named

Scotland. Little did they know that a country that was mocked for its inability to win the decisive battles, that still struggled to regain the independence achieved by Robert the Bruce, was about to take over the world.

The beauty of the project was in its simplicity. One boss, one place of origin, one band. And not just any band. One of the best, as the pamphlets had claimed. Every piper was a true artist, culled from the millions of Scottish men, young and old, for whom the ancient music was almost a religion. They had been raised playing the pipes like all Scottish youth and had earned the right to call themselves the best. The ancient pipes had been an instrument of war, and like the warriors of the great Highland clans of the past, they went into battle believing they were slated for glory.

The piper knew little of the reason behind his selection. He was not a boss; he was exactly what he appeared to be—a much better than average bagpiper from the Highlands of Scotland. His job was clear and straightforward. Play the pipes for the adoring crowds. Meet the contact, exchange the pipes, go home. Do it all again. And again. He traveled around the world sharing the beauty of bagpipes with the uninitiated, and he was paid extremely well for it. It was enough, and he knew that there was safety in ignorance.

The piper was not stupid. He knew that this venture was not entirely honorable, not with all the secrecy. Despite what the boss told them, he understood that danger was ever-present, that the quest could not be noble and virtuous. And in the darkest hours of the night, if he allowed himself to think about what he was doing, he felt dirty, tainted.

He knew that he was emmeshed too deep to ever change his mind, though, so he didn't allow himself to dwell on it too long.

He also knew he was watched. They all were. It was clear to the entire team that they were valued, but only to a point. The pipers were not the only team members under the boss's employ. He ran the business himself and trusted no one with all the information. His lieutenants made sure that every employee did what was required of him, and nothing more. The watchers were shadow men, invisible creatures who were aware of every aspect of the enterprise and made sure that every man knew it.

They were everywhere and anywhere. It would be foolish in the extreme to step beyond the bounds of the mission, to attempt to betray the cause for personal gain or to share the secret outside the cabal. The musicians had been promised all the wealth they could ever want; they just had to wait, and the world would be theirs. The piper could wait.

The announcement was made, and the band began its entrance into the parade ground. Somewhere out there was his contact, a nameless man who would take his pipes and give him others that seemed identical. The piper did not know what would happen after that. He only knew that a sense of relief came over him each time when the job was done, a feeling that he had avoided disaster and could once again become what the world thought he was: a master bagpiper from the Highlands of Scotland.

CHAPTER 4

THE FIVE STAGES OF GRIEF

The tear-stained face of the teenager in the seat across from her should have raised some sort of emotion in Kate, but it didn't. She wanted to lash out at him, tell him just what a little asshole he was. She was supposed to say something helpful, play good cop to Morelli's bad cop. They had honed their routine until it was seamless. Morelli would bark and snarl, frightening the subject and driving him into Kate's sympathetic arms. She would ask gentle questions to draw him out, commiserate with his horrible situation and invite him to cooperate with them. It was a work of art, their interview procedure, and it had garnered them more than one accolade in the past.

That was ancient history. It had ended two months ago with Eddie's death, and Kate simply didn't have the energy to care anymore. Since the accident, nothing seemed to matter. The days went by one after the other in dreary progression. Winter limped into spring. Sometimes it rained; sometimes the sun was out. It was strange, but those were the days Kate hated the most. How dare the sun shine on the world when her life was shattered? How could it be warm when her heart was frozen?

When her mother died from breast cancer five years ago, Kate had received grief counseling from her college guidance department. She had read endless tracts on the five stages of grieving: denial, anger, bargaining, depression, and acceptance. She had attended a support group, learned to share her feelings. It had been hard, but she'd come out at the end of the tunnel having reached acceptance and a kind of peace, and she'd moved on.

This was different. She seemed to be cycling through the first three stages like a hamster on a wheel, and the depression was ever-present. None of the books she had read before mentioned that you could experience all five stages in a single day, every day. They had sent her for counseling again, but she'd refused to go back after the first time. She was barely eating, existing on short spurts of exhausted sleep. Her anger was a living thing, fighting the need to get out and do something, anything, to show the world what a load of *shit* it was. The effort of repressing her feelings was eating her from the inside out. She wasn't sure how much longer she could last, and she didn't care.

They would never have the children they'd planned, all the little Bianchis with rusty hair and brown eyes just like Eddie's. Never take that trip to Italy. Never see another sunrise together on the beach in Sea Isle City. Never hold each other while they watched reruns of old westerns and ate pizza. It had all gone in the blink of an eye. She was drowning, and she wanted desperately just to let go, to sink beneath the waves of anguish and allow the darkness to fill her soul.

Kate knew Eddie would not want this for her. He would never want her to mourn him until she became sick. Her husband was the most generous human being she had ever known, and he would want her to move on, find peace, love again. Sometimes she thought she could hear his voice, telling her that she would never forget him, but she must learn to live without him. She answered the voice by telling him, with fierce pride, that it would never happen. There had never been anyone else for her and there never would be. He was it—she was done.

"Kate?"

"Bianchi!"

Kate's bleary gaze returned to the room. "What?" she said. "I'm listening." Looking around, she realized that she and Morelli were alone in the interview room; the tearful young drug user was gone. When had that happened?

Rob Morelli's patient voice held an extra note of sadness this morning. "No, Kate, you're not. You haven't been listening for a long time." He focused his brown eyes on hers, and she noticed that there were dark circles under them, and wrinkles she didn't remember being there before. His eyes drooped at the corners, making him resemble the old basset hound her father had loved when she was a child. *He looks old*, she thought. *When did he get old?*

"You can't go on like this, Kate." His voice was gentle. "You're no use to yourself, and you're a danger to the task force when your mind isn't on the job."

"My mind *is* on the job!" she said fiercely. "It's all I care about! I have to make this work, Morelli! Eddie was so proud of me!" The last was almost a wail. She could hear it in her head, and she knew the part about caring was a lie. She didn't care about the task force, about the damn drugs, about anything. Eddie was gone and her anger was a raging thing, consuming her from the inside out.

All the danger inherent in her job—the domestics turned deadly, the kids determined to kill themselves with drugs and alcohol, the horrible things people insisted on doing to each other—and it was Eddie who had died. Just a stupid work accident, a shift in a beam, wrong place at the wrong time, and his life was extinguished in a moment. She hadn't even had the chance to tell him she loved him one more time, to say goodbye. Two months, and it seemed like yesterday she'd gotten that call from Fitz. It just wasn't fair.

Morelli was still staring at her, and she squirmed under his gaze. Why couldn't he understand? She *had* to go on with the task force. Once it had meant so much to her to be chosen for such a prestigious unit, and she had basked in the sunshine of Eddie's pride. That pride had gone with him, but the job was all she had now to take her mind off the long sleepless nights in the bed that was now too big and too cold.

She had to pull herself together. She would do

better, try harder to pretend she gave a fuck about Regicide and the idiots who allowed themselves to be controlled by drugs until they were used-up husks. *They* were the ones who deserved to be dead!

Morelli's right, you know. The voice in her head was soft, apologetic, almost as if it were afraid of her. *You're no use to the force like this. You're going to get someone hurt.* She shook her head in denial, but she knew it was true. She hadn't been pulling her weight, had been floating in the netherworld like a ghost, just going through the motions.

She'd rejected the sympathy, hated the pitying looks sent her way. She had flashes of anger so strong that she envisioned herself screaming at everyone just to leave her alone. She was frightened that someday she would give in to the impulse to lash out and petrified that a part of her wanted that day to come.

And then the problem was taken out of her hands.

"Mulgrew says you need to take some time off," Morelli was saying, his voice low and measured. "He says you need to get away from the job, get your head together, take care of yourself. He cares about you, Kate, and he's worried."

"He's *firing* me?" She gaped at him in horror. Surely her performance hadn't been that bad. Yeah, she'd missed some important contacts, hadn't been putting the pieces together as well as she usually did, but it wasn't that bad! She'd thought she was covering it pretty well, hiding the worst of her grief. She'd do better. A wave of mortification swept through her. She'd do better!

"He's not firing you, Kate. He's putting you on leave, just for a few months. He's giving you time to grieve. You need that. You need to take care of yourself, honey."

He never called her honey, not on the job. In their workplace, Morelli had always been the consummate professional with Kate. Off the job was another story; when not working they were family. And it was the endearment that told her this was real. *They weren't on the job anymore.* Not partners. It felt like the end, no matter what he said.

"But what am I supposed to do?" She looked at him, tears in her eyes. "The job is all I have!"

"That's not true. You have Fitz, and me, and you have Aubrey over in Scotland. People care about you, Kate, and they're worried about you. Let them help." Morelli's voice was a plea for understanding.

"I'm glad they care. That's nice of them. But tell me, how will worrying about me help?" Kate's words were low and filled with frustration. "How does caring about me make this go away?"

He fixed her with his sharp stare. "Have you given them a chance? When's the last time you talked to Fitz?"

Kate shrugged. "I don't know. It's been a while, I guess."

"You haven't talked to your best friend since the funeral."

Her partner's words were like a slap. She blinked at him. Was that true? She hadn't spoken to Fitz since it happened? That couldn't be. Did she blame her for the call? Was she killing the messenger? A feeling of self-loathing began to work its way into her mind, chilling in its veracity.

"And what about Aubrey? Have you called her since that first day when you told her?"

"She's busy," Kate mumbled. "Anyway, she's getting ready for her wedding. I told her not to come over. I don't want her to be sad just because I am."

"Do you realize how stupid you sound?" Morelli's eyes had darkened with frustration. "They love you! You're wallowing in self-pity, destroying everything you've worked for and refusing to let the people you love throw you a lifeline. I never took you for a coward, Kathleen Bianchi!"

His words stung, leaving her breathless with rage. How dare he? He of all people knew what Eddie had meant to her. The two men had been like father and son, hanging out on Sundays to watch the Eagles games, going hunting together every fall and coming home laughing hysterically about the one that got away. How could he have forgotten so quickly?

"I loved him, too." Morelli was reading her mind, as he so often did. His eyes were damp, and his voice trembled. "Don't you ever think I would forget him! You're not the only one who's grieving."

Kate stared at her partner, her mind a whirling vortex of sadness and anger and resentment, and suddenly it all broke. She threw herself into Morelli's arms in the silent interview room, felt his hands patting her back as she let it out, great wracking sobs coursing through her body. He said nothing, just held her. When she had nothing left, she pushed herself back, sniffling.

"S-sorry. I'm usually better at keeping that under control. Didn't mean to unload on you."

Morelli handed her his handkerchief. "Whadya think I'm here for? And see—that's the problem. You only *think* you're keeping it under control. You've been letting it all build up until there's no room for anything else. Believe me, Kate, I know."

Kate looked at him, confused, and then it dawned on her. "Damn it," she whispered in a stricken voice, shame filling her where there had been no room for anything but self-pity before. "Alice. I'm so sorry." He made a negating gesture, but she saw the flash of pain in his eyes. Morelli's wife had died of ovarian cancer years before Kate had met him. Though he reminisced about the things they had done together, the fun they'd had, he never talked about her death. But she knew, and she should have been more sensitive. She wasn't the only person in the world who had lost someone. She began to cry again, but this time in remorse. *I really am a mess. A horrible, selfish piece of shit.* Morelli said nothing, just watched until she finally sat back and made an attempt to pull herself together.

"Okay," she said. "You're right. I've been a drag on the task force, on our partnership. I've put myself in a hole and I have to figure out some way to climb out of it. I don't know how, but I think it's going to take some time. And you're right, I can't do it myself." Her voice wavered. "I'll call Fitz and Aubrey, I promise."

"You'll be back on the task force before you know it." Morelli's eyes were damp. "I have faith in you."

She handed back his handkerchief. "Okay," she said again. "There's not much I can do about being suspended. But one thing pisses me off. I didn't think Mulgrew was that much of a coward. He couldn't even tell me himself!"

"He would have, but I wanted to do it." Morelli said. "I wanted you to hear it from me. He's one of the good guys, Kate, and the good guys look after each other."

She nodded, only half hearing him. Panic was rising again, thoughts swirling in her aching head. *What am I going to do now? I can't go home to that empty house and just sit there! I can't stay in Harrington, not right now. I need to get away from here, do something, or I'll go crazy. Maybe I'm already going crazy!*

She took a deep breath and sat up. "Well," she said, in a thick voice far removed from her own. "I guess I should go. But I'll be damned if I know where."

"How about out to the lobby?" Morelli stood and pulled her to her feet, turning her to face the door. "Someone's waiting for you."

She swung and looked at him, startled, but his expression was bland. A frown creasing her forehead, Kate allowed herself to be pushed out into the hall. She walked the familiar corridor without seeing it, trying to comprehend what had just happened. People passed, eyeing her warily. Did they all know what a failure she was? *Suspended.* No matter how nicely Morelli tried to put it, that was the truth of it. She had been suspended for poor work performance for the first time in her life. She was a loser. The shame threatened to take her down again, but then she saw something that brought her up short and drove all other thoughts out of her head.

In the lobby two figures rose to greet her, tentative smiles on beloved faces. Kate's eyes filled again as she felt the wave of love they were sending her way. They stood waiting, their presence a balm to her battered soul. Fitz watched her with worried eyes, clutching in her hand a brown bag from Baglioni's Market. Beside her stood a pale-faced Aubrey.

"Come on," said Fitz, her voice shaking just a little. "We're going to my place. We have plans to make, and I've brought the ice cream."

CHAPTER 5

THE ROAD BACK

inn met them at Edinburgh airport. Without a word he took Kate into his arms and hugged her, giving the American girl the gift of his empathy, support, and understanding. His eyes met Aubrey's over Kate's shoulder, and she nodded, tears in her eyes. It was exactly the right thing to do.

They separated and Finn pulled up the handle of her carry-on. "How was your trip?" he asked carefully, as they walked the corridor to baggage claim.

"I slept!" said Kate. "I haven't slept in weeks, and in that horrendously uncomfortable airplane seat I went out like a light. I think"—she felt her face with her hands—"yes, I think I might just possibly be human."

"She snored, too," Aubrey confided in a loud whisper. "Drowned out the jet's engines. Aren't you going to ask me if I slept?"

"I don't snore," said Kate, in that tone reserved for

people who will never accept the possibility.

Finn smiled. Maybe it wasn't as bad as he'd feared. Aubrey had been beside herself after Kate's call, the day they were about to visit Dunebrae Castle. They hadn't done the tour, of course. After the horrific news, the joy had gone out of the day, and they'd turned around in the car park and headed back to Inverness, frozen with shock. Aubrey had been sure Kate would need her support and she wanted to be there for her, but Kate hadn't called again, and when Aubrey tried to contact her the calls went to voicemail.

As time went on, Aubrey's worry had grown. She talked to Fitz daily, but Fitz told her that Kate was avoiding her too. Finn could see the toll that Kate's rejection was taking. When Fitz told Aubrey that Kate's partner on the police force had called and begged her to step in, Finn sat his fiancée down and told her to go home.

"She needs you, Aubrey. Both of you." He picked up her hand and held it tightly in his own. "You and Fitz won't be able to rest until you've tried everything you can to help her. I know you, and I know what that imagination is spinning right now." His smile was rueful. "I need you too, but I'll be okay for a while. I have classes to teach, and maybe I'll be able to get some work done on the book while you're gone without you distracting me all the time." He grinned at her.

Aubrey's eyes had lit up. "Really, Finn? You think I should just go hunt her down?"

He pulled her in for a long kiss. "I'll be right here waiting. Go get her. Bring her to Scotland if you need to. It worked for you, didn't it?"

And so she had gone back to Harrington, met up with Fitz, and together they'd formed their battle plan. When Morelli called Fitz to tell her that Kate was being put on leave, they were ready and waiting for her. She was going to Scotland with Aubrey, they told her, and there would be no argument. She had nothing to hold her in New Jersey right now, and Aubrey could use her help to get ready for the wedding.

"I'll be along in a few months for the ceremony," Fitz told her. "You just soak in that wonderful Scottish weather, eat some haggis, drink some whisky. Harrington is not where you need to be right now, so get out!" And she'd hugged Kate as if she might never see her again.

As a plan it was full of holes, and they were somewhat surprised when Kate capitulated without much of a fuss. All it had taken was a gallon of Rocky Road ice cream and three bottles of wine.

Now as they waited for her suitcase to come off the carousel, Finn could see the change in Kate—the hurt, the dark circles under her eyes, the despair at life gone horribly wrong. Despite her initial attempts to join in the joking, she was shattered. Empty. A far different person from the woman he had met when she came over last year and Aubrey had been the one who needed help.

Kate was the matter-of-fact member of the trio, practical, somewhat cynical, endlessly self-confident. She was also the one who had thought he was the right choice for her best friend. Aubrey had told him that Kate was firmly "Team Finn," and for that he'd always have her back. Looking at her drawn face, he knew he'd done the right thing in encouraging Aubrey to go to her.

Bags collected and stowed in the Audi, they began the three-hour trip to Inverness. Ever the tour guide, Finn kept the conversation impersonal and informative, but he could have been talking to the gear shift for all the response he got from Kate. Undaunted, he pressed on. He'd had tour groups that were duds before and he had learned never to quit, but grieving widows were another thing entirely.

"That's Stirling Castle, up there on that wee bit of rock," he said, pointing. To their right, a huge volcanic outcropping sat dwarfed by the immense stone structure that had been the home of every Scottish king since the Wars of Independence. It perched above the rock like a beacon, seeming to have grown out of the very rock upon which it sat.

"The castle wasn't always Scottish, though," Finn told them. "From 1296 to 1356 it changed hands a great many times. It was considered quite a plum, strategically located as it is, and men were prepared to die to conquer it. Nobody held it for long, though.

"Do you see that big tower on the hill across the valley from the castle? It's the Wallace Monument. Built for the great Scottish patriot, William Wallace. Started in 1861 and took eight years to build. Construction wasn't what it is tod—" Finn stopped, stricken.

"I'm sorry, Kate," he said. "I didn't mean—"

"Oh, just stop coddling me!" Kate spoke for the first time since they'd left the airport, her words clipped and angry. "Eddie's dead! He didn't die in

1861 building the Wallace Monument, he died two months ago in New Jersey building some damn modern building, with all the safety protocols that laws can provide!" No one spoke. The silence in the car deepened and spread, weighing them all down.

Then Kate spoke again, more softly. "I'm the one who's sorry. I'm such a bitch, I shouldn't have snapped at you, Finn. I just hate it when people tiptoe around me." Her voice was bleak, defeated. "I can't seem to control my anger anymore. The smallest thing sets me off, and I snap at people I care about. Forgive me?" Her eyes were shiny with unshed tears.

"Nothing to forgive, lass." His voice was gentle. "But it goes both ways. You have to let yourself explode now and again without feeling bad about it. You're safe to do that with Aubrey and me. That's why you're here, aye?"

"Aye," she said, with a rush of gratitude.

Things threatened to get rough again when they reached Inverness.

"I can't face those nosy housemates of yours, Aubrey!" Kate's voice was panicked. "They're spooky. I thought it was fine when it was you they were stalking, but that's just not me! I'm not sweet like you, I'll say something mean and they'll judge me. I'll be stuck living with people who hate me."

"You do know you're being ridiculous, right?" Aubrey said. "I'll grant you the Owls are kind of spooky, and they can be a bit intrusive, but they won't hate you. Well, not unless you tell Old Harry that the English did the right thing at Culloden, or tell Maxine that you think she's put on weight." She giggled at the thought and Finn gave her a look of mock horror.

"Besides, we're not going straight to Nessie's. You have a bigger mountain to climb. We're going to see Angus." She laughed outright at Kate's look of panic.

At three o'clock in the afternoon on a Saturday, Mackintosh Book Shoppe was doing brisk business. A young man checked orders, sold books, and ran around looking for titles that customers could only find here. Angus was not at the front desk, but the door to his inner sanctum stood slightly ajar. On the outside of the door was the plaque that had once hung in *Angus' Auld Books* in Harrington. It depicted a mountain lion with its paws raised in defiance and the words "*Touch not the Cat Bot A Glove*" circling the edge. "Touch not this cat without a glove," the Clan Mackintosh motto. Angus was every bit the proud Highlander.

Aubrey knocked and called out, "Angus, it's me. I've brought company."

"Brin' 'er on in, lass! Ah hope ye brooght yer braw lad wi' ye, too," bellowed the nearly incomprehensible Scots of Angus Mackintosh. "An' it sae happens Ah've got a surprise fur ye, too."

As they entered the workroom, three people looked up. Two of them were smiling.

"Mr. MacGregor!" Aubrey exclaimed in delight. "I haven't seen you in weeks, have you been wandering?" The old man stood to give her a hug, and they all caught the familiar whiff of unwashed clothing and too much Yardley's English Lavender. Kate wondered if he got the stuff from Gladys Chesher, who seemed to bathe in it. Both of them seemed to exist in blissful unawareness that a little goes a long way.

Today, Alastair MacGregor was wearing ancient brown corduroy trousers, another faded blue button-down shirt, and a tartan bow tie in shades that no clan would ever claim. The result was somewhere between hobo and absent-minded professor. He was one of the smartest people any of them had ever met and also one of the wealthiest, living off royalties from his many glorious travel books, which the castle gift shops couldn't keep in stock. The definition of "don't judge a book by its cover," Alastair MacGregor was unique.

The second smiling man introduced himself as Chief Inspector Alan Brown of Police Scotland, up from divisional headquarters in Edinburgh. Kate hadn't met him before, but she knew he had been instrumental in saving Aubrey's life a year ago, so she was prepared to like him on sight.

CI Brown looked like a lost soul in his rumpled trench coat and grey suit, which matched his grey hair and eyes. An unremarkable man. He was the kind of person one might pass in the street and be unable to describe later, which was exactly the effect he wanted. With her detective's intuition, though, Kate saw through the exterior to the shrewd mind behind the bland grey eyes. He smiled at her again, and it was a gift.

The third man was someone else she'd never met, but he was the opposite of CI Brown in appearance.

Even though he was sitting down she could tell he was tall, probably at least six-two, and slim. Dressed in black trousers and a white dress shirt and black tie, he looked as if he'd stepped out of the movie *Men in Black*. His thick dark hair was combed back from his forehead and held there as if by sheer force of will, framing an angular face anchored by startling green eyes. An honest face, and one that might be quite handsome if it weren't scowling. He gave the group a curt nod and then went back to the paper he'd been reading when they came in.

An uncomfortable pause settled over the group. Was someone going to introduce the mystery man? Angus could be expected to ignore the formalities of simple etiquette, but it seemed that the rest of them had been infected by the same bug. Or was it a Scottish thing? Brown saw Kate's expression and gave her a benign smile.

"Ladies, Mr. Cameron, I'd like to introduce DI Jack MacDonald, out of the Edinburgh office. He's going to be helping me up here on a case." Another short nod from the curmudgeon, and then he returned to ignoring them.

At Brown's invitation, Finn scrounged three more chairs and they all gathered around the table.

"I can't tell you specifics, but DI MacDonald and I are up here because of a new drug that's been devastating Europe," Brown told them. "It's supplanted ecstasy as the street drug of choice, and it's spreading. A hallucinogen and highly addictive, its hallmark is that it changes the user's personality. It makes him feel that nothing can go wrong in his life, that he is a king and has power over everyone around him. Very dangerous, as you can imagine. And it's coming from the Highlands."

Kate's eyes snapped to Brown. "Regicide!" she said.

His regarded her with surprise. "Yes, that's what law enforcement is calling it."

"And how do *you* know about Regicide?" asked DI MacDonald, speaking for the first time. "The public hasn't been told about that name. I don't understand why we're even talking to civilians about this," he complained to Brown.

Kate bristled at his tone. "I know the name because I'm not a civilian!" she snapped, unable to curb her irritation at the arrogance of the stranger. "I *am* law enforcement."

"Kate was on a special task force to fight the drug in New Jersey," Aubrey announced, pride in her voice. "She's the best."

Kate winced, and the movement was not lost on MacDonald.

"*Was* on a task force?" he said, his voice a sneer. "Then why aren't you in New Jersey, doing your job? Did you get the sack?"

The color drained from Kate's face. Aubrey glared at the detective and put a protective hand on her friend's arm.

Kate didn't seem to notice. Two spots of color dotted her cheeks as she stared the man down until a flush came up in his own face.

She felt something shift in her mind, as if a key had turned in a lock and released her from a dark cell. The jerk was right, she had gotten the sack, but she didn't have to give up and crawl away. It was time to take her life back, to come out of the shadows and prove herself.

Her eyes met his impossibly green ones. She turned to look at CI Brown, and her voice was calm and sure.

"I'm on leave for a few months. I'm here to help Aubrey with her wedding, but I'd be happy to aid you in any way I can."

Brown considered her, and then he smiled. "Glad to have you," he said, "welcome to the team." Something about his calm surety settled Kate's stomach and revived her courage. She could do this. Here was the purpose she needed.

She ignored the soft snort from MacDonald. He was unimportant—who cared what he thought? She gave CI Brown her best smile.

"'At's th' way lass!" Angus slapped his gnarled hand on the table. Kate stared at Aubrey's old Scot and a feeling of warmth swept through her. It was a feeling that had been missing for a long time. Maybe it was a hint of the last stage of grieving—acceptance. *Okay,* she sent a thought to Eddie. *I'll try.*

The people you love become ghosts inside of you, and like this you keep them alive.

Rob Montgomery

SCOTLAND 1644

Why was it always about religion? How many men had died at the hands of their fellow man, simply because their faith did not suit the politics or the time? The world was such a beautiful place, and yet men with swords and righteous anger in their hearts could never see it. Kings came and went, each bringing his religion and his conviction that he was anointed by God—his own God. And underneath it all ran the greed of men, the need to subjugate and dominate. It was the one constant in an ever-shifting world.

Charles I was no different from those who had preceded him. It was all about money. More and more taxes on the poor, cloaked in the robe of the Anglican faith—as if God really cared how people worshipped him. And now Charles had brought the fight to Scotland, to the Highlands, and the clans were at war again.

The piper's own clan, the MacPhersons, had sided with the king against Parliament, whose members now called themselves Covenanteers, and joined forces with the more powerful clans in their march on castles and lands owned by their enemies. In the tides of war, Clan MacDonald helped the MacPherson chief in a tight battle, and in gratitude for his timely assistance the chief of Clan MacPherson awarded the MacDonald chieftain his greatest treasure: the clan's own piper.

Thus had Gawen MacPherson, born to a farmer but possessed of a rare talent in music, become piper to Clan MacDonald. He slogged along with his adopted clan as they marched into greater and greater struggles against the Covenanteers, piping them into a frenzy before each battle as the men of his kind had done for centuries. They marched northward toward destiny, and during the days and nights on the road, Gawen became a part of his new clan, trusted for his loyalty and revered for his music. He grew to love the clan chief as he had his own father, long dead of a wasting sickness. In everything but name, Gawen was now a MacDonald. He knew he would give his life for his clan, and with that knowledge came purpose and peace of mind.

On a dark night as they sat around the campfire celebrating the outcome of the latest skirmish, his chief told the men that they were changing tactics. No more the hit-and-run forays into the enemy stronghold, the attacks by night and melting away into the heather by day. They were marching to face the most powerful clan in the north, the Campbells. They were going to take Dunebrae Castle for the crown.

Gawen, seated apart as he prepared his bagpipes for the next day's march, listened with a growing feeling of trepidation. For the first time, his pride in his adopted clan was overlaid by a fear that he could not dispel. Gawen's mother had been thought to have the sight, and perhaps she had given a little of her gift to her son, for into his mind came the vision of a terrible pain, an agony as much of the spirit as of the flesh. Somehow, he knew that this campaign would be the death of him. He bowed his head in acceptance. Such was the way of war. He would be ready.

CHAPTER 6

THE PIPES THEY
ARE A-CALLING

"So, shall we try this again?" said Finn. They had been unable to schedule another visit to Dunebrae Castle until now, what with Operation Kate, as Aubrey called it privately to her fiancé, but time was biting at their heels and the wedding was only five months away. So on this brisk April morning, all three of them stuffed themselves into the Audi for another try.

"Well, if this one doesn't suit, we'll be spending our honeymoon at Nessie's," Aubrey said. "The Owls would love that; they could give us instructions on how to make children properly."

Kate choked in the back seat, understanding only too well what Aubrey meant. She herself had weathered her interrogation by the housemates with better luck than she'd anticipated, giving as well as she got and narrowly avoiding the temptation to tell them all that it was none of their damn business. With her new insight, she could even appreciate the underlying affection with which the advice had been given.

"My dear, I can't begin to understand what you're going through," Gladys had said, her cultured English voice gentle and soothing. "My George gave me many wonderful years and lovely memories. And of course, he gave me my Ronald." She beamed at her son, who smiled and nodded but as usual said nothing. "But I will say that you were lucky to find a man like your husband. Treasure the time you had with him; not many find that kind of love in this world."

"I did not," Maxine agreed. "When I was dancing in Paris, I had the choice of many suitors, but I was young and foolish, and I chose a man for his money. It was not a good marriage." She shook her head. "There was never another."

Old Harry stumped in from the hallway, a cup of tea in his hand. "Any friend o' oour Aubrey is a friend o' mine. She's family, an' so ur ye. Whitever ye need, we're haur fur ye." And with those words, he marched to his chair and retired behind his newspaper.

Unaware that her friend had received the same sort of sympathetic acceptance only a year ago, Kate was nearly overcome by the warmth of these relative strangers. Behind her Aubrey sipped her tea, smiling.

Kate pulled herself back to the present as the Audi rolled on over the narrow roads. "So Finn, tell me why you're so interested in this particular castle."

"Well, back in the seventeenth century, the castle

was owned for a while by the MacDonalds, who were the Lords of the Isles for a long time." Kate nodded, not having the faintest idea what the Lords of the Isles were but content to let Finn carry on with his history lesson.

"Also," Finn went on, "there's a ghost story that comes with the castle."

Kate groaned. "Of course there is. Do tell."

Finn sniffed. "Believe or don't, you'll not offend me. But for as long as the castle's been open to visitors, people have reported hearing bagpipes late at night."

"Bagpipes? Oh, my God! Bagpipes in *Scotland*? I don't believe it."

"Shut up," Finn said, unruffled. "Do you want to hear about it or not?"

"Oh, I do, I do. I'm sorry, Finn, please go on." She tried her best to look contrite, but the smirk on her face sabotaged the effort.

"Humph. Well, the MacDonald chief was a mighty warrior, and he took Dunebrae Castle from the Campbells for his own. He wasn't content to stay and enjoy his spoils as it was a time of war, and he had other clans to parlay with, so he left a garrison—that's a French word that means 'defend'—and sailed away to his meetings. He also left his piper behind, because he wasn't going to fight and didn't need the man to lead him into battle with his music." He shrugged. "It was a mistake. Soon enough the Campbells came back and retook the castle. They killed all the men of the garrison but spared the piper because of his station."

"What was his station?" asked Kate, sitting up straighter. Aubrey was right, Finn was a gifted story-teller. "Why would that save him?"

"Ahh, a very astute question," Finn told her. "The piper was not a warrior, but he was the most important member of the clan army. Bagpipes are an instrument of war, you know? They filled the men with hope and urged them on to fight. A good piper could sometimes make the difference between winning and losing in battle. He was valuable, so the Campbells decided to keep him for themselves."

"So he was kind of a slave," said Kate. "But wait. Wasn't it kind of stupid for the MacDonald chief to leave his piper behind if he was so valuable?"

"The chief of the MacDonalds," said Finn between clenched teeth, "was not stupid. He left for only a while and it wasn't to do battle. He had no idea that the Campbells would return so quickly. They're a wily lot, the Campbells. Anyway, he decided to come back early and attend to his new castle, but the Campbells were waiting for him, ready to massacre the clan when they walked into the trap.

"The piper knew this, and so he went to the topmost turret of the castle and watched for his clan. When he saw them coming, he began to play his pipes with everything he had in him. You see, the battle songs played by pipers have a meaning, each one of them, and the one he chose was a warning to the clan. 'The Piper's Warning to His Master.' It told them something was wrong, so the MacDonalds heard the music and knew what it meant. They heeded the warning and turned around, retreating to the sea and safety. Unfortunately, that meant leaving the piper behind to pay the price for his bravery.

"To face the music, you might say," said Kate, an

innocent look on her face. But Finn refused to rise to the bait.

"Aye. The Campbells saw their quarry turning away, and they heard the pipes playing. It didn't take much imagination to figure out what the man was doing up there on the turret, so they went up and grabbed him."

"What happened to him?" This time it was Aubrey who asked. She hadn't heard this one before.

"No one knows. He was never seen again. Probably killed, because he'd cost them their victory over the MacDonalds. There are a lot of examples of pipers giving their lives for their clans. History doesn't say what happened to this one—it's a mystery. But guests who stay at the castle sometimes swear they hear bagpipes playing late at night.

"But Finn, didn't you tell me the owner of the castle is captain of a pipe band?" Aubrey asked. "It would be natural to hear bagpipes, wouldn't it?"

"Aye, he is, and of course they do. Duncan Munro lives at the castle, and that's where the band lives during the season and where they practice. But not at night. Besides, it's only one piper and he always plays the same song, 'The Piper's Warning.' It's not one that is played by pipe bands today. Look—we're here."

As before, the castle rose out of the ever-present sea mist like a specter. Something about the huge black hulk sent a chill down Kate's spine. She looked at Aubrey.

"You want to have your honeymoon *here*?" she whispered. "This place gives me the willies."

"To be honest, it makes me want to run for the

hills," Aubrey whispered back. "I'm kind of hoping it's awful inside and Finn won't like it. But I really don't care where we go. I just want to get married and live happily ever after. Oh!" She stopped, stricken. "I—"

"Shhh," Kate put a gentle finger to Aubrey's lips. "It's all right. That's what I want for you, too. So let's check this place out."

Dunebrae Castle was not awful, not even a little bit. On the inside it was charming, all warmth and brocade and tapestry, with portraits of Campbells and Munros from ages past adorning the walls. The hallways were carpeted in what must be the Munro tartan, and huge chandeliers hung in every room. It reminded Kate of storybook castles in the fairy tales she'd read as a child.

They were met at the door by a handsome middle-aged man in a kilt who introduced himself as Hector Munro, son of the owner. Friendly and seemingly unaffected by the glory of the massive place he called home, he led them on a personal tour for the next hour, explaining in depth the most beautiful castle they had ever seen. His pride in his heritage was obvious and charming. Kate looked at Aubrey and saw that both she and Finn had stars in their eyes, and she understood. This was Scotland in all its medieval glory.

As they emerged from the rooms that were designated the "honeymoon suite," Kate saw a woman dressed in period costume glide across the hall and disappear into a room. Seeming not to have noticed the woman, Hector Munro called to someone at the end of the corridor, and turning, they saw two men in conversation. One wore the uniform of a chef, but it was the older man who commanded their attention. Like Hector, he was dressed in the Munro tartan, but his kilt was topped by a formal wool jacket decorated with ornate buttons down the front and sleeves. Satin lapels and epaulettes finished the regal look of the jacket, which was worn with a tie that matched the tartan of the kilt.

"Seems a bit much," Kate muttered to Aubrey.

"Shhh!"

Finn, who had overheard, explained in an undertone that the man was wearing the equivalent of a formal tuxedo in kilt wear.

"It's called a Prince Charlie jacket," he said, "and yes, it is somewhat formal for a weekday. Usually they're only worn on special occasions, like weddings. The old boy must be somebody special."

The man left his companion and joined them.

"Duncan Munro, at your service," he said in a cultured brogue, with a small bow toward Aubrey. "I hope you're enjoying my humble home and are perhaps considering staying with us for your honeymoon."

Finn looked at Aubrey, who nodded. "Yes, I think we may very well be," he said, with a calm tone that belied his excitement. "Could we discuss it further?"

"By all means, I was hoping you'd say that," Duncan replied, and they were led to a well-appointed office on the ground floor that had three lush armchairs in front of a huge walnut desk which looked to be at least two hundred years old. Hector Munro left them there to return to his duties at the front of the castle.

"It's a charming touch to have people dressed in

period costumes," Kate told Duncan Munro as they sat down. He gave her a blank look and then laughed.

"Oh, you must have seen one of the castle's ghosts," he said, eyes twinkling. "An old woman in a lavender gown?"

Kate nodded, avoiding eye contact with Finn. The guy had to be kidding. Was everybody in on this ghost stuff?

"She wanders around the castle quite openly, said Munro. "No one knows who she was, although historians think she must have been the wife or mother of one of the early lairds. She's not the only ghost here," he added. "We have a bagpiper who is never seen, but guests have heard him play." He broke off, looking with some concern at Aubrey and Finn. "I hope you're not put off by ghosts?"

His guests looked at each other. "Not at all," Finn assured him. Aubrey gave a wan smile. Kate kept her expression blank.

Within minutes, with the innate ability of men to scent their own kind, Finn and Duncan Munro were deep in conversation about bagpipes.

"So you're in a band," Munro said. "Which one, might I ask?"

Inver Caledonia, Finn told him. "I heard House of Munro play at the Worlds last August. You're amazing."

"Not amazing enough to win this time, unfortunately," Munro said. "Came in second, as you know. But your band is rather good too. Out of Inverness, correct? Didn't you place in the top ten?"

"Aye, we did. Eighth." Finn's answer was simple,

but Kate could hear the pride in his voice. Here was this man whose pipe band placed first or second in the World Pipe Band Championships every year, and he was complimenting Finn's band! It must be like meeting the Beatles, Kate thought. She was happy for him, even though bagpipes were one of the world's great mysteries to her.

"It's a treat to find another piper to talk the trade with," Duncan Munro said. "For the band it's all work, and Hector doesn't know or care the first thing about bagpipes. My son's passion is the castle and its history—he does all the tours." He shook his head, but the three visitors could hear a father's pride in his voice and found it touching.

Dusk had fallen by the time they walked toward the car park. Mist had completely covered the hillside above, hiding the castle from view. Finn turned to Aubrey. "Well, what do you think?"

"I love the castle, Finn, I really do. And the honeymoon suite is spectacular. Mr. Munro is lovely, and so humble. As if he's fully aware that he's fortunate to own this marvelous place, but not carried away by it. He reminds me of the Mackenzie, Earl of Castle Leod. His son is sweet, too." She gave him an anxious look. "Can we afford to stay here, though? The prices Mr. Munro was throwing out were pretty high."

"I've been saving," Finn assured her. "We can swing it. I'm glad—"

He never finished what he was going to say. A sound rose on the air, coming from the direction of the castle. A long, mournful wail of sorrow and loss, it raised the hair on Kate's arms and caused her heart to pound in her chest. She was frozen in place where she stood next to the Audi.

"What the hell?" she gasped. "What is that?"

"It's bagpipes," Finn said.

"Why on earth would Munro's pipe band be practicing at this time of day?" Kate asked. It's nearly dark."

"I don't think it's Munro's band," Finn said quietly. "It's only one set of pipes. And it seems to be coming from one of the towers."

The music died away, and Kate recovered her equilibrium. "Oooh," she said, her voice sarcastic. "Do you think it's the ghost?"

"Might be," Finn answered in a voice that trembled with excitement. "That song was 'The Piper's Warning to His Master.'"

Kate was quiet on the way home. While Aubrey and Finn chattered about their host, the glories of the castle, and the possibility of a bagpiping ghost, she stared out the window at the darkening Scottish sky. For some reason she couldn't name, she didn't feel like talking about the other ghost at Dunebrae Castle. No one else had seen her, after all, and she wondered why that made her happy. She felt a strange kinship with the old woman in the lavender dress, as if they shared some sort of secret, and she didn't want to share. The old woman was hers. Ridiculous, but there it was.

Kate sighed. *Scotland.*

CHAPTER 7

TENDER SPIRITS

"Finn's taking us on a tour!" Aubrey announced.

Kate groaned. She didn't want to stop what she was doing to play tourist. Two weeks had passed since the trip to Dunebrae. She'd been working with CI Brown and the surly Jack MacDonald on the Regicide mystery, but nothing at all had happened in the search for the mysterious drug's origin. They had set up a sort of "Reign Board" in Angus's workroom at the bookshop. Similar to the link boards that her partner Rob Morelli favored in his investigations, it was a mind map, featuring locations where the drug had been identified in quantity and people of interest in the case, with yarn lines pinned to the top to be used when they found links. *If* they ever found one.

So far, the board was depressing. There were precious few pictures, and the yarn lines hung straight down waiting for connections to be made. The simple truth, Kate thought, was that although they knew Regicide had originated in Scotland and begun its malicious journey in Europe, there were no connections to anything. No one knew how it was transported or where it might be manufactured. For a small country, Scotland might have been the size of Siberia for all the progress they had made in finding its source. Until they identified the origin of the natural substance that was the base of the drug or its method of dispersal, they were dead in the water. Or buried in the peat bog or whatever it was here. There were no leads, no breaks, and tempers were beginning to fray.

Temper, not tempers. CI Brown was always the consummate professional. The chief inspector never betrayed impatience, or much emotion at all for that matter. Not that he was cold, not at all. He was kind to Kate, listened to her ideas. Her presence on the team was reflected on the board, evidence that *someone* valued her ideas.

Jack MacDonald was another story. Most of the time he acted as if she weren't there. Not overtly rude—at least that would have been something. He just ignored her, and when she did catch him looking it was a brooding stare. He might be the most unpleasant man she had ever met, Kate thought. Total waste of good looks.

"Kate? Earth to Kate. Are you listening to me?"

Kate pulled herself out of her own head and focused on her friend's face. *Does anyone have the right to look that happy?* she thought. Always cheerful, Aubrey was a positive Pollyanna these days. It was grating on Kate's nerves.

"I can't take time off for a vacation, Bree. We're close to a breakthrough, I feel it, and I want to be here when it happens. This is important! I have to be right here."

"I met CI Brown on the way in, and he said it's fine for you to take some time off. He has to go to Edinburgh this afternoon, and he's taking DI MacDonald with him. So there's nothing for you to do here for the rest of the day. You're free." Aubrey gave Kate a triumphant grin. "What's your next excuse to avoid fun?"

Kate gave a defeated sigh. "I got nuthin'. So where are we going?"

"To a castle!"

"Not another castle!" Kate moaned. "Haven't you seen enough castles? Is this another possible place for your honeymoon? I thought you were set on Dunebrae."

"We are. You can't stay at this one. It's uninhabited, but you can visit. Eileen Donan is one of the most beautiful castles in Scotland. We passed it on the way to Skye last year, remember? That gorgeous keep out on the loch?"

"If you say so," said Kate. The truth was, the trip to Skye had been marred by her worry for Aubrey, who had been showing more and more interest in the big Scot who acted as their tour guide. She herself had never trusted Connor MacConnach, and her fears had been borne out later when he'd turned out to be a criminal. Fitz, of course, had thought he was perfect for their heartbroken friend, but Fitz had always had legendary bad judgment where men were concerned. It figured she'd pick him over Finn Cameron.

She supposed she could forgive Connor his sins. It was true that he had put her friend in harm's way and nearly gotten her killed, and he'd been part of a conspiracy to cripple the Scottish independence movement through sabotage and murder. But in the end, he had tried to protect Aubrey, and his betrayal had earned him a grisly end at the hands of his fellow conspirator. MacConnach's late game heroics hadn't mattered anyway. Aubrey had already fallen in love with Finn Cameron, and now her life was perfect.

As Kate's had once been.

She could feel herself slipping into that grey place where she'd lived since Eddie's death, and pushed herself to rise above it. She could usually do that now--pull herself back from the edge of black despair and return to something resembling normalcy. She knew she'd been better lately. The task force had given her something to do, a feeling of purpose, and she'd begun to show signs of her old self-confidence. She knew she was smiling more, her brown eyes sparkled as they once had. But then someone would say something, or she would be reminded of something she and Eddie had done together that would never happen again, and she'd be right back in the swamp, in danger of being strangled by the weeds of grief and pulled under.

Ever alert to Kate's moods, Aubrey jumped in. "Finn says that Eileen Donan is the most photographed castle in the country and a symbol of Scotland."

"Well, if Finn says," said Kate. Her tone was lightly mocking. She knew what Aubrey was trying to do and appreciated her friend for the effort. She didn't want to go back to that dark place in her mind, either. Maybe a day out among other people led by the most charming tour guide in Inverness would clear out the cobwebs. She stood up and stretched, and then stopped with her arms extended over her head and glared at Aubrey.

"Wait a minute! Does this castle have a ghost?"

"Of course it does. More than one, I think. You're in Scotland, Kate!" Aubrey turned and left the workroom, laughing. With a sigh of defeat Kate followed in her wake. To be honest, Scotland was beginning to creep her out. She hadn't mentioned the old woman at Dunebrae, the one dressed in period costume who seemed to glide rather than walk, but she hadn't stopped thinking about her. Couldn't stop wondering why she was the only one who seemed to have seen the woman. More of the weirdness, and Kate didn't do weird.

The tour bus wound north and west, through shadowed mountains covered in bracken and sheep. The heather was not in bloom as it had been the last time they'd come this way, but the ancient hills still exercised their magic, calling to the hearts of the people who passed through them as they had for centuries. Even Kate's practical soul was captured by the power of the Highlands.

Finn, in his element, had his headset on as he drove the small bus along the narrow road, pulling over when he needed to make way, surging by when it was the other car's turn to wait. And all the time he maintained a discourse about his native land, his smooth brogue enchanting the younger, female members of the tour as it always did.

"Mr. Cameron," said one of a pair of girls in the seat across from Kate and Aubrey, "can you tell us the truth?"

Here it comes. Kate winced. The Question.

"The truth, lass?" Finn caught Kate's pained look in the mirror and grinned.

"Yes," the girl said, giggling, "what *does* a Scotsman wear under his kilt?"

"Weel, noo, lassie," Finn broadened his brogue wickedly as he winked at Aubrey, "I'd tell ye, but I've got my future wife on board t'day an' I ken she wouldna approve o' my sharin'."

The girl followed his eyes with thinly disguised envy. "Oh," she said, disappointed. An older couple in the seat behind her laughed.

"You keep looking, dearie," the woman said, "and maybe you'll find a nice-looking Scotsman yourself. But a word of warning. I've been on a lot of tours, and that question gets asked on nearly every one. Funny thing, too--the answer's always different!" Everyone on the bus laughed.

The tour bus pulled into the car park and the banter was forgotten as they all stared in awe at the castle perched on a spit of land in the loch. Finn took off his headset and stood up to give his flock their instructions before releasing them.

"Eileen Donan sits at the point where three great lochs meet," he told them. "There has been a keep here since the sixth century and a castle since the thirteenth, but this one is the last of four to stand on this site. Fires, battle, and the elements are not kind to the achievements of man, ye ken?"

Kate stared at the ancient stonework, amazed. "Who owns it?" she asked.

Finn raised his voice to take in the entire bus. "Eileen Donan is the ancestral seat of the MacRae's," he told them, "and they still own it to this day.

"Please stay with me so I can check you in at the kiosk, and then you can walk across the stone walkway to the castle. Movie buffs might recognize the walkway from the film *Highlander*—the one with Sean Connery." There were gasps of delight from some of the older members of the group.

"And speaking of movies, when you get to the courtyard, you'll see the Coat of Arms of Clan MacRae along with their motto, in Gaelic. Now, you *Outlander* fans will be happy to know that one of the strongest alliances for the MacRaes was a clan called . . ." He paused for effect. "Fraser." He waited for the exclamations to die down and then added, "in fact, the motto translated means, 'For as long as there is a MacRae inside there will never be a Fraser outside.' I think you lassies can appreciate that, aye?" He winked at the girls in the front seat and turned to lead his group to the ticket kiosk.

Aubrey and Kate mingled with the tour group and met up with Finn at the castle entrance. As they followed him through the arched portcullis gate and the huge wooden castle doors, they passed into history. The three spent the next hours going through the restored rooms of the castle, each of which had its own guide. They found the banqueting hall and stood for a while admiring the portraits and period furniture on display there.

"To the right, through here," whispered Finn, "is a Piper's Gallery. It's still used during wedding ceremonies."

"Did you ever play here?" asked Aubrey.

"Once, when one of our drummers got married here. It's quite an experience. But now, let's skip to the part I think you'll like, he said to Kate, leading them to a room filled with weapons. Her eyes widened as she took in the rifles, dueling pistols, and cannonballs on display.

"Ohh," she said, her voice reverent. "Knives!"

Finn laughed. "Knew she'd like it," he said to Aubrey. He raised his voice so Kate could hear. "I'm never going to make her mad, not the way she's ogling those dirks!"

Kate ignored him, in rapt study of the wicked looking twelve-inch blades, resplendent in their cases. *This is what it's all about.* She was glad she had come, grateful to both Aubrey and Finn for pulling her out of Inverness. She'd needed this distraction.

"And now," Finn's voice was innocent, "let's see if we can find the ghosts."

"Damn," Kate muttered. "You two go, I'll meet you outside."

"But one of them is Mary, Queen of Scots," said

Finn. "Don't you want to see her? She was a prisoner here, as well as several other castles. In fact, Mary's ghost haunts so many castles in Scotland it's a wonder the poor woman gets any rest."

"Well, if she's a ghost, she probably doesn't need much rest," said Kate, refusing to rise to the bait.

"Aye, you have a point there," Finn acknowledged. "But there's also the ghost of a Spanish soldier who wanders around without his head. I'd like to see him."

"I'll pass," said Kate, her eyes fixed on a beautifully decorated dirk. But as Finn and Aubrey walked away, wrapped up in each other again, her mind returned to the subject of ghosts, and she felt the familiar depression closing in.

At the appointed time, they all met back at the tour bus, everyone tired but satisfied with their experience at Scotland's iconic castle. While they waited for stragglers, Kate wandered off by herself to sit on the stone wall of the walkway, and that was where Aubrey found her, staring at the castle with that lost look on her face.

"What's the matter, sweetie?"

Kate pulled herself out of her trance and looked at her best friend.

"Bree," she said, "I've been wondering. There are so many ghosts in Scotland—" she stopped.

Aubrey cocked her head, waiting.

"Well, you know I don't believe in ghosts, but supposing you and Finn are right, and they are real—why?"

"Why?"

"Why are they here? Why don't they just go to

Heaven like they're supposed to? Why are they hanging around?" Her voice was plaintive.

"Well," Aubrey said slowly, "I've only seen the one ghost, so I'm no expert. But I think they stay behind because they have unfinished business, something they have to set right before they can move on. Someone they loved, maybe, who needs their help. That's the way it was at Rait Castle. Why?"

Kate didn't answer. When Aubrey looked, she saw tears in her friend's eyes. "Kate! What is it? Please tell me."

"Well," Kate said softly after a long while, "if ghosts are real, and they stay for someone they loved, why haven't I seen Eddie? We never got to say goodbye. Damn it, that's unfinished business, isn't it? Do I have to believe in ghosts for it to happen?" Her face was etched in pain. "I miss him!"

Aubrey took Kate's hands in her own and looked her friend in the eye.

"But Eddie didn't *have* unfinished business, darling. He loved you with all his heart, and you loved him the same way. His life on earth was complete. You made him so happy, there was nothing he needed to fix in this world, was there?"

Kate looked at her, eyes shining with unshed tears. "Do you really think that's true, Bree? Because if it is, I think maybe I could begin to move on, too. If I knew he was okay."

"I know it's true," Aubrey said with conviction, and Kate nodded slowly. They walked back to the bus in silence, each thinking of her own ghosts.

CHAPTER 8

THE WAGES OF SIN

It was beginning to rain, but what else was new in Scotland? Hugh Ross leaned against the brick wall on the corner of Inglis and the High Street in Inverness and let his thoughts brood. It had been a hellish day. He looked down at the box that held the pound coins, euros, and quarters and sighed. He was better than this pathetic collection of the world's cast-off coinage, and soon everyone would know it. Soon *he'd* be the one tossing pocket change at some poor beggar who huffed up a lung for the crowd's entertainment.

In another week he'd be expected back up at the castle, practicing for the European Pipe Band Championships, getting ready for the Worlds. Most of the band was there already, but Hugh felt himself drifting away from them. He knew he was putting space between his mates and himself, working toward the time he would be leaving that life forever. Maybe he felt guilty; perhaps that was why he was selling himself on the streets of Inverness like an itinerant musician, but he knew it was more than that. He was leaving a life he loved, forever.

He glanced down at the pitiful pile of change and his eye caught the corner of a piece of paper that was wrapped around an American quarter. Curious, he stooped to pick it up. Unfolding the small square, he saw that it was a cartoon, something likely ripped from a magazine. A bagpiper stood against a wall, pipes at the ready, and a sign at his feet proclaimed, "Pay or I'll play." Very funny. Everyone was a critic, and those damn Americans were the worst. They had no idea of the history behind the sound they mocked, no idea how much work went into producing the music that had moved armies and inspired men to charge into battle through the centuries.

The idiot who had tossed this joke into his box didn't understand history because he had none. Perhaps he'd come to Scotland searching for his roots, chasing some mythical ancestor who had once lived in the Highlands. Most likely got his ideas from that damn *Braveheart* movie. Somewhere in his DNA, there might once even have been a piper who led his clan into the fight, who produced the mystic notes that rang over the mountains and created victory out of sure defeat, but the fool had no idea. To him, bagpipes were stereotypes of Scotland, like kilts and whisky, to be laughed at and joked about back home in ridiculous parodies of Scottish accents as the eejit strutted around his local bar.

They certainly had no trouble imbibing the whisky, these tourists. That was part of the problem. They weren't used to the heady distillation; it went to their heads and gave them Dutch courage, the impetus for their mockery of their host country's customs and culture. It wasn't only the Americans, either, if he felt like being fair. He had just selected them today as the target of his frustration because of the quarter. The tourists were all the same. They saw him as nothing but a clown, a street performer, and he agreed with him. He deserved their scorn.

But that was all going to change, and soon. Thinking of the future, brilliant in its possibilities, Hugh straightened and shouldered his pipes. He was a musician, and a good one, but soon he'd be able to put away his pipes and live an entirely different life. The information he carried would assure he'd never have to work another day. After tomorrow's meeting he could quit the band and live like a king, master of his own fate.

Ross had never envisioned himself as a turncoat. The promises given when he'd accepted membership in the enterprise were grand, and he'd thought himself content. But the glory was always in the future, always dangled just a bit too far ahead. He wanted to start his new life *now*, not in some distant time he might never see. The man he was about to meet had named a fortune and promised it would be in his hands tomorrow. All of it. There was really no decision to be made.

Hugh snapped himself back to the present moment, back to the crowded High Street and the tourists standing around in knots, eager to hear him play his music. Tomorrow he'd be done with them, but for now he was a bagpiper, and a good one. He loved his craft, and he was going to give them the best he had, whether they knew it or not. Today they would be getting the best of Hugh Ross, piper.

As if in recognition of his improved mood, coins began dropping into his box with greater frequency. Small clusters of tourists gathered around his corner to listen as he puffed and squeezed and forced incredible music out of a sheep's stomach. It was enough, for now.

The man in the black leather jacket stood among a group of tourists, listening to the performance on the street corner of Inverness. Just one of many such musicians, but this one was different. The man had been sent to take care of some business with this particular musician, but it could wait. The man in black knew his bagpipes, and this piper was truly good. It would be a shame to waste all that talent, and he had all the time in the world. He joined in the clapping for "Highland Cathedral" and waited for the next song to begin.

As the sun sank behind the purple hills beyond Inverness, the stores on the High Street began to close their doors for the day. Tourists wandered away to dinner at Johnny Fox's or the Fig and Thistle, and the crowds thinned, leaving Hugh Ross alone on his corner. He lowered the instrument from his shoulder and unscrewed the drone pipes from the bag, placing them carefully in their straps in his battered case. Pouring his day's earnings into a zippered leather pouch in his instrument case, he secured the case and wandered up towards View Street in search of a dram at the Castle Tavern. Maybe some Neeps and Tatties, too—Lord knew he'd earned it.

Two hours later, Ross emerged from the pub, stomach full and mind a bit foggy from the tavern's good whisky. As he trudged up Castle Street toward his rooming house, he felt the dusk settle like an old familiar cloak around him and thought again that this was the best place in the world. Who cared what the tourists thought? There was no place like the Highlands of Scotland, and there was nothing as good as a piper's life. Except for the life of a king.

A dark shadow separated itself from the stone wall along Castle Street, following Hugh at a distance. As the piper turned into his own street, a low whistle pierced the quiet night, and Ross stopped and turned, startled. Sensing danger, he backed away. Too late. He felt a sharp, agonizing pain in his side, then a pervasive weakness. A searing burn spread under his ribs, causing tears to well up in his eyes.

Ross staggered, reaching for the stone wall next to him and missing. Curiously, his legs no longer seemed able to support his weight, and he felt himself sinking to the pavement, vision blurring. Confusion filled his mind as he groped for the source of the excruciating pain, and his hand came away wet in the dark. A metallic tang filled his nostrils. Something was seriously wrong, but he couldn't make his brain focus on the problem. He could no longer feel his arms or legs. A chill that had nothing to do with the weather spread through him, and he could feel his senses evaporating as the cold intensified, and he began to shiver uncontrollably.

The man in the black leather jacket bent down and whispered in Hugh's ear. "This is what comes to traitors. Hope the devil likes your music as much as I did." He patted Ross's head and wiped his blade on the piper's jacket before placing the dagger into its sheath on his belt. The man picked up the bagpipe case and opened it, extracting the leather money pouch. Unzipping the pouch, he shook out the coins onto the quivering body, watching as they rolled off and down the street. He tossed the pouch aside and tucked the case under his arm, walking away without a backward glance at the forlorn kilted figure lying in a spreading pool of dark viscous liquid.

Hugh Ross stared in shock and disbelief at the retreating figure. He wasn't cold anymore and the pain had subsided, but there was no comfort in it. He knew what this was. As his vision dimmed and the shivering subsided into a feeble twitching, he heard a plaintive voice in his mind wail, *it isn't fair!* Darkness chased the voice away, thickening and expanding until it pulled him into the void. His body shuddered a final time and was still.

A small white piece of paper caught on the piper's belt before drifting away on the wind, its words barely visible in the growing dark. *Pay or I'll play.*

CHAPTER 9

YOU DON'T KNOW JACK

On Saturday morning, Kate wandered into the kitchen for a cup of coffee. Nessie looked up from spacing tattie scones on a tray and smiled her little garden gnome smile.

"So, feelin' a bit better, lass?"

"Yes, I am," Kate said, knowing it was partly true. The events of yesterday had driven everything from her mind for a while. She'd felt freer than she had since that February morning before the call from Fitz that had shattered her life in a raw second. Getting out of Harrington and coming to Scotland had been the right thing to do. Somehow, seeing that woman at Dunebrae and hearing that ghostly piper had made her feel closer to Eddie. It seemed that this magical land understood, that it had been through all this a thousand times and had made peace with its ghosts. As must she.

And then she had awakened this morning in a blind panic, unable for a minute to picture his face. Her heart clutched as she lay rigid, summoning his warm brown eyes, his wide smile. Shame coursed through her at the realization that his image was no longer as clear as before. Was she that shallow, that disloyal? Or was this just another step in the dance of widowhood? Still, she didn't feel the stab of guilt as much as she had before, and her conversation with Aubrey yesterday had somehow buoyed her, given her an odd sense of hope.

"It's all right tae let him go, dearie," Nessie said, her dark little bird eyes fixed on Kate's face. "He'll always be there," she pointed to Kate's heart, "But he wouldna want t' be stuck in yer head, ye ken?"

"How do you *do* that?" Kate asked, her eyes wide. "You and Angus. How do you read minds like that?"

"Ah dinna ken what ye mean, lass," Nessie told her, turning away to slide a tray of black puddings into the AGA.

"Um, Nessie?"

"Yes, lass?" Nessie put her hands on her hips and faced Kate again.

"Have you ever seen a ghost?" She should have felt silly just saying that, but somehow it seemed a perfectly normal question here in Scotland.

"A ghost? Aye, o' course. Hasna Aubrey told ye?" She looked surprised.

"Yes, she told me the story about Rait Castle, but . . . I didn't really believe her. I thought it was some sort of romantic thing her imagination cooked up to explain how she felt about Finn. I mean, it's impossible, isn't it? There's no such thing as ghosts, really." Kate looked at Nessie out of the corner of her eye.

Nessie looked at her, shocked. "Where've ye been, lass? O'course there's ghosts! Angus was there at Rait Castle, he'll tell ye. Ye mean ye never saw th' book?"

Kate shook her head. She knew the book to which Nessie was referring, and a shiver went through her at the memory of a gabbling Aubrey going on and on about a magic book that talked to her and smelled of rotting flesh and tasted of blood. But Aubrey had been hungover on Angus's Talisker whisky at the time and mourning the defection of Marc Russo. Kate had just assumed that she was letting her wild imagination run away with her as usual.

Still, something *had* happened to Aubrey in Scotland. Something terrifying and incomprehensible and wonderful. She had been sent by Angus to "break a curse on a clan and find a Mackintosh," as Aubrey had put it, and she had met Fionnlagh Cameron, a Mackintosh by birth. It was a coincidence, of course. Scotland was a small country, and there were a lot of people named Mackintosh—but Aubrey had not only found one, she'd fallen in love with him. Deeply in love. The real thing. And she'd sworn that she'd met a ghost. Not just any ghost, either, the ghost of an ancestor. Once Kate had thought it was all just nuts, but now she wasn't so sure.

Kate did not have a wild imagination. She was practical to a fault and had always prided herself on being the sensible, grounded member of their trio. Aubrey was the dreamer, Fitz the tender romantic, and Kate the one who tethered them to the Earth, provided the reason and the explanations. Somehow, the three of them worked.

Were all Scots floating around in the ether like Nessie and Angus, she wondered? Almost every one she'd met took the idea of ghosts seriously, even Finn. But then, according to Aubrey, he'd seen the Rait Castle ghost, too. If all of this was to be believed, he'd been the ancestor of the Mackintosh that the ghost was in love with! Even thinking about it was crazy, but *they* believed it. They all believed. It made her feel left out of a big wonderful secret.

Well, there was one Scot who didn't seem to buy into the ghost business. That Jack MacDonald oaf was too dour and sullen to be swayed by anything that couldn't be proven. It was the only good thing she could say about the guy, but it was something. She wasn't too sure about CI Brown, but Aubrey had told her that Brown was there at Rait when the ghost had appeared, and he hadn't discounted the story. She snorted. This country! How did they ever get anything done here?

Aubrey had left early to meet Finn for some wedding-y conference and Kate felt at loose ends, so she decided to walk off another of Nessie's full Scottish breakfasts. She hadn't really seen much of Inverness on her last trip, only what the hop-on, hop-off bus provided, and she hated tours, so this would be a perfect time to scope out the place for herself.

It wasn't raining, but a look at the overcast sky told her it was bound to do so at some point today, so she ran back upstairs for her trusty windbreaker and set out up the steep hill. She passed more rooming houses, some with renovation signs and others offering bed and breakfast. Reaching the top of Castle Road, she started down toward the High Street and the tourist area. Inverness Castle loomed in the distance halfway down the hill, its warm tan stone standing proud above the River Ness and the city center.

Kate stopped. An alley just off the street was sealed with blue and white tape, the word "police" emblazoned along its length. Different from the black and yellow crime scene tape back home, but its meaning was unmistakable. Something bad had happened here, and recently. She peered over the barrier as she passed and saw a large brown stain on the pavement near a stone wall. Someone had been hurt. Most likely killed, with that much blood. Kate sighed. Even in Scotland people did unspeakable things to their fellow human beings. Peace was an illusion, no matter where you were.

A sudden pain surged through Kate at the thought of what she should be doing back home. She missed her job, needed to get back and redeem herself. An image of Rob Morelli came unbidden into her mind, and she stumbled, righted herself, forced her leaden feet to move past the barrier. What was he doing? Who was partnering with him now? She felt tears close to the surface and brushed at her eyes.

"Miss Bianchi!" A voice hailed her, and she turned, startled. Damn, it was that odious DI MacDonald.

"Mrs." she corrected him, her voice as cold as she could manage.

"Oh, pardon me," he responded, face tightening at her tone.

"I'm a widow," she said. Had no one told him? It sounded odd, as if she were describing someone else. *She's a widow. That woman over there is a widow. Her husband died, poor thing.*

"I'm sorry for your loss." MacDonald offered the standard response of policemen the world over. She'd said it many times herself, knowing how lame it was, but it was all they had.

"Thank you." She moved to walk on, but he fell into step beside her.

"Would you like a cup of coffee?"

Kate stopped, startled again. Was the man trying to be civil? It certainly seemed so. She was curious. Why, after the way he had acted up till now, was he bothering?

"Uh, sure," said a voice that she recognized as her own. Damn, now she'd be stuck making small talk with someone she'd disliked on sight, someone who obviously felt the same way about her.

They passed a coffee shop on the High Street, but he continued on down the street. "Too many tourists," he said in a terse voice. Turning right on Church Street, he led her down past a music store and several restaurants, finally turning into a narrow alley which led to a set of double doors.

"I know this place!" Kate said, gazing at the ornate red arches overhead. "The Victorian Market—Aubrey brought me here on my last visit. There's a knife store around here someplace."

MacDonald laughed. "It's a kilt rental shop, but I know the place you mean. Lots of lovely sgian dubhs. Fancy knives, do you?"

Kate forgot she didn't like the man as she turned shining eyes on him. "Oh, yes!" she breathed. "There's nothing like a good sharp blade. That's a real weapon!"

"Don't you Americans prefer guns?" he asked her. "Holsters and six-guns, ten-gallon hats and all that?"

"That's out west," Kate said, "and it was about two hundred years ago. Nowadays, pardner, we prefer AR-15s. Nothing like a good assault rifle to mow down your enemy!" She laughed at his expression.

"Nope, I do carry a handgun on the job, but I collect knives. And look at those gorgeous things!" She pointed to the array of blades in the window of the kilt shop, sighing at the filigreed handles on the short daggers. "Saw them last time, but I didn't have time to buy one. Can't exactly carry it onto the plane in my sock, you know. But I'm definitely ordering one this time and sending it home."

"Well, those are more for show," MacDonald told her. He guided her to a seat at a small table in front of a cafe next door to the kilt shop. "The men carry them in their stockings for special occasions like weddings, when they're wearing the kilt. A sgian dubh'll do the job, if you need to use one, but you'd have to be close."

The waitress appeared, and MacDonald ordered two flat white coffees and a plate of scones. While they waited, he continued his lecture on Scottish blades.

"For serious killing," he told her, his green eyes narrowing, "you'd want to be using a Scottish dagger, or a dirk. It's about eleven or twelve inches long, easy to conceal, very lethal. There was a murder two

nights ago right up the road. One of the street performers, a bagpiper. Killer likely used a dirk."

"I saw the place!" Kate said. "Up the road on the
hill, right? Crime scene tape's still there."

Jack nodded. "Weird case. The man's pipes were
stolen."

"Why on earth would someone want to kill someone for his bagpipes? Aren't they pretty easy to come
by? Who did it, a rival bagpiper or something?" The
image of two kilted men going at it over a set of bagpipes appeared in her mind, and she giggled.

"Think it's funny, do you?" MacDonald asked,
frowning. "The man's dead. Maybe you find that
amusing in the States, but we take murder rather
more seriously here."

Now, there he was. The Jack MacDonald she had
met the first time. Not the charming, lighthearted
imposter who had lured her into having a cup of coffee so he could browbeat her and make fun of her
country, and then accuse her of making fun of his!
The man glowering at her over the table was the real
one. The oaf was back.

"Chill out, will you?" Kate said, exasperated. "I'm
not making fun. Well, not really. I'm sorry," she added,
not sounding sorry at all. She stared at him. "Why
are you so prickly?"

He glared back at her, and then his mouth twitched
and he let out a bark of laughter. "I am not prickly!"
he enunciated each word. "I'm just—just—"

"Just prickly." She folded her hands and glared at
him. "Do you have something against Americans," she
asked, "or are you just naturally grouchy? Or is it me?"

His mouth opened, but whatever retort he'd been about to make was interrupted by the arrival of the waitress with their coffee and scones. An uneasy silence settled in as they made a great show of sipping and chewing.

"I'm sorry."

Kate blinked. "What?"

"I'm sorry. I think we got off on the wrong foot, that's all. It's not you. Or it's mostly not you." MacDonald was staring at the shifting patterns in his coffee.

"*Mostly* not me? And pray tell, which part of it *is* me?"

"I'd rather not talk about it, if you don't mind. Tell me about your husband."

Kate's coffee sloshed into the saucer as she slammed the cup down. Her eyes widened, color flooding her cheeks. "M-my husband? You don't want to talk to me about your problem tolerating me, because you definitely have a problem, buddy, but you think it's appropriate to ask me about my *husband*? That's your idea of a topic of conversation? Well, he's dead! He died in a construction accident two months ago! Is that good enough for you? Damn you!" Kate pushed her chair back and stood, holding herself together with a every ounce of strength she possessed.

"I think this conversation, such as it is, has gone on long enough. Goodbye, DI MacDonald." She whirled around and walked the length of the corridor to the street door, repressing the urge to look back.

The nerve of the man! The unadulterated,

unmitigated gall! Where the hell did he get the brass balls to browbeat her, insult her, and then ask her about Eddie? Tears filled her eyes and she brushed them away with her sleeve as she walked toward the High Street. It was raining. Perfect.

A hand grasped her arm and swung her around. She jerked away and stood with hands fisted at her sides, glowering.

"I'm sorry!" Jack MacDonald stood in the street, his brow creased. "I'm an arse. I didn't mean to say that. I don't know where it came from. I don't seem to know what to say to you, it comes out all wrong. You affect me somehow—I can't explain it. I'm really sorry!"

The green eyes bored into hers, leaving her floundering for a reply. Kate gathered herself up and stared back at him, heedless of the people hurrying to get out of the rain.

"It—it's all right. Maybe I overreacted. It's just so new and raw, this being alone—you couldn't have known. I don't know how to talk to anybody except Aubrey and Finn. My social skills are gone. And you're not much help, you know," she added with a touch of asperity.

He took a deep breath. "Let's start over," he suggested, holding out his hand. "I'm Jack."

"Kate," she said, taking his hand and shaking it. "Nice to meet you."

"May I walk you home?" he asked. "See, I can be civil."

"Hmm, we'll see. Yes, Mr.—Jack, I guess you can walk me home."

Neither of them said another word as they walked back up Castle Street and down the path to Nessie's. By the time they reached the front door, the silence didn't feel uncomfortable or awkward anymore. It just felt . . . new.

CHAPTER 10

THE NEW BOSS

Without being asked, Angus had given over his workroom to the Regicide task force, such as it was. Brown had wanted to keep the investigation close to the vest for the time being, and that meant the local police department was out. For now, their team consisted of CI Brown, DI MacDonald, and disgraced American detective Kate Bianchi. But that was about to change.

"I have to get back to Edinburgh," Brown told them. "I'm leaving Jack in charge, and Mrs. Bianchi, you are his deputy. I trust that you two will get the job done up here until I can free up another officer to join you. I have the utmost faith in you, Jack. And you, Mrs. Bianchi."

"Please, sir, call me Kate," she said for the hundredth time, turning a full wattage smile on the chief inspector. "I won't let you down."

"Sir, may I have a word?"

"If it's to tell me that you'd prefer to work alone, no." Your partner for the foreseeable future is Kate Bianchi here, and I trust to your professionalism to make it work." He gave both of them the eye. The unspoken addition to his comments was, "or else." MacDonald looked militant but said nothing.

Kate let out a sigh of relief. Despite her rocky relationship with the surly detective, she needed this distraction. And she had an ulterior motive. If she was instrumental in helping to get to the root of Regicide production in the Highlands, where it had all started, she'd be able to fly back to Harrington with "success" written all over her record. Her job reinstatement would be assured.

Of course, she wasn't about to let New Jersey get off that easily. She would make them beg, just a little, before graciously accepting their offer of a promotion and a pay increase. The thought of Mulgrew's face as he begged her to come back was a balm to her wounded soul. She could almost taste her triumph.

"Are you with us, Detective Bianchi?" Jack MacDonald's disapproving face swam into her squad room in New Jersey, causing her to jump and return to the present. Not New Jersey. She was in a bookshop in Inverness, Scotland, and her partner was a brusque Scot whose manners ran from tepid to cold. It was as if someone had thrown water from the deepest waters of Loch Ness over her head. She rolled her shoulders and faced her adversary. She would have to make this partnership work, no matter how obnoxious Jack MacDonald could be.

Kate had hoped that the fragile truce she thought they'd achieved last month when they'd had coffee and he'd walked her home would hold, but apparently not. No blood had been shed, but that seemed to be as good as it was going to get. What the hell was wrong with MacDonald? She had no illusions that she was a femme fatale, for God's sake, but she cleaned up pretty well, and men didn't exactly run away when they saw her coming, did they?

To be honest, she had no real idea what men thought of her, because she'd been with Eddie since fifth grade. She had no real experience with other males of the species. Maybe she was repulsive. Maybe Eddie had been the exception to the rule, and she was just a turn-off to men.

Kate winced, hearing Sister Ellen's voice in her memory.

"Don't you fret, dear. Bradley only threw that rock at you because he *likes* you. That's what boys do when they like girls. Now go help Sister Agnes clean the rectory with the other girls, that's the way."

Kate snorted at the memory. How would an ancient nun know what boys thought? Sister Ellen had been about a hundred years old! *Bradley Miller threw rocks at me because he was a miserable little shit, and it gave me great pleasure to arrest him two years ago for drunk driving. He sure didn't like me then!*

As for Jack MacDonald, she was convinced that the problem was with him, not her. The jury was out on whether he had thrown rocks at girls when he was a kid, but she'd bet if he did, it wasn't because he liked them.

"Now that we've got that squared away," CI Brown said, his voice breaking into her memories, "I have something concrete for you two to work on. We may finally have a lead. The autopsy results are in on that bagpiper who was killed last month . . ."

They waited.

". . . and they tell us nothing new."

Kate and Jack looked at Brown. "But?" MacDonald said.

"Hugh Ross, the man's name was. A well-known piper from the north, attracted a nice little crowd at lunchtime. Not famous, himself, nothing out of the ordinary except for his talent.

"However," Brown went on, "as you know, his bag-pipes were missing." He paused. "And that *is* out of the ordinary. His money pouch was nearby, all the coins dumped out around him, but the case and the pipes have disappeared. And I find that more than a little interesting." He stopped and gave them a level look. Before Kate could ask how any of this constituted a lead, Brown continued.

"A very good piper takes care of his instrument, treasures it," he told her, "and from all accounts, Ross was one of the best. The pipes would have been made special to his needs, and his alone. You see? They would have been important to *him*, but they would have meant little to anyone else. Pipers do not normally covet each other's instruments. They have their own." Brown was adept at hiding his thoughts, but now that she knew him better Kate could see the glint of excitement behind the gray eyes.

"So why, I have to ask myself, would anyone want

to steal a set of bagpipes? And what was there about those particular pipes that someone was willing to kill to get them?"

Kate felt her pulse quicken. It still didn't make sense, but detective work was a puzzle. Rather than looking for the pieces that fit, the police spent just as much time trying to find that one elusive piece that *didn't* fit. This was why she had become a cop. Searching for that "aha" moment that made it all worth it. All the wild goose chases, the abortive interviews with uncooperative witnesses, the leads that ended with brick walls—they all led to this tingly feeling she had right now.

"What do we know about the killing?" she asked.

"Stabbed once, killer used a Highland dirk or other long-bladed weapon. With a blade that effective, once was all that was necessary. Not immediately fatal; he bled out on the street. It was almost as if the killer wanted him to know what was happening to him, and why. Personal. Leaving his earnings scattered over his body is curious too. An act of mockery, it could be said."

"Was it a lot of money?" Kate asked.

"You'd be surprised at how much can be collected by a street performer in Inverness," Brown said. "We're the capital of the Highlands, and a lot of tourists pass by the pipers and other artists during the course of a day on the High Street. Ross, by all accounts, was quite good. He was a member of The House of Munro Highlanders, which has won or finished in the top five at the World Championships for the past four years." Brown frowned. "Yes, he collected a fair amount of money. But I can't imagine it would be enough to justify killing him."

Kate's brow furrowed. "Why was he standing out on a street corner playing for the tourists, if he was that good?" she asked. "I mean, I know next to nothing about bagpipes, beyond what Finn's told me, and to be honest I sort of tune him out sometimes when he gets going on it, but I thought it was only the kids who played for the tourists."

"Well, you're both right and wrong there," Brown said. "Often it is the younger members or novice category pipers, as they're called, who play for the tourists in smaller cities like Inverness.

"However, when bands start coming to town to get ready for the European Championships, which will be held right up the road in Forres next month, the pipers often use the opportunity to practice and make a little spare cash. It's not that unusual for a member of a championship pipe band to be doing just that. Like any artist, pipers crave an audience. We just don't know what motivated Ross."

Something had been bothering Kate. "But, sir," her voice was hesitant. "What does a murdered piper have to do with the Regicide investigation?" Jack MacDonald had been silent, but he flashed her a look of something that might have been approval. It was clear he had been wondering the same thing.

"Very possibly nothing," was Brown's reply. "But our investigation has focused on following the drug trail *backwards*. We haven't found the original source of the drug, but we know it begins as a powder of some sort, and then is mixed with other, innocent substances. We've intercepted people passing the drug along the pipeline at various stages."

Brown sighed. "None of the people we've picked up are talking, and we suspect they may not even know anything beyond their step of the process. So, we began looking at what else was going on in the area at the times of interception. What we've discovered is that the trail of Regicide production has nearly always coincided with a bagpipes championship or demonstration held at the same time. It's happened too often to be a coincidence."

He shrugged. "It's a long shot, of course. We have the drug, we have bagpipes, and we have a dead piper. It may mean nothing, but it's an anomaly. We're focusing on the likelihood that our Mr. Ross saw something he shouldn't have, or angered someone, or perhaps threatened them somehow. It may not even be a connection, and nothing we've found in his background gives us a clue, but we're going to tear his life apart until we find out which motive resulted in his death. And that's where you two come in.

"I want you to follow the trail. The House of Munro Highlanders are based at Dunebrae Castle, and that's only an hour north of here. In another week or so Ross would have moved up there to train for the season. So for now, start on the High Street and continue working backwards to Dunebrae."

"I was there!" Kate exclaimed. "Dunebrae is on the short list for Aubrey and Finn's honeymoon, and we visited it just last month. Gorgeous place. Has a couple of ghosts." She sat back, embarrassed, and waited for the expected snort from Jack MacDonald. But he said nothing.

"I know the story," Brown told her. He gave her an odd look. "An old lady and a bagpiper, if I'm not mistaken."

"Yes, Kate said. She shouldn't be surprised that Brown would know that. "And," she hesitated, not wanting to find herself on the receiving end of MacDonald's mockery again, "we heard him. The bagpiper's ghost."

Both men stared at her. Then the snort came.

"I'm sure that the castle provides canned bag-pipe music for its guests, so that they can go home to Rubeville, USA and tell all their friends they've experienced a real Scottish ghost!" Jack's voice was caustic.

"Stop making fun of me!" Kate challenged him, face red. "I didn't say I believed it was really the ghost! I knew there was a pipe band there, and I fig-ured it was them. But Finn wasn't so sure, and I trust *his* opinion." *More than yours, you pompous ass!*

"Now, children, let's see if we can keep it civil, shall we?" Chief Inspector Brown seemed more amused than annoyed. He stood up to leave. "Now, is it safe for me to go, or should I call for backup?"

"Sorry, chief, we'll be good," muttered MacDonald. He stood up as well. "Kate, shall we get down to the High Street and see if we can scare up some wit-nesses who might have seen our dead piper before he became dead?"

"Sure," she answered, "but give me a minute. I wanted to ask Angus something."

"Meet you outside, then." Campbell strode away in Brown's wake.

Kate followed, stopping at the front desk where Angus sat almost hidden behind piles of books.

"Angus, when we were at Dunebrae Castle, we heard bagpipes playing in a tower, and Finn seemed to think it might have been . . . might have been . . ."

"A ghostie? Aye, probably was. Dunebrae has a coople a' them. Why d'ye ask?"

"Because there's no such"— she looked at the weathered face—"oh, never mind."

Angus smiled his beautiful smile. "Noo yer learnin', lass."

Kate was shaking her head in bemusement when she joined Jack MacDonald on the sidewalk. They fell into step and walked toward the High Street, neither saying a word.

"I think," Jack said as they stepped onto the bricked pedestrian crossing, "that we need to find out where Ross stationed himself on the day he died. You'll usually find the performers spaced along the walkway and down as far as that pub by the bridge. I say we split up and go in opposite directions, and then meet up back here." He indicated the edge of the walkway where Castle Street rounded the corner and became the High Street. Cars whizzed around the corner at high speed, barely slowing down before making the turn. Visibility was further hampered by the huge baroque Town Hall building that dominated the far corner and threw the roadway into shadow even on a sunny day.

MacDonald pointed toward the bridge. "I'll take this end, you do the tourist walkway. After all, you are one, maybe they'll relate to you." Without waiting for an answer, he turned and walked toward the river.

"Yes, boss," Kate muttered, and made her way up the street.

It wasn't difficult to narrow down the place where Hugh Ross had set up for business, even a month out. He seemed to be a favorite of many of the locals, who came out to listen to the performers during their lunch hour when the weather permitted.

"He came once every few weeks for a couple of days, and he was always right here," a woman wearing a red beret perched on spiky orange curls told her. "I like—liked—to come out and have my sandwich while I sat on that bench right there and listened. He was one of the best, poor man. Can't think why someone would want to hurt a piper; he was just making music."

"Did you notice anyone in particular hanging around, or following him when he left?" Kate asked her.

"Wasn't here when he left. Had to go back to work. Besides, everybody just hangs around, don't they, when the music's playing? They're listening." Her expression said that the American's questions were silly.

Kate sighed and thanked her for her help. She moved up the street, asking shop owners, tourists, and locals but got no further help for her persistence. *Well, at least I found out where he was stationed. Top that, Oscar the Grouch!* She reached the edge of the pedestrian walkway and stood in thought. She knew she wasn't being fair. MacDonald wasn't really being bossy; he had been polite if not friendly since they'd left the book shop, and he *was* the boss now that Brown was gone. Maybe she should try a little more patience.

"Look out!" a woman screamed, and things happened all at once. Kate heard the screech of tires and turned to see a large black sedan rounding the corner at high speed. Frozen in shock, she watched it miss the turn, jump the curb, and head directly at her where she stood on the edge of the sidewalk. Time slowed as the vehicle barreled onward. She could see the driver's horrified face suspended in the car's windshield like a fright mask. *He's out of control—he's going to hit me!*

And something did hit her. Jack MacDonald sprinted across the sidewalk and bowled into Kate, throwing them both out of the way and rolling her up against a bench as the car made the turn on two wheels. She cried out in pain as her arms scraped along the concrete and her head hit the hard wood of the bench. For long moments they lay clutching one another, allowing the adrenaline to drain out of their bodies. Kate could feel Jack's heart beating a frenzied rhythm in time with hers, could see his wide green eyes staring in shock. The perfect hair was falling onto his forehead, making him look like a small, frightened boy.

He saved me. He just saved my life. God, his eyes are gorgeous. Oh, dear.

*Love really is worth risking everything for.
And the trouble is, if you don't risk anything,
you risk even more.*

Erica Jong

SCOTLAND 1644

I t was time. Gawen MacPherson picked up his pipes, settled them on his shoulder, and waited for the signal. It came not a moment later. He took a deep breath, put the chanter reed to his mouth and began to play his clan into battle. The ceòl mòr, the great music of the Highland bagpipes, rose on the air. Its simple theme swelled, calling the men, stirring their hearts. As Clan Donald began to move across the uneven ground, the notes became more and more complex, louder and more frenzied. Dancing, swirling, the music became the men themselves, mirroring their courage and the grace of their movements on the battlefield. Every soul was touched, every man knew that victory was at hand. That was the gift of the piper to his brothers.

As dawn crept into the wild northland, the men surged forward at the call of their piper, moving as one, feeling invincible with the power of the music. They marched in time as they had done so many times, as their ancestors had done for centuries before them. Each soldier carried his hope for the future of the clan, his understanding of the Highlands code, and to a man they followed the pipes without hesitation.

Awakened by the blood-chilling call of the bagpipes, the Campbells were caught unprepared. Teams of men scattered to stations on the battlements, readying the great culverins, the cannons that belched out seven-pound balls at the rate of ten shots per hour. The Donalds had no fear of the great beasts; they had seen the like many times before and knew them for the ponderous frauds they were. The pipes swelled above the steady throb of the culverins, challenging their power.

Men poured out of the doors of the castle now, armed with broadswords and halbards, the giant battle-axes that could take a man's head off cleanly with a single swipe. But Clan Donald was ready. They drew their pistols, sighted carefully, and fired once, throwing the weapons to the ground to be collected later. Then like a horde of locusts, they swarmed over their opponents, cutting and stabbing with their dirks, the long blades finding tender flesh under arms, biting into necks, opening throats. And all the time Gawen stood at the center of his clan and played the great Highland pipes.

As they neared the castle walls, men emerged from the mist with scaling ladders which they threw against the ancient stone, climbing like monkeys and ducking the rocks thrown down at them from the parapet. Some fell, but most made it to the top and began pitched battles with the castle defenders.

In the end, the Campbells were forced to surrender and beg for their lives from their sworn enemy. They would claim that it was the surprise attack, the mist over the sea, and the failure of their great cannon that caused the defeat. But the Donalds knew the truth, and Gawen's clan gathered in their new great hall to toast their piper's health. Of all the modern weapons on the field that morning, the Highland Bagpipes and the ceòl mòr—the great music--had been the most effective.

The Campbell chief and his family sat at table with their conquerors and supped with them, watching as the Donalds ate their stores of food and drank their wine. On the morrow they would be turned out of the castle with all their men, but for tonight Highland chivalry demanded that they be treated with respect.

At the height of the celebration, Gawen was called to play. He chose the song his clan chief loved best, "Tiodhlac a 'Phìobaire"—"The Piper's Gift." As he played, his eye swept the crowd of men before him and his heart swelled with pride. And then his eyes met those of another, sitting with her family at the end of the high table. Daughter of the Campbell. As he looked into those astonishing blue eyes, a feeling he had never known before swept through him, and though he knew she was leaving this place and he would never see her again, Gawen MacPherson's heart was lost. Maybe this was the death he had foreseen. If so, he welcomed it with every fiber of his being.

The men of Clan Donald swore their piper had never played with such passion as he did this night.

CHAPTER 11

HAGGIS, NEEPS AND TATTIES

hat the hell?

Kate lay on the ground and stared up at Jack MacDonald's shocked face. There was a buzzing, the sound of a thousand insects, but the world had narrowed to the brilliant green eyes inches from her own. Somewhere in her consciousness she was aware of a warm body pressed against her, of a heartbeat that thrummed in rhythm with hers. It felt exactly right. It couldn't be—she knew she wasn't thinking straight, but she wanted this moment to go on for the rest of her life.

And then the world crashed in around them, and the spell was broken.

"Sir? Miss? Are you all right?"

"God, that crazy idiot nearly killed you!"

"Didn't even stop! What's this town coming to?"

"Do you need a doctor?"

Jack sprang to his feet, looking embarrassed. Kate sat up, and he reached out to pull her to her feet. She noticed that his hand was shaking—or was it hers?

"No, no, I'm fine," she told the concerned onlookers. "Just a few scrapes and a headache. I've had worse."

She looked down at her arm and saw a patch below the elbow where the skin had been rubbed off, leaving a raw and angry wound. A twin scrape decorated her other arm. Blood welled to the surface and ran down toward her wrist, bringing with it the knowledge of pain that was oddly comforting. A drum corps was practicing in her head, keeping time to the wild thumping of her heart. She hadn't felt so alive since Eddie died.

"Really," Kate assured the crowd of curious onlookers. "I'm all right."

Jack snorted. "Stop being brave; you look like hell. Come on." He hadn't let go of her hand, she noticed, and now he pulled her across the walkway and into the Poundland.

Poundland, she giggled, feeling the first signs of incipient hysteria. *Scottish for 'Dollar Store.'*

Jack found the first aid aisle and snatched up a roll of bandages, some sterile wipes, adhesive tape, and a bottle of something called "Paracetamol." He dragged her to the checkout, grabbing a bottle of water on the way, and then back out onto the High Street, heading for a bench a few feet away. Pushing her down on the seat, he knelt in front of her and studied her arm. Kate struggled to regain a modicum of control.

"Um, you can let go of my hand now," she said. "I got my first aid badge in Girl Scouts when I was twelve, and therefore I can patch myself up. Being a big girl and all." She could hear her voice shaking, giving the lie to her pronouncement.

It didn't matter anyway. Jack ignored her, moving to sit on the bench as he dumped out his purchases and began to sort through them. She felt laughter welling from some place deep inside and let it come, knowing that her hilarity was more a reaction to the shock she had just had than to the situation, which was not all that funny. He was really being quite chivalrous, in his own way, she observed in amusement. Who would've thought?

Jack narrowed his eyes and reached again for her arm, holding it out straight while he carefully swabbed the scrapes. She watched in silence as he wrapped the bandages around her arm and secured them with the tape. By the time he had finished the second side, Kate was shaking with suppressed laughter.

"Where did you get your medical degree?" she asked, trying to keep the giggles from bursting free. "The Archaeological Institute? I look like a mummy!" And now tears were rolling down her cheeks as she gave in to the hysteria and it plowed her under. She leaned forward and put her head on Jack's shoulder, clutching his shirtsleeves in white-knuckled fists as the events of the past few minutes flooded through her memory.

"I almost died!" she blubbered. "That maniac nearly killed me, and you—you—"

He clucked at her. "There, there, you're just having a bit of a reaction, it's perfectly normal. It's just the shock." It was the uncharacteristic kindness in his voice that brought her back to reality. Kate sat up straight, glaring at him through a watery haze.

"I *know* what it is!" she said tartly, pushing him away. "Stop treating me like a child!"

"Now who's being prickly, hmm?" He narrowed those lovely eyes again, but there was a new softness in them that threatened to melt her where she sat.

"Wait a minute," Kate said, widening her own brown eyes. "Is that *humor*? Are you being *funny*?" And then she went off into gales of laughter again.

He sighed and stood up, pulling her off the bench. "Come on. There's only one cure for shock in the Highlands. Haggis, Neeps, and Tatties. And whisky, of course."

Kate allowed herself to be pulled up Castle Street, past a kilt rental place, the ice cream shop, and Inverness Castle. Passers-by stared at the bandages decorating her arms, but Jack said nothing as he dragged her along, keeping a steady pace up the street. Well, Kate thought as she huffed along behind him, he *was* bossy, but for some reason she didn't feel like arguing with him right now. It had been so long since anyone had taken the lead, made the decisions for her, that she thought she might just go along with it for a while. It was probably the shock, but it felt different. It felt good. They could always resume hostilities later.

Just past the castle they came upon a pub called, appropriately, The Castle Tavern. Jack pulled Kate inside and deposited her in a booth in the corner, taking a seat across from her and regarding her with solemn eyes. In the pub's dim lighting those eyes were a soft grey-green, the color of moss in the woods back home.

She shook herself out of her trance and remembered what he had said.

"What's Haggis and Nips . . . ?"

"Haggis, Neeps, and Tatties," he said, his tone serious. "The most Scottish of Scottish dishes, and perfect for whatever ails ye." The waiter arrived and he ordered two plates. "And two Benromachs, quick. The lady's had a bit of a shock, aye?"

The Scots took their medicinal treatments seriously, Kate decided, as the whisky arrived in what seemed like seconds. A tiny amount of golden liquid in a short glass, with no ice. She'd seen Finn drink it like that, and even Aubrey, but she'd never been able to figure out why anyone would pay that much for such a little bit of alcohol.

"How did he know what you wanted in your drink?" Kate asked him.

Jack assumed an appalled expression. "There is only one way to drink whisky," he told her, enunciating his words carefully. His eyes were green lasers. "Neat. You do not. Put. Stuff. In whisky. Ruins it." He shook his head in dismay at her ignorance.

"But I don't like—" she caught the look on his face and stopped.

He nodded. "Right. Good lass."

She reached obediently for the glass, but Jack put a hand over it.

"There's a proper way to enjoy whisky," he told her.

She raised an eyebrow. "Aye?"

"Aye. First, you put your nose in the glass and take

a sniff." He demonstrated, and she nodded, following his example.

"Okay, done. Now what?"

"You might want to do that a few times, until you start to notice the notes."

"Notes? Like musical notes?"

"Like whisky notes, foolish girl. You might smell spices, or wood, or even chocolate depending on the type."

"Chocolate is good," Kate said, perking up.

"Keep your mouth open while you smell it, helps you to understand the whisky, ye ken?"

"Is there a point where you actually drink it, or do you just commune with it, discuss the weather and such?"

"Shut up. Then, you take a small sip and roll it around on your tongue. Go ahead."

She took a tiny sip. To her surprise, the whisky was good. Very good. It went down like ice cream without the cold, coating her throat with a delicious warmth.

"Some people like to chew it," Jack said helpfully.

"Oh, stop it, now you're just messing with me!"

"I do *not* mess about with whisky," he said, affronted. "Chewing just means you let it coat your entire tongue before you swallow it."

She tried to "chew" the next sip—and choked. Jack reached out and patted her on the back.

"You may not be ready for that step yet," he offered.

Kate took another sip. Her glass was almost empty. "But there's not very much of it, is there?" she complained.

Jack laughed. "Oh, there's enough, lass. And there's more in the bottle." He proved his point by ordering another dram. By the time the food arrived, Kate was feeling much better. About the accident, about her life, and especially about the company.

"Okay," she said, studying the concoction in front of her. "What's this stuff?" There were three mounds of mushy things, one brown, one green, and one white, formed into a flower shape. Nothing she could identify, although the white one looked a little like mashed potatoes. One could hope.

"Oh, no, you have to try it first, then I'll tell you. That's the rule."

She took a miniscule bite of the white mound. "Potatoes," she said happily.

"Tatties," he corrected. "Get going, that was easy."

Kate took a sip of whisky to fortify herself, and then tried the brown pile.

"Haggis?" she said hopefully. She'd had haggis every morning at Nessie's, and she was pretty sure she'd gotten that one right.

"Aye."

Taking a deep breath, she tried the green mound. "That's good!" she said in surprise. "Neeps? What are neeps?"

"Turnips," he answered with a triumphant grin.

"But I *hate* turnips!" She took another bite. "Amazing."

"Indeed. Haggis, Neeps, and Tatties. Cures everything." Jack dug into his own plate. "Whisky helps, of course."

The waiter cleared their empty plates, and they

sat, suddenly awkward in each other's company without the food to talk about.

"I was afraid, Kate," Jack said, breaking the silence. "I thought that car was going to hit you, and I was too slow. I didn't think I could move fast enough." His face had gone pale at the memory.

"I thought so too," she said. "I couldn't move at all. I saw him coming, and my feet were just stuck in place!" She shuddered. "You saved my life . . . thank you."

"You're welcome." His tone was ironic, but his eyes had darkened to a deep forest green. Kate was suddenly nervous.

"And you don't even like me," she said, trying to dispel the sudden tension with humor.

A hand came across the table and covered hers.

"I like you." His words were so low she could barely hear them.

"Um hum," she said, but she didn't remove her hand.

"I mean it. I do like you."

Kate stared at him, stupefied. "You *like* me? Well, to be honest, you have a funny way of showing it."

"I know. I'm sorry. You just make me crazy—I don't know why. I act like an idiot around you. I know you're not available, that you just lost your husband, and I shouldn't feel this way. I've tried so hard to leave you alone, but I can't. I don't know what to say, so I lash out. It's stupid. I'm stupid."

Kate's eyes were round. She grabbed for her whisky glass with the hand that wasn't covered by his and took a large swallow. Had this man just said he *liked* her? Had the great Jack MacDonald just called himself *stupid*?

She began to laugh. As he stared at her in bewilderment, she felt the mirth rise up in her and, aided by the whisky, let it spill out. She laughed until she began to hiccup.

A flush rose in Jack's face and his eyes narrowed. He tried to pull back his hand, but Kate grabbed it with both her own, struggling to speak around the bubbles of laughter.

"N-no," she choked, "I'm sorry! I'm not laughing at you. You're not stupid. It's just that I've realized something just now." She took a deep breath, fighting for control.

"Sister Ellen was right," she choked. "All this time, she had the answer. You were throwing rocks at me because you *liked* me!" And she went off in gales again.

The flush receded, although Jack MacDonald was looking at her as if he might be measuring her for a straitjacket. He shook his head in confusion. "I think that'll be your last dram of whisky, lass," he said.

So Kate told him about Catholic school in Harrington, and about how the nuns handled bullying. By the time Jack called for the bill, they were both laughing, and the conversation had returned to something approximating normal, although Kate wasn't sure she'd be able to walk home. Because that was where she was going. Straight home to Nessie's and to bed. She was going to sleep off that whisky and those tattie neep things, and this whole incredible discovery about Jack MacDonald, and when she woke up the world would stop turning so fast, and she could get off.

She stood up, swaying, and Jack put his arm around her to steady her.

"I'll be walking you home, lass," he said, and he maneuvered them around tables and out into the hazy sunshine and chilly air of a Scottish summer day.

"It's still daytime!" Kate said in wonder. So much had happened today, and it was still light out.

They walked up the street to the top of the hill and down the path to Nessie's as they had a month before, but this time when they got to her door Jack turned her to face him, and suddenly she was pressed up against him, and he was kissing her. Without allowing herself to think, she returned the kiss, her arms going around his neck and her fingers twining in his hair. She felt unsteady, and the whisky had only a little to do with it.

They broke apart, arms still wrapped around each other's waists, chests heaving. For a long minute they simply stared at each other, eyes wide with discovery and a new understanding.

"Don't throw any more rocks at me, okay?" Kate said, her voice husky.

"I won't," Jack promised. He smiled at her, and Kate thought that the sun felt a little warmer.

"I had a good time, today," he said finally. "Not so much the part where you almost got run over, but the rest of it."

She laughed. "Me too. We didn't get much work done, though."

"There's tomorrow," he shrugged.

"There is." Kate turned at a movement from the house behind them and saw the curtain fall back into place. She turned back, regarding him with pity.

"Your honor is ruined," she said. "The Owls are watching."

CHAPTER 12

IT'S IN THE BAG

e know it has something to do with the bagpipes."

"We have no proof of that! It's just a hunch."

"Well, Brown thinks it's a viable lead, and he's usually right. Why did they steal the man's pipes and leave the money? And the way it was just thrown all over him, with the money pouch. Almost like a taunt. You said yourself that was weird."

"Maybe they were trying to send a message to someone else. A colleague, a jealous rival. Someone who crossed them. That's the problem, it could be anything. I don't know!"

Jack raked his hands through his hair in frustration. They had been going round and round the subject for an hour, getting nowhere. Round and round, always ending up at the same place. Jack's normally perfect dark hair was standing on end. Kate pulled her thoughts out of the memory of her hands running through that hair as they had kissed yesterday and stood up.

She marched to the whiteboard that they had set up in the workroom, picked up the end of a string of yarn, and attached it with a piece of tape to the picture of Hugh Ross, their murdered bagpiper. She held the other end out.

"Pick something. We have to start somewhere, don't we? We're not getting any further just sitting here arguing."

Jack sat back. "Okay." It was grudging, but a start. "Follow the money."

Kate held other end of the yarn to a word card that read "money."

"Killed for his money? Maybe there was a bigger stash hidden in that case with the bagpipes?"

She wrote a question on another notecard and tacked it to the board. *What was in the bagpipes case?* She pinned the card to a space beside the photograph of Ross and stood back.

"Okay," Jack said again, his eyes fixed on the board. He stood up and tacked another piece of yarn to the picture of Ross. He stretched its other end to a picture of a pipe band that Angus had found for them in a magazine. He stood back, frowning, and Kate picked up on his thoughts. It was the only other connection they had, but it made no sense.

Ross had been in a pipe band. So what? Was someone in the band jealous, or angry? Had Ross crossed one of his bandmates somehow, betrayed him in a business venture or stolen something from him? Was his murder simple revenge? Payback for an affair with another band member's wife or girlfriend? Or was it somehow connected to Regicide? Brown had given them the slimmest of connections, a gossamer thread leading from the interception of drug carriers to the presence of pipe bands in close proximity. Was it just a coincidence? There was no way to know. Yet.

Brown's team in Edinburgh had already interviewed most of the band members, but none was able—or perhaps willing—to provide a clue. Ross had no enemies, was the standard response. Well, people who had no enemies usually didn't end up bleeding out on the street from a dagger wound, did they?

They had precious little information on Hugh Ross. Twenty-six years old. Born and schooled in Inverness, he'd excelled at the pipes from an early age, moving up in the ranks, playing for more and more prestigious bands. He had no family, no special girlfriend, although his open friendly face and outgoing manner seemed to attract young bagpipe groupies when he entertained on the High Street. Everyone they'd talked to sang his praises.

"He was a good lad, always ready to lend a hand. Smart in school, too."

"Didn't really care much about sports. It was always about the pipes with Hugh."

"Had a kind of fan following on the High Street, and some people followed the championships because of him."

"Always told people that someday he'd be rich

and famous, all from playin' the bagpipes. He really wanted to make it big, poor lad."

"He deserved better than t' be killed on the street and left there like yesterday's rubbish."

The responses were the norm when someone met with an untimely death; nobody wanted to speak ill of the dead. But the truth was, someone *had* wanted Ross dead, and from the look of it the killing had not been a random act of street violence. On the contrary—the money thrown onto his body indicated that it had been personal and vicious.

"Mmmm. Let's try something else." Kate moved the picture of Ross to the center of the board and placed the other pictures and word cards in a circle around it. She pinned the ends of several yarn pieces to the picture in the center, and then tacked the other end of one string to the picture of the pipe band.

Jack stared at the board, arms folded across his chest. "That's a better visual. But something's missing. He grabbed a card and scribbled *House of Munro Highlanders* on it. Then he strode to the board and tacked the card above the picture of the pipe band.

"What if it has to do with the actual band he was in, not just any pipe band? What if his bag wasn't the only one worth stealing?"

Kate's eyes widened. "Yes!" She grabbed another word card and wrote *Dunebrae Castle*, and then added it to the circle of cards around the picture of the murdered piper. She attached a string of yarn to the card, and then took another string and ran it from the castle card to the picture of the pipe band. Now there was a pathway between the dead piper, his band, and the castle. A castle in the north of Scotland, in the middle of the Scottish Highlands.

Through the thrumming of blood in her veins, Mulgrew's words from three months ago came back to her. *Regicide seems to be coming from Scotland. The Highlands, to be precise.* She looked at Jack. He was grinning at her.

"Good job, Kate." He stared at the board. "I think you're right. I'll bet it *is* all about the bagpipes—or at least about this particular piper. You're a natural with crime boards."

Kate flushed at the praise. She wasn't used to it, not from Jack MacDonald, but things had changed between them since yesterday, when he'd rescued her from the runaway car and taught her about whisky, and made her eat that Haggisy Neep stuff, and . . .

She shook herself back to Angus' workshop. *The case. Stick to the case.* But she couldn't help the smile that spread over her face.

"Morelli, my partner back in South Jersey, used to swear by crime boards. Most of the detectives in my department prefer to work on the computer. They thought that the board took up too much room and belonged on TV, but he insisted that the old-fash-ioned way was best. 'You see the picture much bet-ter,' he said, and that's how he taught me."

But Jack was not listening to her. His eyes were fixed on the board. "What if—?" his voice held sup-pressed excitement. He picked up a new card and drew a huge question mark on it. He put it at the very top of the board, above the circle of pictures.

"What might fit into a bagpipe case?" he asked. "Something small, but valuable enough to be killed for?"

"Jewels?" said Kate. "Money, of course." Her eyes met his. "Drugs."

Jack nodded. "Let's say there was something besides bagpipes in that case," he said. "It would have to be very small and very well hidden. Seems pretty brazen if he's carrying contraband of some kind. Could something have been hidden in the lining?" He paused to think, and shook his head. "But I don't think he'd leave the case in the street while he was performing if it carried something valuable. Seems kind of careless. It just doesn't make sense."

Angus waddled into the workroom.

"Someone's aut haur tae see ye. Says he foond somethin' 'at micht be important." He gave a gaellic snort. "Good lad, but probly wants a reward. Dae ye want heem?"

"Send him in," Jack told him. "Can't know less than we do already."

The man who came into the workroom was familiar, but Kate couldn't place him. She'd seen him somewhere, though, and very recently.

"Hello, sir. Hello, ma'am," he said. A sly grin eased across his face when he looked at Kate. "Hope you're feelin' a mite better."

Kate gawked at him, and then it came back and a slow flush crept up her neck and deposited itself in plain sight on her face. He was the bartender from the Castle Tavern. The one who had been so delighted to keep serving her wee drams of whisky until she could hardly walk. She glared at him, hearing a snort of laughter behind her.

"I'm fine. You have something for us, Mr.—?"

"Murray. Donal Murray. Well, sir—ma'am, I might. I heard you're lookin' into that murder a few nights ago?"

Kate and Jack said nothing. The man's smirk faded, and he shuffled his feet.

"Well, anyway, I was throwin' out the rubbish in the skip bin out back o' the pub this mornin', and I saw somethin' shiny under a whole lot o' junk. Thought it might be somethin', um, useful, if you get my meanin'. I know yer busy, but I thought it might be important."

"And why did you think it might be important to the police?" Jack's voice was soft. "And to us, in particular?"

"Well, I know Angus, ye see, an' I heard he's got detectives here lookin' into that murder. So when I found this . . . important thing, I thought I'd bring it to him, see if he agreed."

"Come, man, what is it? As you say, we have work to do."

The bartender flushed. "Right. Well then, here." He thrust a large object in their direction.

Jack and Kate looked at each other, shock mirrored on their faces.

It was a bagpipes case. Made of leather, old and well-traveled, but it had once been expensive, and the buckles on the straps were indeed shiny. Someone had valued this case.

"So, did I help?" The bartender's face was eager. "It's important, right? It's the one Hugh Ross had when he got hisself stabbed, isn't it?"

"You knew Hugh Ross?" Jack's voice was sharp.

"Oh, sure! He lived in town when he wasn't stayin' up at the castle. He came in lots o' nights after playin' on the High Street, just to relax before he went home. Came in that night he was killed, too."

His eyes widened. "Hell, I might o' been the last one t' see him!" Murray gave them a look of surprise, and then the excitement drained from his face and it turned a light shade of green as the realization set in. He gulped and stepped back.

"Thank you, Mr. Murray. You've been very helpful." Jack reached into his pants for his wallet and pulled out a fifty-pound note. "Here's something for your trouble, and I'd like you to keep your eyes and ears open. There might be more."

The man's face brightened. "Thank you, sir, thank you. I always wanted t' be in the polis . . . now I can tell my lass I sort o' am!" Donal Murray backed out of the room, his grin as wide as the doorway.

"That was a lot of money you gave him," Kate murmured.

"Well, if this is what it seems to be, it was worth every penny," Jack said.

They carried the case to the worktable and stood staring, almost afraid to open it. Their first big lead, really their only lead. It was made of black nylon, with a large zippered compartment and a canvas shoulder strap. Around the case was wrapped another canvas strap like a belt, with a shiny metal buckle, and a zipper went around the entire top flap. The case was old, but it had been lovingly cared for.

"Go ahead," Kate whispered, and Jack released the

strap and unzipped the case, his movements slow and deliberate.

The case was empty, except for a large black bag which lay, deflated, in its bottom.

"The killer took the pipes," Jack said softly. "He left the bag and took just the pipes. Now why the hell would he do that?"

"And what kind of pipes are worth killing for?" asked Kate.

Jack shrugged. "Well, we do know something more now." He pointed to the label inside a plastic window in the roof of the case. *Property of Hugh Ross* had been written on it in black ink.

They studied the case, went over every inch inside and out, but came up with nothing. The lining had not been tampered with. The case was empty except for the bag itself. The drone pipes were gone.

"We were thinking that something small might be concealed in a bagpipe case," Kate said, staring at the Reign board. "But now we have two possibilities. Either the killer removed the contraband from the case before he threw it in the Dumpster, or the *pipes* were what he really wanted. Because why else would he take them? And how can that even be? Nothing can be stored in the pipes themselves, can it? Aren't they kind of like flutes? All air and holes, right?"

"Could the pipes have belonged to someone else, and Hugh Ross stole them?" Jack was mumbling, talking more to himself than to Kate. "No, that's ridiculous, pipers on the level Hugh Ross was on have their own pipes, they'd never take someone else's! None of this makes any sense!" He raked his hands through his hair again, making it stand up on his head like a ferocious hedgehog.

Kate walked over to the coffee pot that Angus had thoughtfully provided for them. Pouring herself a cup of too-strong coffee, she wandered back to the display and stared at it. Then she tucked her hair back behind her ears and approached the mind map they had created only minutes before. She pulled the picture of Dunebrae Castle off the board and put it at the top, attaching a piece of yarn to the image. Rearranging the circle to form a line, she pinned the other end of the yarn to the picture of bagpipes. There was now a series of strings with a beginning and an ending. The sequence now read *Dunebrae Castle, Munro Highlanders, Bagpipes,* and *Hugh Ross.*

Kate looked at the picture of the piper, and followed the sequence in the other direction, from the bottom to the top of the board. That made more sense. If something was in those pipes, it had been put there before it had been given to Hugh Ross. And the place where Hugh and his fellow pipers, the House of Munro Highlanders, were trained and where their bagpipes were assembled, was Dunebrae Castle--home of Duncan Munro and probable honeymoon venue for Aubrey and Finn.

Jack MacDonald came over and stood beside her, studying the board.

"Fancy a wee trip to a castle?" he asked.

CHAPTER 13

HIGHLAND ROYALTY

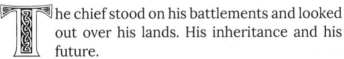he chief stood on his battlements and looked out over his lands. His inheritance and his future.

The castle had seen its share of violence over the years since the first stones were laid at the edge of the North Sea in the thirteenth century. Men had long fought to take it, but none had held the keep for long. Until now.

From where he stood on the parapet of his castle, the chief could see far out into the sea. He could imagine the men of clan Donald marching toward the castle they had left months before, secure in the knowledge that their own garrison held it for the return of their chief. He could see their banner flapping in the wind, the sign of a rampant cat rippling in the ceaseless wind. *Per mare per terras.* "By sea and by land." Ridiculous motto. What did it even mean?

His own clan's motto was "Dread God," so much more appropriate. Because he felt like a god. His kingdom was the world, his subjects all those weaklings who existed to serve him and add to his wealth.

He wasn't really the clan chief, not in the eyes of the law. A chief was the laird of the entire clan, and he was certainly not that. He was merely the custodian of a huge, ancient castle, a pile of stones that fought nature to keep itself from crumbling into the sea. He was chief in his own eyes only, but that was enough. His power was going to be greater than that of any chieftain in history.

He remembered the beginning, those first heady days after the castle had become his legacy. So much expectation! He had thought to live in splendor for the rest of his days in his keep at the edge of the sea. How foolish he had been then. Oh yes, he was inheriting a castle—along with its debts. He had discovered all too soon what it took to keep a pile like this running in the modern age. Taxes, heating, electricity, plumbing, the list went on. Not to mention landscaping and keeping the roof intact. He had begun like other castle-owners by allowing tours, and then by letting some of the rooms for weddings and conferences as so many in this modern age were forced to do, but those efforts were a drop in the bucket. Finally, he had faced the unthinkable—the castle was going to be lost to a different kind of invasion.

And then he had experienced a reversal of fortune, a serendipitous turn of events caused by a discovery on his own lands. His head groundskeeper had literally stumbled into a cave, falling through a cleft into a dark hole on the edge of the sea that had been concealed from human eyes by a rockfall centuries ago. The man had come back to report his finding to his boss, who had sent him back to explore. People loved caves, maybe they could add this one to the tour. Marketing was everything in tourism—it never stopped. The man with the edge was the one who survived.

After a time, he had noticed a change in the groundskeeper—subtle at first, but then unmistakable. Ordinarily cheerful and jovial, the man became truculent, abusive of his subordinates, ordering them to accomplish tasks beyond their job description or ability. His behavior became more and more bizarre until one day he challenged his employer and was fired. But it did not end there. The disgraced groundskeeper kept coming back, trespassing on the property and hiding himself in the cave, until one day he attacked one of the guards who had found him attempting to remove a bag from its interior. In self-defense, the guard had been forced to shoot and kill the crazed man.

The bag had been taken unopened to the chief, who found that it contained fungi of some kind. The strange discovery sent the castle's overseer himself to the cave, and there he found a strange fungus growing all over rocks in the deepest part of the cave where almost no light penetrated. It emitted a strange sort of green glow that was weirdly beautiful. When the bag was brought out of the cave and into the light, the fungus crumbled into a brownish powder, its eerie beauty gone.

Why had this man been so desperate to have a fungus that couldn't live outside the cave? The chief did not like mysteries, not on his land, so he took some samples back to the castle and began to study them. There was nothing unusual about the weird plant, nothing at all. He was about to give up, until he began to notice a change in his own attitude—a building of confidence, a persistent euphoria that was at odds with his normal character. He remembered the change in the groundskeeper's personality, and the pieces fell into place.

Unlike the unfortunate employee, the chief did not allow himself to fall under the spell of the strange plant. Instead, he chose a small group of his employees and—without their knowledge or consent—began to experiment on them. He added the crushed powder to the cigars he presented as thank-you gifts for their service, stirred it into the whisky served for special events. And the results verified his suspicions. The powder was a hallucinogen. Absorbed through the skin or ingested, it caused such happiness in his subjects—for that was what they were, after all—that their work production was increased by leaps and bounds. He experimented further and, over the next five years, learned exactly how much could be ingested before the negative effects of the substance began to emerge.

He understood that in time the removal of the substance caused distress in his subjects, and a panicked need for more. He practiced the amounts he dispersed until he knew how to create the perfect dose. He had discovered a new drug, and the ramifications of that discovery were astronomic. All he had to do was learn how to disperse his product to a larger public. The chief realized that he needed to educate himself on the methodology of the world of illicit drugs. His new world, the salvation of his empire. And he had to find allies who were not only greedy, but loyal only to him. A delicate balance.

One day, as he sat at the head of the huge dining table listening with half an ear as his latest crop of houseguests waxed poetic on the wonders of his castle, his attention was caught by something one of them said.

"We heard him," the young Englishwoman said, her eyes shining. "Landon and I. We're in the west tower wing, and last night we were in bed—um," she blushed as only a newlywed can.

Stupid cow, the chief thought, even as his face displayed a benign pleasure in her comments.

"Anyway," the woman went on eagerly, "we heard him. The ghost piper. It made the hair stand up on my neck, I'll tell you." She looked around the table at the other guests, who stared back with varying degrees of interest. The French and German couples with their rudimentary English seemed confused, while the American couple could barely contain their excitement. *This was what they had been promised. A Scottish castle with a real ghost! A bagpiping ghost!* And the piece fell into place with such a click that the chief wondered how his guests hadn't heard it.

Their host gave the group his standard patter about the history of the castle's ghosts, but his mind was whirring. As soon as he could do so without seeming rude, he excused himself and went to his rooms in the private wing of the castle, throwing himself into his armchair by the fire and staring into its flames, unseeing.

Bagpipes. The word sounded over and over in his brain. He knew he had it, the method for dispersal of his drug. He would give the powder to a select group of his employees and send them out to spread the new treasure to various parts of Europe. He would have to let some of his people in on a part of the secret, of course, but he already knew which of them possessed the necessary combination of loyalty and greed to serve his purpose. He would put middlemen in place, people who were only too eager to be in on the ground floor of a new venture like this. They would collect from his minions and pass the drug along to the dealers eager for new ways of appeasing the weak, and thus his product would find new parasites on the streets of Europe.

That had been two years ago. Because it took a miniscule amount of the drug to form the base of a dose on the street, and a hundred times that amount could be transported by one disciple, the new offering of evil to the world was soon the rage on the streets of Europe. And now, thanks to the growing popularity of his country's iconic symbol, he had reached America. His empire had placed a footprint in the New World, and his worries were over. He was no longer a mere chieftain: he was a king.

CHAPTER 14

WEDDING JITTERS

"I don't see how this is going to work, Jack."

"What? You want to dump me so soon before the wedding? I'm devastated."

"Shut up." Kate resisted the urge to punch him in the arm, but only because they were on that narrow winding road again and she didn't want to cause an accident.

"I mean, they've seen me. I was with Aubrey and Finn when they came up in March to see the place."

"So?" he shrugged. "They've seen you. You loved the castle so much when you toured it with your dear friends that you talked your beloved—that's me—into looking at it for our own honeymoon. It's perfect." He batted his eyelashes and gave her what was probably his idea of a loving smile. It looked more like a leer, and Kate laughed.

It *was* perfect, though. She already knew from her previous trip as a third wheel tag-a-long that the owner of the castle, a charming old gentleman named Duncan Munro, would insist on the full sales pitch. It would entail a tour of the castle and a bit of the grounds, and then a long interview in which Munro would grill his prospective clients on their Scottish forebears and financial wherewithal, while offering them a special tea that was supposedly imported from Timbuctu or some other exotic locale. She had to admit that she'd really liked the old man, despite his elitism.

She knew that she herself would never pass the Scot Test, but that wasn't a problem. Jack was a MacDonald. His ancestors had *owned* the place hundreds of years ago. She stifled a giggle at the thought of Jack MacDonald and Duncan Munro squaring off against each other, claymores at the ready to fight for their ancestral seat. They would be wearing their clans' kilts and screaming at each other in Gaelic. Jack would win, of course.

What's happening to me? she thought. *Is Scotland rubbing off on me, or am I channeling Aubrey's imagination?*

The ancestor conversation was just the owner's way of showing off his pride in his own heritage, she suspected. It wasn't to vet his guests as much as to add to the mystique of the castle. She remembered that there had been couples from more than one foreign country in the great room that she, Aubrey, and Finn had passed through on their tour, and she doubted that snobbery would be allowed to interfere with the collection of cold hard cash, whether it be in the form of pounds, dollars, euros, or yen.

No, Duncan Munro seemed to be exactly what he

portrayed. A Highlander whose family had managed to avoid the strangling poverty that had afflicted so many of his countrymen after Culloden and the clearances. One who was justified in his pride of clan and of his ancient home.

And his bagpipes. The trip was, after all, about the bagpipes. They hoped to get a look at the place where House of Munro Highlanders had their instruments made to order, where Hugh Ross might have had his particular set of pipes put together.

A little judicious research had yielded the information that House of Munro Highlanders had all their pipes made on-site. The drums were manufactured elsewhere and brought in, but this was where the band lived during championship season, where they practiced, and where the instruments were all stored between engagements. Ground zero. If something had been put into Ross's drone pipes, there was every likelihood that it had been done here.

"I just can't figure out how something could have been put into the drones without affecting the sound, and that's something that would never be allowed to happen," Jack mused, as he urged his ancient red Mini Cooper through the tortuous bends and hills of the northern Highlands. "I mean, Munro's band is consistent in its quality. How would any significant amount of contraband, whatever it might be, fit inside the pipes without threatening that?"

Kate sighed. "I know. Maybe we're on the wrong track altogether. Maybe Ross was just killed because he romanced the wrong bandmate's sweetheart or couldn't meet a gambling debt or something. But that still doesn't explain why they stole just his pipes and threw away the rest."

"No, it doesn't. And that's what we came to find out. So put on your most loving face for your dear fiancé, darling—because we're here." Jack pulled the Mini into a spot between a Porsche and a Citroën.

The huge front door was opened by a younger version of Duncan Munro, a handsome man in his late forties. Kate remembered him from her last visit as the owner's son, a charming, unaffected man. She'd liked him and his clear devotion to his family home.

"Welcome to Dunebrae," he said, smiling at them and extending his hand to Jack. "Hector Munro. My father is waiting for you in his office." He gave Kate a puzzled look but said nothing.

"Jack MacDonald, and this is my fianceé, Kate Bianchi. You have a lovely home, sir."

Hector's smile faltered for a second, and as quickly was back in place. "Thank you. I'm thrilled that you've considered us for the most important event in your lives." Hector Munro's smile was infectious. "I feel confident that you'll want to stay at Dunebrae after you've taken the tour. It really is the most marvelous place, and I should know. I grew up here." He winked at them.

He led them back to the sumptious office that Kate remembered from her last visit and took a seat next to his father. This time there were only two chairs in front of the great desk. *The personal touch*, she thought. *This place knows how to do things right.*

"Welcome, please make yourselves comfortable," Duncan Munro said, smiling that lovely smile that he had passed down to his son.

"Would you like a cup of tea? It's a special blend made just for Dunebrae, and we're rather proud of it." Without waiting for an answer, he rang a bell and a man dressed in tails and a bow tie entered and took the order.

Munro took a second look at Kate. "Do I know you?" he asked. "You look familiar."

"Yes, sir," she smiled back. "You have a good memory. I was here with my friends, Aubrey Cumming and Finn Cameron. They were visiting with the idea of spending their honeymoon here."

"Ahh, yes. Lovely couple. Then you probably know that they did indeed decide to stay with us. He's a piper, you know. Fine lad."

Kate chuckled to herself. She wasn't sure if Finn had been a "fine lad" before Munro had found out he played the bagpipes, but it was obvious that he now had cachet with this delightful old Scot. She caught Hector Munro's glance, and he winked and rolled his eyes almost imperceptibly.

"Yes, he is," she agreed loyally, "and a good one, too, or so Aubrey tells me. I'm sorry, I know next to nothing about bagpipes." She tried to look apologetic.

"And you, sir? Do you play?" Munro's voice was hopeful.

"I'm afraid not, sir. I was more into the drums in school."

"Oh yes, well, the drums are a fine instrument too. The House of Munro Highlanders, my own band, has some of the finest drummers in Scotland. They're not practicing today, or I'd take you around to hear them."

"I may not play myself, but there's not a Scotsman

worth his salt who hasn't heard of Munro's Highlanders, sir. The best, in my opinion."

Kate caught Jack's eye and blinked. *Don't lay it on too thick, dude.* He gave her a loving smile, and she succeeded with some difficulty in keeping her own eyes from rolling.

The waiter, or butler, or whatever the black-suited man was, returned with a tray on which sat an exquisite teapot and matching china cups. He poured, and they all took a moment to savor the aromatic brew.

"But back to what we were saying," Kate turned back to Duncan Munro, "I was so impressed when I visited here with Aubrey and Finn last February that I told Jack he had to see it for himself. She turned a brilliant smile on Jack, taking his hand and caressing his fingers. *I missed my calling. Should have been an actress.*

She felt his pulse quicken at her touch. He put his other hand on hers, squeezing a little harder than necessary. "My lass may be an American," he said, winking at Munro, "but she loves Scottish history, and especially castles. I trust her choice completely. But I wanted to see it for myself, and I must say she was spot on. Good call, darling."

"A MacDonald is always welcome at Dunebrae," said Duncan Munro. He smirked at a snort from Hector.

"My son has an issue with Clan MacDonald," he explained to Kate, "The Munros and the Campbells were allies, and therefore the MacDonalds were the enemy. But that was all long ago—for most of us." Duncan smiled affectionately at Hector, who grinned back at him and then at Jack. Apparently, this was a favorite topic of banter for father and son.

"You see," he went on, "Clan MacDonald held this castle against the Campbells for a while during the seventeenth century. Then the Campbells took it back and managed to keep it for about fifty years. Sometime in the early seventeen hundreds, the castle fell into disrepair and was sold to clan Munro, and we've had it ever since." He thickened his brogue, speaking to Jack but looking at Kate to assess the impact of his performance. "Ye willna be thinkin' o' tryin' to take it back now, will ye?"

Jack laughed. "No sir, my branch of the MacDonalds wouldn't be able to raise the necessary cash to buy the car park!"

"What exactly is it that you do, Mr. MacDonald?" *Ahh*, thought Kate, *here it comes*. Translated, his question meant, "can you afford to stay here?"

"I own a small software company out of Edinburgh," was the rehearsed answer. "We work on website design for a lot of the tour companies there and in the Highlands. We're thinking to expand, so I'm currently based in Inverness. It's where I met Kate," he said. "She was planning a tour, and I swept her off her feet. Didn't I, dear?" He beamed at her.

Kate was prepared with a spiel about her new career as an accountant, but she knew it was unlikely that she'd need to pull it out for Munro's inspection. His age and pedigree practically guaranteed that he would focus on Jack as the presumed head of their future household. For once, she didn't mind the chauvinism.

"Well, that's lovely. And now if you're ready, I think you should begin your tour," said Munro. "Hector's the best guide you could want," he said, turning them back over to the younger man. Kate and Jack thanked Duncan and rose to follow his son out of the office.

They were led through beautifully appointed rooms. The lighting was soft but not dim, hidden fixtures giving the effect of old-world candlelight but without the smoke and smell. The bedrooms were carpeted in a beautiful dark blue, green, and black tartan—Black Watch, Hector told them for Kate's benefit.

"It was the name given to the official tartan of six Highland companies formed after the first Jacobite risings in 1725 to patrol the Highlands. One each of the Munros, Frasers, and Grants and three of the Campbells."

"I thought the Frasers fought with the Jacobites," Kate said, recalling her favorite television program.

Hector Munro smiled at her. "Aye, they did, but that was in the Forty-five. Fraser of Lovat switched sides as often as some men change clothes, and it ultimately cost him his head." He smiled. "But the Munros stayed loyal to the Crown, which turned out to put us on the right side of history. We wouldn't have this castle if we'd supported the Jacobites, lass."

He led them into the great hall, where several couples sat in comfortable wing chairs before a blazing fireplace. Kate heard German and French, and even an accent that had to be from somewhere in the deep south of her own country. Dunebrae was a popular destination, and Hector had every right to be proud. Kate had seen every luxury a fairytale castle could provide. What she hadn't seen was an old woman dressed in a lavender gown from centuries ago, and she was surprised at the disappointment she felt.

The tour finished up without a sign of bagpipes or anything to do with a band. They had expected as much, assuming that the band trained away from the tourist areas and their workshop would be in a separate part of the castle. Like good little future newlyweds, they returned to the great hall murmuring to each other about the wonders of the castle, and as Munro turned to lead them back to the office, Jack made his prearranged move.

"Can you direct me to the toilets?" he asked Hector, adding to Kate, "I'll catch you up, darling."

"Through that hallway there," their host said. "Can you find your way back to the office?" Jack nodded and disappeared into the corridor. As soon as he was out of sight, he began to walk quickly toward a door he had seen earlier, one that must lead to a private part of the castle.

He was right. He slipped through the unlocked door and into another world. It was darker here, the lighting more mundane—all semblance of elegance gone. This was a working area, a place that tourists and guests were not privy to. Exactly what he wanted. No one seemed to be present at this time of the afternoon, and he proceeded unhindered past room after room, some with open doors showing boxes, furniture, and fixtures. No bagpipes.

Suddenly, a door opened near the end of the hall. Jack melted back into the shadows as a man emerged from the room carrying a set of bagpipes. He turned and entered a combination, locking the door behind him. *Bit of overkill for a music room. Are bagpipes that valuable? None of the other doors have locks like that.* His pulse quickened.

The man turned in the opposite direction and disappeared around a corner. Jack's time was up; he needed to get back to the main part of the castle or they'd send out a search party. But at least now he knew where the workroom might be.

He rejoined Munro and Kate and soon afterward they took their leave, promising to be in touch as soon as they'd made their decision.

"We can't come back," Kate said. "Aubrey said that they had to make their decision right away and put down a hefty down payment on their second visit. I don't think Brown is going to be too keen on funding our fake honeymoon, especially since we didn't find anything."

"Something's going on back there, why else is the bagpipe area locked up like the Royal Mint?" Jack said. "We have to get into that room!"

"I know, we can have Finn look," Kate said. "He and Aubrey have to come up to make their last payment soon. I'll bet Duncan Munro would be delighted to show Finn his bagpipe room, since he's such a *fine lad.*"

"I don't know. Finn's not a detective. I know he helped Brown before, but I'd hate to see him get into trouble when he's not trained for it. Ross was murdered, Kate."

"You're right. But we wouldn't be asking him to sneak around like you did. If he asks, and Munro won't bite, then there's no danger. And then we'll *know* that he's hiding something, because I can't imagine that old codger being able to resist showing off for another piper."

Jack gave her a worried look. What she said made sense, but he had a really bad feeling about this whole enterprise. His gut was telling him there was something fishy about Dunebrae Castle, although he had absolutely no proof it was anything other than the magnificent old keep it seemed to be.

"Sure," he said. "What could possibly go wrong?"

CHAPTER 15

WHISKY AND BULLETS GANG TOGETHER

t was raining. Of course it was, what else would it be doing in Scotland in July? Kate blinked the misty drizzle out of her eyes, tightening the cord that held the hood of her rain jacket in place, and looked around at the chaos that heralded the European Pipe Band Championships. She was freezing.

No one else seemed to mind the cold and damp. Adults stood with steaming cups of coffee, animated hands gesturing as they talked in melodious Scottish voices. Children ran around in their raincoats and wellies, jumping in puddles and sliding on the wet grass. All the members of the pipe bands were wearing the same style of long black caped raincoat to protect their kilts, but no one had a hood or hat.

The sounds of bagpipes being tuned rose on the air from all sides of the park, sounding to Kate's ear like the howls of a million dyspeptic hounds. Drums throbbed and droned in her head and sank into her soul. Kate could imagine the devil keeping time as all the demons of Hell wailed and pounded their homage. How did anybody ever stand this? She had a headache already.

Finn and Aubrey stood together off to the side, their heads together and arms around each other's waists. Under his black cape, Finn wore his performance kilt, and to Kate's eye he looked much as a Mackintosh piper might have in centuries past as he prepared to lead his clan into battle. Aubrey was dressed in jeans and a modern raincoat, but somehow she fit into the picture as if she were wearing a long gown and a—what did they call it in *Outlander*?—an arisaid, that was it. The tartan shawl that proclaimed a woman's allegiance to the clan. This was Aubrey's life now; she belonged here as she had never belonged in New Jersey. Kate felt a surge of affection and happiness for her friend.

She watched them for a while, entranced and somewhat envious of the love flowing between two of her favorite people. Aubrey had once told Kate that she had known Finn was the one last year at this very venue when all the pipers began to play at the same time. Listening to the horrific noise rising into the wet Highlands air, Kate tried to imagine the scene. It did indeed sound as if all the pipers in Scotland had shown up to play at the same time. *Is that what Aubrey was talking about in such glowing terms—this awful din? If that's romance in Scotland, I'll pass.* But she knew she was lying to herself. She'd had romance, she knew how it felt to be loved and to love in return. And she knew she wanted that feeling again.

As if she had conjured him with the word "romance," Jack MacDonald strode up and grinned at her. He was wearing a wheat-colored aran sweater and jeans, and a tweed flat cap covered that amazing dark hair. No raincoat. He looked edible. His green eyes sparkled at her as if he knew exactly what she was thinking.

"Isn't this great?"

"Um, yeah. Great."

"What do you like best so far?" He was giving her that smirk that made her want to hit him . . . or kiss him. *When did I become so violent? And why does it feel so good?*

"The . . . the rain?"

Jack burst out laughing. "You're such an American!" he chortled. "Did I tell you I played the drums in our school's pipe band?" He raised both hands and executed a complicated twirling motion in the air before swinging them down again to simulate the striking of a drum. Kate rolled her eyes.

"Seriously," he said. "Aren't the drums amazing? So dramatic, so primitive."

"*Your* drums are amazing," she said. "Want to know why?"

He gave her a narrow look. "No."

"Because they're quiet," she told him. "You are therefore my favorite drummer. And my favorite bagpiper is that kid over there." She pointed at a young boy, perhaps twelve or thirteen years old, who was silently fingering his pipes with his eyes closed as if committing a melody to memory.

"Humph!" Jack said. "Well, I can't be bothered to stand here trying to convince the uncultured, so let's go find something you *do* know about. Oh, look! There's the whisky tent, and they're serving Benromach, your favorite. The distillery is right here in Forres." He grabbed Kate's hand and pulled her toward the huge canvas tent with a large sign that read "Sample the best of the Highlands—Forres' own Speyside - Benromach."

A small crowd seemed to have put down permanent roots in front of the tent, although when they got closer Kate could see that the mob was moving in a slow circular motion in and out of the large tent, emerging holding tiny plastic cups the size of large thimbles. They would make short work of the contents, then join the line to go through again.

"In Scotland, free whisky is always popular," Jack said, urging her forward. "And since you're marrying a Scot, you're included."

"I am not marrying a Scot," she said automatically, but a strange feeling had lodged in her chest at his words.

Jack yanked her out of the line and around the side of the tent and then held both of her arms in a vise as he stared at her, his green eyes stormy.

"What kind of detective are you, anyway?" he hissed. "We're maintaining a cover, remember? Don't they teach anything in that backwater you come from?" The old Jack MacDonald was back, and suddenly the irritation broke free and took over.

Kate jerked her arm free and slapped him in the face. His eyes widened. He put his hand up to the place on his cheek that was already reddening in the shape of a handprint, and then he put both hands in his pockets as if he didn't trust himself not to hit her back if they were free. He backed up.

"I—I'm sorry!" Kate's face was redder than his. "I'm not like this, I'm not! You were right—I don't know why I did that!" Her throat thickened as she fought back tears.

He stepped closer to her again. "No, it's my fault. I'm sorry, I shouldn't have made fun of your country. Stay here," he ordered, and disappeared around the corner. When he returned, he had a sample dram of whisky in each hand.

"Looks like we just had our first fight as an engaged couple," Jack said, handing her a cup. "Let's celebrate."

Kate took the tiny cup and downed the whisky in one gulp. When she dared to look up, he was smiling at her.

"So, *darling*, shall we amble on over and find out where Munro's band is stationed?" She nodded, grateful at his willingness to move on, not trusting herself to speak. He took her hand. A shiver went through her at the touch, but she didn't pull away.

"One little thing first, *my love*," she looked at Jack from under her lashes. "I think I need one more wee dram, for fortification."

He grinned and fetched two more of the plastic cups, and they walked in silence toward the grove of trees where Finn had said Duncan Munro's pipe band was tuning up.

The House of Munro Highlanders had gathered behind a group of tents which offered such varied products as tweed bags, hats and scarves from the

Isle of Harris, tartan table runners and book covers, and Celtic silver jewelry.

"Oh, Jack, look!" Kate breathed in delight. "Knives!"

"On the way back. We have work to do."

"Yes, Dad," she said in a mockingly obedient voice.

"Look, their truck is parked next to that tent," Jack whispered. "Keep a lookout, I'm going to go have a peek. He disappeared in the direction of the trees and the band tent before she could tell him to be careful.

Without Jack there to distract her, Kate realized it had stopped raining. A weak sun was struggling to reach through the haze as the band members moved into a circular formation and began to practice. They were *very* good, even she could tell. The drummers were making those weird gestures that Jack had imitated, lifting their arms to the sky and then twirling their wrists so that the pom poms on the ends of their drumsticks danced in dizzying figure eight patterns, looking like the batons she had envied back in eighth grade. She saw out of the corner of her eye that Duncan Munro and two of his bagpipers had left the circle and were making their way toward the tent and the truck parked next to it.

Jack! She needed to warn him that someone was approaching, so he could make his escape before it was too late. He was probably in the tent now, poking through the pipes and the cases. There would be no way he could explain his presence if Duncan or his band members came upon him snooping through their things.

"Mr. Munro!" she squealed, sounding to her own ears like a pig running from an axe-wielding farmer, "I was hoping to see you here!" *God, could I be more lame?* But it worked. On the point of entering the tent, Munro and his pipers stopped and turned. Kate was too far away to see the wince that surely must have crossed his face at her shrill tone, but she knew it had to be there. Munro said something to the men with him and crossed to greet her where she stood by the craft tents. The two men waited, and Kate held her breath.

Had she given Jack enough warning to get out? She had no way of knowing, but the men stayed outside waiting for their captain, which was encouraging.

"Why Miss Bianchi, how wonderful of you to come to see the band!" Gracious as ever, Duncan Munro showed no evidence of annoyance at being interrupted.

"And where is your handsome fiancé? Have you lost him somewhere in the chaos?"

"Here you are, darling." Jack approached them from the direction of the whisky tent, two small cups in his hands. He winked at the band leader. "I believe we've made a whisky drinker out of my future wife, Mr. Munro."

Kate took the cup and sipped it, wondering how he had managed to come from the opposite direction of the tent. She had been watching. *How did he do that?* It was simply uncanny sometimes, the way he was able to be right where he needed to be, like when he'd been right there to push her out of the way of that car. Jack MacDonald, she was beginning to realize, was a man of many talents.

"He treats me too well," she said, batting her eyelashes at Jack.

"Well, it's our turn soon," Munro told them. "Why don't you find a place in the stands? You'll be able to see everything much better from up there." It was a dismissal, albeit a gracious one.

"Let's do that, darling," Kate gushed. "Good luck, Mr. Munro."

"A piper makes his own luck, my dear," said Munro, smiling that beautiful smile as he turned and made his way back toward the trees and the band members, who had stopped playing now and were beginning to form up into rows.

"You almost gave me a heart attack!" Kate hissed at Jack as they made their way back toward the parade grounds past the tents. "How did you get out of there without them seeing you? And did you find anything?"

"I have to have some secrets," he told her with a grin on his face. Then he sobered. "And no, found nothing. If something is being stashed in those pipes, it's happening at the castle. I guess we're going to have to recruit Finn, after all.

"Thanks for creating that diversion, though," he added. "While those dulcet tones won't win you a singing contest, you might have a future in hog calling." He laughed at the expression on her face, and then became serious. "There was nothing except what you'd expect to find in that tent. Drums, sticks, bagpipe cases. I guess this was a wasted trip. Ready to go?"

Kate was staring at him. No, she wasn't ready to go. She wanted to wander around the parade grounds and the craft booths, eat some haggisy things, and all right, yes, listen to some bagpipes. She wanted to continue holding Jack's hand as if they were a real couple.

"Shouldn't we at least listen to Finn's band?" she asked. "And I don't think they've run out of whisky in that tent yet."

He shrugged. "Sure, this day's done as far as work, anyway. Let's go buy you some Scottish souvenirs."

The t-shirt tent offered pithy sayings about what Scots might or might not wear under their kilts, pictures of thistle and Celtic symbols, and shirts with the European Pipe Band Championships logo. "Finn has that one," she said, pointing to a plain gray shirt with the words "Whisky and Bagpipes Gang Together." Think I'll buy you one."

"Don't you dare!" Jack growled. "I hate those stupid things!"

She put her hands up in surrender, and then gasped in delight. "There's the knife tent. I just want to look." Without waiting for him, she moved into the tent and was soon lost in the wonderful world of sharp weapons.

Jack leaned up against a tree at the edge of the concourse and watched her for a while, smiling at her childlike delight. *I'm going to buy her a sgian dubh of her own.* He wondered if it would be an appropriate gift, and if he should be buying her gifts so soon. There would be a time, though. He wanted very much to see how far this relationship could go. He wanted to see her beautiful brown eyes shine for him, run his fingers through those springy dark curls, wanted—

He grinned at his fantasy. He should get a picture

of this, capture her excitement so he could tease her about it later. He twisted away from the tree to reach for his phone, and as he did he heard a pop from somewhere behind him in the trees, felt a sharp pain in his shoulder, and looked down in surprise to see a spreading red stain on his jumper. Odd, where had that come from? He realized that his back was beginning to ache, and he couldn't move his left arm. He should think about this; it might be important.

"Help!" shouted a faraway female voice. "That man's bleeding! I think he's been shot!"

Shot? I'm a cop, I should look into that. In a minute, though. I think I'll just rest for a while.

And then Kate was there, huge-eyed, calling "Jack! Stay with me!" She was holding him, keeping the ground from coming up and hitting him in the face. That was nice of her. He put his head on her shoulder and closed his eyes, and the world went away.

The devil's agents may be of flesh and blood,
may they not?

Sir Arthur Conan Doyle

SCOTLAND 1644

They came at night.

Silent as cats, the Campbells placed their scaling ladders against the walls and climbed to the parapet of the castle. The long dirks made short work of the garrison's guard as they stood along the wall; one by one the defenders were dispatched by the cunning shadow men. Their weapons undrawn, the MacDonalds slipped to the stones, clutching at their throats as their life's blood poured out onto the parapet. The invaders had learned from their enemies, and there had always been stealth and deceit in the Campbells.

The intruders slithered like eels through the castle hallways they had been forced to abandon only a month ago, treading passages they knew well, finding and slaying the sleeping men as they lay dreaming. Their silence lasted until they reached the great hall, where the ten men not on duty or asleep nodded into their cups.

The MacDonald men were bored. Never able to be still for long, their chief had left a garrison of soldiers to hold the castle while he went further west to seek out other Royalists. He would return in six months, he had told them. He was also leaving his piper to entertain them as music would not be needed for a journey that did not involve battle.

The Clan MacDonald men were not used to an idle life, and they did not like it. Their attention began to waver in the long nights without challenge or women or adventure. At least they had music, food, and wine, and they made good use of the castle's stores. It had only been a month, they lamented over their trenchers, how were they going to last for five more?

Into their midst came a nightmare. Twelve men dressed in dark clothing broke their silence with bloodcurdling yells, brandishing the lethal Highland blades that knew so many ways to kill. Most of the men died in their seats, sliding boneless to the cold floors, their eyes fixed open in surprise at how easily they had been killed. One or two managed to stand, even to draw their weapons, but they lasted only a moment longer as there was nowhere to go, no escape from the killing blades. Not a single Campbell was touched. It was over in minutes.

Silence fell onto the hall, as the Campbell men realized that they had taken back their castle without a single casualty. Cheers broke out and the castle doors were thrown open to admit the rest of the victors. The Campbell followed with his family, looking around in satisfaction at the carnage in his hall. The corpses of the enemy would remain where they lay until morning, as a tribute to the clansmen who had killed them. Normally their heads would have been placed on pikes along the castle walls, but not this time. The chief of clan Campbell had something else planned for his enemy, and it would not do to show his hand too soon.

A Campbell warrior came forward to greet his master, pushing a young man before him.

"The piper, my lord. He is not a soldier, so we did not kill him with the others. That decision, of course, is up to you."

"No! Don't kill him! Hasn't there been enough killing?"

Gawen MacPherson's head came up at the words, uttered in a woman's voice. He was looking at the girl he had seen a month ago, the one he had thought never to see again. The one who had stolen his heart. She did not take her eyes off him.

The Campbell looked at his daughter and considered.

"What is your name, young man?"

"Gawen MacPherson, my lord." Gawen kept his voice low and even.

"Not Clan MacDonald, then," the Campbell murmured. His sharp eyes ranged over the piper for long moments, and then he spoke.

"My daughter speaks true. I will spare this man. He can entertain us now, and he will be given the respect due his station." He looked at Gawen, and then at his men. "But he is not to be trusted and will be watched until he proves himself worthy. That is my decision."

So, Gawen thought. She had saved his life. This was not the appointment with death that he had foreseen. Not yet. But it was coming, he knew it with a certainty that belied his escape from his clan's fate. He had seen it in the deepest recesses of his mind, and it was not far off.

CHAPTER 16

POINT OF CHANGE

amn! My arm hurts! What the hell?

Jack opened his eyes and squinted against the sharp light. No bagpipes, so he wasn't at the pipe band championships. He wasn't even outside—no rain. For a few minutes he lay still, trying to figure out where he was. The wall across from him was a soft blue, and there was a television mounted high on the wall. Hotel room? No, there were monitors on a cart next to his bed. A line crawled across the screen, undulating like a snake.

His bed. He was in a hospital bed, and there was an IV attached to his right hand. Kate was asleep in a chair next to the bed, curled up with her head on her arms. He could see the dark circles under her lashes, the streaks of dried tears on her face. He moved to reach out to her, and it all came back with a rush of pain. The crowd, the whine, the screams—Kate's frightened face.

He'd been shot! At the European Pipe Band championships in Forres. In the middle of a crowded festival, someone had shot him. It was crazy, and if he weren't lying here in a hospital—Raighmore, he guessed—he wouldn't have believed it. He examined this new knowledge again.

Someone had shot him, in broad daylight with people all around him. And that was just plain ridiculous. People didn't get shot in Scotland. Well, of course they did, but it was rare, and usually domestic, and never in a crowded area where the shooter might have been seen by any number of people! He sat up and yelped as an excruciating pain shot through his left arm.

"Damn it! *Ow!* Oh, shite!"

Kate's eyes flew open. She jumped to her feet and looked at him with a relief that was mixed with something else. "You're awake," she breathed. Her voice was tremulous, thick with emotion. "Thank God. I was a bit worried there for a while. You need to keep still. You lost a lot of blood, Jack." She sucked in her breath with an effort. "The doctor says you're incredibly lucky—the bullet nicked a blood vessel, but not an important one."

"It was important to *me*," Jack snarled. "It was *my* blood vessel, and it's my fucking arm, and it hurts!" His hair stood up all over his head, his pale face needed a shave, and he had dark circles under his eyes. His face was drawn with pain, but Kate wasn't thinking about that. She was thinking that he looked adorable with his stubbly visage and grumpy expression. She should have known Jack MacDonald would not be a model patient. A wide smile of relief and affection spread over her face. She didn't much care *what* he looked like, as long as he was alive.

"What are you grinning at?" he demanded. "You think this is funny, do you? Well, you just try it then, see how much *you* like it. Who the hell shot me, anyway? Did they get him?"

"He got away," said Kate. "Just blended into the crowd and disappeared. Witnesses said it was a tall thin man in a black leather jacket." She sighed. "Or a man of medium build wearing a black trench coat. His hair was black. Or red, or brown. Speaking of Brown, he's here," she added. "He's waiting for you to wake up and tell him how you managed to get yourself shot at a pipe band championship."

Jack narrowed his eyes. "Enjoying this, aren't you?"

"Hey!" Aubrey came in, with Finn behind her. She smiled at Jack in sympathy and then looked at Kate. "I know you don't like bagpipes much, Kate, but isn't this a little bit extreme? You could have just told Finn you didn't want to hear him play! You didn't have to go all postal and take it out on poor Jack. I apologize for my friend, Jack."

Kate laughed. "Shhh, don't give me away. He thinks a stranger shot him!"

Jack glared at both of them.

Next through the door was CI Brown. "Apparently hospital rules say you're not supposed to have more than two visitors at a time," he said, "but I brandished my badge and told the nurses you were a dangerous criminal who had to be watched very closely. So, how are you feeling?"

"It hurts," Jack muttered. "And no one seems to care."

"Quit yer whingin' an' greetin', laddie.Yoo're a Scot!" came a rough voice from the doorway. Angus waddled in, kilt flapping around his bony knees, and plunked a bottle on the bedside table.

"Angus, he can't have whisky!" Kate protested. "You'll kill him!"

"It's nae fur heem, lassie, it's fur th' rest o' us 'at haf tae pit up wi' heem!" the old man snorted. He gave Jack a fond look. "Jist yer wing, then? 'At's nae sae bad. Yoo'll be up in nae time at all. Ye were lucky."

"Och—!"

At an outraged gasp, they all turned to look at the doorway. A nurse came in, fisted her hands on her hips and gave them a furious look. "What is going on here? This man has been seriously injured! He's to have rest, not a party! Out, the lot of you!" She shooed everybody except Kate and Brown toward the door. "You can all sit in the waiting room until the doctor sees him." She picked up the bottle from the table. "Honestly!" Shoving it into Finn's hands, she assumed a battle stance next to Jack's bed until they had all left.

"Now, sir," she said to Brown. "I don't care who you are, you are not to tire this poor man out. Do you hear me?"

"Yes, ma'am," said Brown with a very good imitation of a penitent look.

The nurse plumped up Jack's pillow, took his vitals, and patted him on his good arm. "There, now, dearie, the doctor will be in as soon as he finishes his rounds. Try to get some rest. If you're in pain, just press that button." She glowered once more at Kate and Brown and swept out the door.

"I like her," said Jack.

Brown snorted and pulled the room's other chair up beside the bed. "Now, *dearie*, if you can bring yourself to concentrate on your job for a wee bit, I'd really appreciate the effort. You're still on the clock, after all. Do you think you can give some thought to a few rather mundane things? Like however did you get yourself into a situation where someone would take a potshot at you in such an unusual venue?"

"I know exactly why someone shot at me," Jack said, his voice calm. "They saw me hanging around the House of Munro's tent. Had to be that. There's no other possible reason, is there?"

"Well, there's your charming personality," Kate murmured, and grinned when he speared her with a narrow-eyed glare. She couldn't stop grinning. He was alive.

"Children?" Brown's voice was verging on dangerous. They returned to business.

"So, you didn't get out as fast as you thought, after all," Kate said after a moment. "And that means we must have been right about Munro. He's not as sweet and cuddly as he'd like us to believe." She put her chin in her hand. "But even if they saw you there, why would they take such a drastic step? Now they must know we're on to them!"

Brown intervened. "It seems likely that they thought you saw something worth killing for in that tent, Jack, but I think shooting you was a spur of the moment decision. The bullet they dug out of you was from a small caliber pocket gun—probably a Browning or a Colt. Not a very effective choice for an assassin, although it certainly would have done the job if it had gone in another inch to the right. More a weapon of opportunity, I'd say. The shooter saw his chance and took it, and he nearly succeeded. Can't you remember anything unusual?"

"Nothing." Jack sighed. "Maybe it'll come to me after I get out of this place, clean myself up and start to feel a bit more human. I just don't know. I'm sorry."

Brown waved his hand in dismissal. "No worries. You're my best man, Jack. If anyone can solve this mystery, it'll be you. Along with your intrepid deputy here, of course." He smiled at Kate. "I'm truly glad we have your help. We wouldn't be as far as we are without you two working so well as a team."

Kate blushed at the compliment and glanced at Jack. He was staring intently at her, his expression soft. Kate opened her mouth to say something, thought better of it, and nodded at Brown.

The door opened, and the doctor came in. "I'm going to have to ask you two to leave," he told Kate and the Chief Inspector, "just for a few minutes while I look over our brave boy here." Kate snickered and Jack impaled her with a frown. She and Brown left the room and rejoined Aubrey, Finn and Angus in the waiting room. They passed around the bottle of whisky, celebrating the outcome of this day. The five of them sat for a while in silence putting the pieces back together, each thinking about how close they had come to tragedy.

Jack was meant to die, the voice repeated endlessly in Kate's head. *If he hadn't moved—these people are deadly serious.* She felt the tears welling again at the thought of what the outcome might have been and swiped a hand across her face to blot them. She was on the job, and she had to get it together. *You chose this life, Bianchi. This was what you wanted, and you knew the risks.*

"Listen," said Brown, breaking into her thoughts and echoing her fears, "this puzzle is getting more and more mysterious, and also more dangerous. I wish I could spare another man to come up here and help you out, Kate, but at the moment they're all on the Regicide investigation in Edinburgh." He sighed. "They know the key is up here in the Highlands, but I have bosses too, and they don't think they can spare the manpower right now. Maybe after this they'll think again."

"But until then . . ." He looked at Finn and Aubrey. "Whatever happens, I don't want you two getting involved in any way." Finn opened his mouth and Brown put up a hand to stop him. "I know you put yourself at risk for me last year," he said, "and I didn't feel very good about it then, either. So not this time, understood?"

Brown's normally expressionless face twisted as if he'd eaten a lemon, and he sighed. "Angus here will be my point man until Jack is back on his feet"—Angus nodded, his lined face fierce—"but only because he won't listen to me anyway." Brown shook his head. "Hard-headed old Scot!" Angus beamed as if it was the highest compliment anyone could pay him, and Brown rolled his eyes in exasperation.

Finn tried again. "Well, Jack and Kate already mentioned that they could use a man of my skills and knowledge," he looked at Kate for support, "and it's not a bad idea. Aubrey and I have to go back up to Dunebrae to pay our final installment for the honeymoon anyway. I can ask Munro to show me his bagpipes and the wonderful workshop that turns out those championship instruments, and I'll look around and report anything odd I see. Simple."

"No, Finn," Kate shook her head, "that was before these creeps shot Jack. He's a trained detective and look what happened to him. I don't want anything to happen to you, too. Jack was lucky—we're almost positive they were trying to kill him. I'd never forgive myself if anything happened to you."

Aubrey took his hand, a worried look on her face. "I agree with Kate, darling. They *shot* Jack! It's too dangerous."

Brown stepped in. "Kate's right, Finn. I'm completely serious here. We'll just have to find some other way to find out what's going on up there at that castle. You are *not*"—he gave Finn a severe look—"to get involved, under any circumstances. Agreed?"

Finn nodded, looking a bit disappointed. "Agreed."

The doctor came into the waiting room and told them that Jack was going to be fine. "If he has a good night and there are no complications, he'll be able to go home tomorrow. I've given him something for the pain," he added, "and he's pretty sleepy. I don't think he'll be up for any more visitors for a while. Which one of you is Kate?" She raised her hand. "He's asking for you. Just a few minutes," he cautioned her. "He needs his rest."

Kate wasn't listening. She found it difficult to hide the elation those simple words had brought. *He's asking for me.* She bid the others good night and walked back to Jack's room, her heart dancing. Composing herself before opening the door, she peeked in and saw that he was staring at her. Waiting for her.

"Well, you took long enough," he said in a rough voice. "Come here and hold my hand. I think it might help with the pain."

She laughed, but crossed to sit next to the bed. He reached his good hand out and she took it, and before she stopped to think she kissed it. He grabbed her wrist and pulled her closer, and suddenly she was holding his face in her hands and kissing him as if her life depended on it, the tears running down her face and onto the white hospital sheets.

"You could have died, Jack," she whispered. "They *meant* for you to die. And I—I don't know what I would have done if you had." She laid her head on his chest, being careful not to disturb the side where the sling and bandages protected his shoulder. One or two inches closer, and he would have been gone. Like Eddie.

"But I didn't die, Kate. I'm right here and I'm not going anywhere. Do you believe me? I'm not going anywhere. Not without you." She raised her head to see him looking at her with eyes like bottomless pools, green and intense, and she knew it was more than the drugs. They had reached a turning point in their relationship. It had happened as she cradled his unconscious body and watched his blood seep through the handkerchief she had pressed to his shoulder, waiting in desperation for the ambulance to arrive.

Something had shifted in that moment, and now she wondered if she were ready for this, if she could learn to love again, to *feel* again. *Oh, hell, that ship has sailed, girl.* And then Jack pulled her down again and kissed her until she thought she might break with the desire to jump into that bed with him.

Sometime during the next few minutes, she felt his grip slacken on her hand. His eyes were drooping, the muscles in his face growing soft. Kate stood and watched him, still holding his hand in her own as those beautiful eyes closed and his breathing became even. After a few moments she laid his hand on the white hospital sheet and backed away. She needed to get back to Nessie's and get some sleep herself. It had been a very long day, and she had a lot to think about.

She turned to leave.

"Kate?" She turned back. His eyes were still closed.

"I love you," he whispered.

CHAPTER 17

NORTHERN HOSPITALITY

"I won't ask him, Aubrey, I promise." Finn grinned at his fiancé. "I know how your mind works. I promised Brown I wouldn't ask to see the bagpipes, and I won't. Probably won't even come up."

Aubrey eyed him suspiciously but said nothing. Having met Duncan Munro, she found it difficult to imagine that sweet old man as a criminal, but clearly CI Brown and Kate suspected him as a possible factor in Jack MacDonald's shooting, and they were the detectives. She was not going to let anyone mess with Finn's life. After finding him and almost screwing it up with her damned uncontrollable imagination, she was taking no chances with her man.

Her eyes softened as she studied his profile. His light brown hair fell onto his forehead as usual, just the way she liked it. His blue eyes were fixed on the road, but she knew how lost she could be when they were focused on her. And his lips . . .

Those lips curved into the lopsided smile she loved so much.

"What's going on in that head of yours, love?" he said, still focused on the hairpin turns. "I can feel the thoughts going around, and I'm scared."

Aubrey laughed. "You don't want to know. Or maybe you do, but if I told you your head would swell up and you wouldn't be able to get out of the car."

Finn pulled into a passing place to let an oncoming car pass and took the opportunity to lean over and deposit those wonderful lips on hers. Aubrey sighed as he removed them to pull out onto the road again. Her imagination was telling her that it was dangerous to love someone this much, but she ignored it because that was just stupid. She searched for a distraction.

"Finn, what do you think is going to happen with Kate and Jack? They seem to be getting *really* close lately, have you noticed?"

"Oh, aye, he's in love with her," Finn said. "I don't know if she knows it, but he is."

"But what about her?" Aubrey asked, as much to herself as to him. "Is she ready to move on? And is he the one to make it happen? Does she even know how he feels? They're always arguing, trying to one-up each other. Sometimes it seems as if they can't stand to be in the same room together!"

"Well, not everybody can be like us, darling." Finn glanced over at her and grinned. "For some people, arguing is a way of life, but it doesn't always mean that's bad. Both of them are opinionated, stubborn people, and neither is going to want to admit the attraction, but it's there."

He shuddered. "I wouldn't want to fall in love with Jack. He's a cranky bastard, but to each his own."

"Well, that's good. I feel much better knowing I don't have to compete with Jack for your affections." Aubrey laughed.

"Kate's not my type either," he went on, ignoring her. "Too focused, too practical. I love her to death—after all she did have my back with you—but *my* type is a woman who sees the magic in the world, who loves history and romance, who has blonde hair and gorgeous hazel eyes like a loch on a spring day. Come to think of it—a woman like you."

For a moment, Aubrey's eyes filled with tears. She wanted the best for Kate, but she knew without a doubt that *she* had won the grand prize. She was the luckiest woman in the world.

The Audi pulled into the Dunebrae Castle car park. It was one of only four cars there; the others probably belonged to honeymooners or other guests staying the week. The castle opened for tours at ten o'clock, and Munro had suggested they come early so he could give them his undivided attention. Such a nice man. He *couldn't* be what Kate and Brown suspected—it was impossible.

As before, they were met at the huge arched doorway of the castle by Munro's son, Hector. Aubrey remembered seeing a man in butler's livery the last time they were here, but heaven knew what his job was. He never seemed to be around except when tea was served. Of course, other than television Aubrey had no idea what butlers did, but it seemed that answering the door would be a part of the job.

Or were they just honored to receive the attentions of Duncan Munro's son because of his father's band? Maybe because of Finn's status as a piper they were considered special guests by the old man. He had certainly treated them with deference once he'd recognized a fellow bagpipe aficionado on his property, but she'd assumed that his charm was just a part of the castle's old-world hospitality.

Aubrey wondered about Hector's role in the running of the castle. He wasn't part of the pipe band, and Duncan had indicated that he had little interest in his father's passion. He had shown them around when they were here the last time and then left to lead another tour, so maybe that was his function here: while his father handled the guests who stayed in the sumptuous rooms on the second floor. He certainly seemed to know his stuff and seemed quite proud of his ancient home and its history.

Their tour had only included the ground floor, and it was restricted to this half of the castle. The other half was where the family lived and where the pipe band musicians stayed, and she knew that there were more floors above that were off limits. Aubrey kept her eyes open for any of the castle's purported ghosts, but nothing spectral made an appearance. Maybe they'd get to see more when they were actually staying here for their honeymoon. Finn would want to explore, to learn more about the ghosts that Hector seemed so proud of.

Today there would be no tour. They were here to

sign the paperwork for their honeymoon and make the final payment. They would sign and pay and leave, then be back on the road. That was the plan. If Duncan Munro was operating a human trafficking ring or selling porn out of his lush office, she didn't want to know about it because she didn't believe it for a minute. Even her wild imagination rebelled at the thought. Jack and CI Brown were just paranoid, and they'd sucked Kate into their world of intrigue and menace.

Hector deposited them in the lovely office where they had first met the owner of Dunebrae Castle and told them that his father would be with them shortly. "I have to get ready for the tours," he told them with a smile. "An innkeeper's job is never done." As he left, he held the door open for his father, just coming in. Dressed as before in a formal Prince Charlie jacket and tartan tie and kilt, Duncan Munro shook their hands and sat down behind his ship of a desk.

There was something different about him today, but Aubrey couldn't put her finger on it. She'd only met him once, but there was something about his eyes this time, a distracted air as if he wasn't entirely there with them.

Duncan blinked and smiled at them. "Well, this is it, then. You've decided to stay with us, and I think I can say with real satisfaction that it is the best choice you could have made. You'll be here for a week, which includes unlimited access to every part of the first two floors of the castle on this side. The doors are well-marked, so you won't have to worry about accidentally straying into the parts marked off for the family or the band, don't worry about that. The grounds are also at your disposal, and I know you'll love the gardens, Miss Cumming. There's horseback riding and skeet shooting, and you can even try your hand at fencing or falconry classes if you wish. Your happiness is our goal.

"I would caution you not to wander too close to the cliff edges nearest the sea," he said. "There is no access to the beach and only the bushes to keep you away from the edge. We don't want you to end your romantic time with us by a tragic fall onto the rocks."

He laughed loudly and gave an exaggerated wink. "Of course, you may choose not to leave your room at all."

Aubrey flushed, embarrassed. *Well, that was a bit inappropriate, coming from him.* Now that she noticed, Munro's eyes seemed bright. That was it, they seemed *too* bright, a bit unfocused. Was it possible he had been drinking, this early in the morning? Then he smiled his wonderful smile, and the sensation passed. Imagination again.

He produced the paperwork, they signed, and Finn wrote the check and passed it over. It was done; they could leave. Aubrey realized she'd been holding her breath.

"Mr. Cameron," Munro said, standing again. "I heard your band perform at the Europeans last month, and I was very much impressed."

"Thank you, sir, that means a lot coming from you," Finn said. "Of course, I listened to House of Munro as well, and if you can get any better, I don't know how."

The older man nodded acceptance of the compliment. "I was wondering," he hesitated, "if you'd like to see where the magic begins. I'd love to take you on a personal tour of the bagpiping facility here. It's not something the tourists get to see, but as you're an expert yourself I thought you might be interested. Your lovely fiancé could explore our wonderful library while she waits for you." His eyes glinted as they returned to Finn. "Perhaps you can take a practice session with the band one day while you're staying with us."

"Um, well . . ." Finn glanced at Aubrey. "I'd love to, but we do have to get back to Inverness."

Munro looked disappointed. "Of course, I understand." He looked so sad that Aubrey felt her heart go out to the old man. What could it hurt? Nothing could happen to Finn while she was right here waiting for him, could it? And he'd promised to avoid being a detective.

"Go ahead, darling. We have time to get back. I know you'd love the opportunity." She turned her smile on Munro. "If Finn was a teenager, he'd have a poster of The House of Munro Highlanders on his wall!"

Finn gave her a grateful smile. "Okay," he said to Duncan, "lead on!" They went off together through a side door of the office, and Aubrey sat for a moment by herself, wondering, *did I just do something noble or incredibly stupid?* She stood up and left the office, looking at her watch. *I'm giving him a half hour, and then I'm hunting him down*

Finn followed Duncan Munro through a darkened passage that ran behind the office and great hall. It was amazing, he thought, that these two worlds existed side by side, and no one who sat before the blazing fire in the ornate great hall was aware that this other part of the castle existed. Lit by utilitarian fluorescent lamps at intervals on the ceiling, the uncarpeted hallway was bare of any decoration. This was a place where things were done, not shown. The corridor seemed to go on forever.

Eventually, however, they reached a simple metal door with a very modern combination lock pad on it. This must be the door that Jack had seen, Finn thought to himself. Something very important had to be on the other side of such a protected door. All the other doors in the passageway were made of wood and none had keypads. His pulse quickened.

Munro entered a combination and the door swung open, and there, in front of him, was a piper's dream. Bagpipes filled all available surfaces, in every possible stage of construction. Bags lined the walls, and tables in the center were piled with chanters, blowipes and drones waiting for assembly. Bagpipe cases were stacked against the opposite wall, and a table containing polishing cloths, oil, sandpaper, and brushes stood in the far corner. Large metal canisters and tins stood at the back of the table. Finn turned to Munro, his eyes full of wonder.

"Do you make your pipes from scratch here?" he asked.

Munro smiled. "We do. We want to be in charge of the sound from the very beginning, and I think it's worked out well for us, don't you agree?"

Finn nodded, eyes shining. He ran his fingers over one of the drones, feeling its perfection. "It does indeed," he said. "Who is your drone maker?"

Munro's smile grew wider. "That's a secret," he said, holding his finger to his lips like a child. "Can't tell anyone."

Finn looked at him, suddenly wondering. What was wrong with the man's eyes? Was he showing signs of senility? He seemed a bit odd, unfocused. And then the sensation was gone. Finn shrugged. His imagination, probably. Time passed in a blur as he explored, noting the quality of workmanship and organization of the room. He wandered over toward the workbench in the corner. Odd. He'd never seen some of this stuff in a bagpipe maker's shop. Why did they need denatured alcohol? The table was littered with the residue of some kind of flakes. Curious, he reached to touch one.

"Dad?" Finn's eyes snapped to the door, where Hector Munro stood staring in surprise. Finn moved away from the table and back to the doorway of the room to stand beside Duncan Munro.

Hector smiled at his father. "Mr. Cameron's fiancé sent me to find him," he said, looking apologetically at Finn. "Sorry to interrupt, but when women send me on a mission, I don't hesitate."

"I don't blame you," said Finn, laughing. "Your father wanted me to see his workshop because I'm in a pipe band, too, as you know. It's quite an honor, a fantastic place."

Hector shrugged. "I suppose so. Not really my area." He ushered them out the door and waited while Duncan locked it behind them. As they walked back up the hallway, he dropped back to speak to Finn in a low voice. "My father sometimes forgets how much danger there can be down here, he's so used to it. I never come down myself. Dad's so proud of his band, he doesn't stop to think about insurance and liability." His smile was indulgent.

"Of course," Finn said. The men exchanged a smile as they passed along the corridor. In the great hall, he shook hands with both Munros, collected Aubrey from the library, and they took their leave. He was pretty sure he wouldn't be getting any more personal tours of the castle's secrets, and that was fine. At least he'd had a glimpse of the most wonderful bagpipes workshop he'd ever seen, and it was obvious that he was among the select few who had. In fact, he might be the *only* outsider who had ever been inside that room. It had been a rare gift, and one he would treasure.

CHAPTER 18

LOOSE ENDS

The chief sat in his sanctum, looking around at the tools of his trade, and felt his anger building. Nothing had changed, but he couldn't help feeling that it was all fraying, coming apart at the seams. For the first time he could sense the end, a day when he would have to abandon his project, clean house, and give up the riches that were pouring in—at least for a while. He had learned to trust his instincts, and his instincts were screaming at him that his enterprise was in danger.

Where had it started to go wrong? He had chosen his acolytes with such care, had trusted them with just enough information to make them think that each was his favorite. While they went about like puffed up roosters, thinking they had been given the keys to the kingdom, he had monitored their activity and set his spies on them. They were never alone, always watched when they left his sight. They knew they were under scrutiny because he had told them so. He told them it was for their own protection, and they bought it, the fools. It should have been enough to keep them loyal, or if not loyal, at least obedient.

No, he knew exactly where he had begun to lose control. The decay had begun with that damned Hugh Ross. One of the best pipers, Ross's pride in his music and in his status as a member of the best pipe band Scotland had seen in a generation should have guaranteed his loyalty, should have assured that he would do anything to stay in the inner circle. He knew he would be rich someday, wealthy beyond imagining. Why couldn't he have waited? Why had Ross betrayed his master for the promise of a lesser payment now? How could he, the man who knew greed more than anyone else and exploited it so well, have missed the signs of weakness in the man?

The chief paid his employees well. Even those who were not in on the secret made more than any other bagpipers in the trade, and they were well aware of their unique status. Most pipers in Scotland were weekend warriors, forced to take other jobs to pay the bills. For them piping was a hobby, sometimes an obsession to be sure, but rarely a career.

House of Munro Highlanders was the epitome of pipe band achievement. Auditions were held infrequently and crowded with every mid- to upper-level player in Scotland, all hoping to land a lucrative contract with the esteemed band. For those few chosen to join, the band became their life. They quit their regular jobs and moved to Dunebrae during the season. All of them were single. It was a condition of their employment, and none questioned it. There were no women in the band. And for a select few of those fortunate enough to be chosen, the ones invited after a trial period to join the inner circle, membership offered the reward of a lifetime.

But it had not been enough for Hugh Ross, and now the chief had to wonder. Were there more like him? Others who had cast their eyes outside the circle, who had embraced betrayal for a quick payout? He had no way of knowing, but he had ways of assuring that it wouldn't happen again. He had made sure that the piper's execution was public and ugly. The chief had wanted to send a message.

For most of the band, Ross's death was a tragic loss. The man had been well-liked, and his bandmates were shocked at the manner and brutality of his murder. These things just didn't happen in Scotland, they told each other. Bagpiping was a part of the fabric of the country, and to attack a piper seemed an obscenity.

But the inner circle knew the truth. The chief had made certain that the other band members, those deep in the enterprise, knew exactly why Ross had been killed. They understood that he had crossed the invisible line and had paid the ultimate price for his perfidy.

The assassin had returned the drone pipes to the castle. There was no evidence, nothing to point to Ross's profession or his band. The police were stymied as to why the piper had been sought out and stabbed in the very center of Inverness, the capital of the Highlands, but every single man in the inner circle knew why it had happened. It should have been enough.

The police had visited the castle to report that one of the pipers had been the victim of random violence. The chief had been shocked, saddened that Scotland was becoming a place where it was not safe to walk the streets at night. What was the world coming to? he had asked them, with tears in his eyes. And they had gone away satisfied, or so it had seemed.

But the police were not stupid, and they were not finished, the chief knew. His assassin had made a mistake in throwing away the bagpipe bag and case. He had made a further error with his dramatic gesture of throwing the man's money on top of his body. That detective Jack MacDonald had picked up on the oddities in Ross's murder and had realized it was not random violence.

The detective had made the connection to the band and thus to the castle, although he couldn't possibly know the secret of Ross's pipes. He and that American woman had shown up at the castle, posing as an engaged couple. How stupid did they think he was? What had they hoped to achieve with such a masquerade? He had pasted a smile on his face and gone along with the charade, when all he wanted was to plunge a dagger into the man's chest and watch the life drain out of his eyes.

He had sent them away empty-handed that time and thought to be rid of them. And then they had shown up again, nosing around the band's tent at the European Championships. Posing again as a loving couple, that American girl with her awful nasal accent thinking she was so clever, causing a distraction so her partner could search the tent.

And for what? There was nothing to be found. To any observer, House of Munro was exactly what it seemed, one of the premier pipe bands in the world. The special instruments were, to the naked eye, impossible to discern from the others.

But then the assassin had panicked and made his second mistake. He had shot MacDonald. Worse, the detective had survived, and now he suspected that House of Munro was hiding something, which meant that his focus was back on Dunebrae Castle.

The chief sighed. Perhaps it was time to let the assassin go. He had escaped into the crowds at the festival, and the eyewitness accounts were typical of the sheep-like mentality of the general public. Only one or two had come close to identifying him. But the police would keep looking and asking, and sooner or later they would find the man; it was inevitable. And he would talk. They all talked in the end.

It was obvious that MacDonald had sent the other one, that Cameron, to continue where he had left off. The chief did not believe in coincidences, had not survived in the shadow world this long by allowing himself to be played for a fool. But he had gone along with it, permitting the man to think he was special because he played the bagpipes, for God's sake. He had stroked Cameron's ego, allowing him to think he could be privy to the secrets of the band he so coveted, allowing him access to the room of his dreams, watching his hero worship. The fool.

Maybe the police had been skulking around even

before Ross's death. Yes, that had to be it. Cameron must have been involved in the investigation from the beginning, from way back in February when he had first called for an appointment to see the place. Perhaps he and that Cumming woman weren't engaged any more than MacDonald and his partner were. It was even possible that Cameron was a cop too, not a history professor as he had claimed. It didn't matter; he would handle it.

The list was growing longer, the risks greater, but he had it all in hand. The enterprise must not be permitted to falter, the inner circle could not be allowed to suspect the danger. He would have to be careful. He might have to shut down the operation for a while, but first he had to tie up the loose ends, and the first was the man who had committed the unforgivable sin of making a mistake. It was unfortunate. He had been a valuable tool, but other assassins could be bought, and it was time for a changing of the guard.

CHAPTER 19

CONNECTIONS

K ate stared at the Reign board. She'd been staring at it for ten minutes now, and absolutely nothing was coming to her. The pattern was the same: Dunebrae Castle, House of Munro Highlanders, Hugh Ross. The lines of yarn connecting the pitifully few pictures on the board stared back at her as if willing her to understand. *Here we are*, they said, *it should be obvious. You're a detective, so detect.*

They had added a picture of bagpipe drones printed out from an article on the internet, but the trail ended there. What was supposed to happen to those drones that Hugh had been carrying when he was killed? Was he meeting someone? But no, he'd seemed to be headed home to his rooming house, his body had been found in his own street. The drone pipes were the key—but to what?

Jack came over with two cups of coffee and stood next to her, staring at the board. He hadn't mentioned his "confession" in the hospital as he was drifting off to a drugged sleep, and she was damned if she would bring it up first. It occupied a warm place in her heart, hers alone, and she would treasure it until something else happened.

I love you. He *had* said that, hadn't he? Of course, he'd been well under the influence, almost out, and probably hadn't even known he was saying anything. He could have been talking to his mother for all she knew—but no, he'd said her name. He'd said *Kate.* She grinned.

"Are you finding something amusing on that board?" he asked, handing her a coffee. "I swear I can't figure out your idea of humor sometimes. Must be an American thing."

"Yes, we Americans think that smiling at least once a month is good for the soul. We should be more like you Scots, all dour and glum. I'll work on that." *There you go again, Bianchi, always ready with the sarcastic remark. He didn't mean anything by that comment. Get it together!* She peered at him over the rim of her cup, but he didn't seem angry. On the contrary, the green eyes glinted with humor.

"Aye, we Scots are dour indeed," he said, thickening his brogue. "Historically we havna been verra successful at things like war or sports, ye ken, so our outlook is a bit dark."

"How's the arm?" she asked him, eager to change the subject. Everything about Jack MacDonald was affecting her these days in odd, delicious ways, and the velvet brogue was close to having her jump him right here in front of the board.

She cleared her throat. "I mean, is it still sore?" It had been two weeks since the shooting. He still wore the sling most of the time, but he had admitted, reluctantly, that the pain had subsided to a dull ache. He was milking it for all it was worth, Kate thought with amusement—carrying those coffees was a huge step forward. For all his toughness, Jack was the absolute stereotype of the helpless male when he was injured. She couldn't wait until he got a cold.

"Well—"

Here it comes.

"—I guess it's getting better, but I still can't lift it higher than this." He demonstrated. "I don't know if I'll ever get complete range of motion back." He gave her a pitiful look and winced.

"Jack, you were *shot*. It takes time." Her voice took on a hint of exasperation. "Just think how much range of motion you'd have if you hadn't moved a second before that bullet was fired? And be glad it happened in Scotland—back home the guy wouldn't have been carrying a little pocket pistol. You'd be one big hole, and we wouldn't even be having this conversation."

"Humph. Your sympathy is astounding," he grumbled. "You're a hard woman, Kate Bianchi. Don't know why I keep you around."

"You keep me around because Brown said you have to . . . and because you love me."

Oh shit! Where did that come from? She kept her eyes fixed on the board until the tension had built to an unbearable level. A veritable crescendo of silence.

"I do." His voice was barely a whisper. Kate spun around and looked at him, her eyes wide.

"What?"

"I remember what I said, Kate. And I meant it." He was studying her face, waiting for her reaction.

"You—you *love* me? Me?"

"I know, hard to believe, right? You're not very lovable, of course, all prickly and mean, but there's something—"

"*I'm* prickly and mean? Why, you—you—"she caught his eye and began to laugh. "You drive me crazy, Jack MacDonald! One minute you act as if I'm the worst thing that ever happened to you and you want to pack me onto a plane back to the States, and then the next minute you tell me you love me! I'll never figure you out." She put her cup down on the table and wound her arms around his waist, being careful not to disturb the sling. She placed her lips on his. There was silence in the room for a long minute, and then she leaned back. "But I suppose I'll have to keep trying, because I think I'm starting to thaw a bit toward you, too."

Jack snorted. "Well, if that is a declaration of affection, I suppose it'll have to do." He pulled her in for another kiss.

A noise at the door to the office had them breaking apart, looking like two guilty schoolchildren.

"Oh, um, sorry!" Aubrey backed out of the open doorway.

"It's okay, Bree," laughed Kate. "Get back in here!"

Aubrey came in, followed by Angus. "Are you two busy? With work, I mean?"

"Never too busy for you, darling. What's up?"

"I need to talk to you. Both of you."

Curious, they allowed Aubrey to draw them over to the chairs around the worktable.

"Um, I may have a problem."

Angus waddled over, a militant look on his rugged face, and stood behind Aubrey as she slumped into the only comfortable chair. He loomed over her as if ready for battle.

That old man loves her like a daughter, Kate thought, looking at Angus's fierce face. He's here to protect her from something. She felt a surge of affection for the old Scot. *We all love Aubrey, Angus. You're not alone in this.*

"What's the matter, sweetheart?" Kate asked her, eyes narrowing at the look on Aubrey's tight face. "Not trouble with Finn, surely?"

"N-no, not trouble *with* Finn, more like trouble *for* him. I think I might have done something really stupid, Kate, and I think I ought to tell you about it so you can reassure me that it's all just my imagination." She took a deep shuddering breath. "It's about Dunebrae."

Kate pulled up a chair next to her friend. "What happened, darling?" She didn't like the ominous feeling that was crawling through her at that name.

"Well, you know how Finn promised not to ask to see where the bagpipes were made? And he didn't!" Her tone was firm. "It was my fault."

Aubrey told them about the trip to Dunebrae to sign the final papers, and about Duncan Munro's invitation to Finn to show him the inner sanctum of House of Munro Highlanders.

"And he tried to get out of it, just like he promised he would, but I could see how much he wanted to see that room, and I told him to go. I just didn't think you could possibly be right about that sweet old man!" She looked at Kate and Jack with tears in her eyes. "But now I'm worried that something might be wrong with him. I keep seeing his eyes when we were leaving, and they were all funny."

Jack and Kate exchanged glances. "Did Finn say anything about what he saw?" Jack asked.

"He didn't see anything. He just said that Hector—Duncan's son—came down and found them there, told him some stuff about insurance. But Finn said he was nice about it and made a joke about his father being nutty about bagpipes. Hector doesn't have anything to do with the pipe band, but Finn thought he seemed kind of worried about his father. Kept watching him out of the corner of his eye."

Jack exchanged another surreptitious look with Kate. "What did you mean when you said Duncan Munro's eyes were all funny, Aubrey?"

"Oh. Kind of vacant, like he wasn't really all there. Finn noticed it too—he told me. He thought there was something off about him that day. Like he was on something, kind of spacy." She looked up into Kate's face. "What if he's not what he should be, like you thought? Like senile or something?" Aubrey paused to think. "Only it didn't seem like that. He seemed to weave in and out of the conversation at times, and I don't remember getting that feeling the first time we were there."

She looked up at Jack, worry darkening her hazel eyes.

"What if I put Finn in some sort of trouble for being there? Finn says I'm just being silly, and he's probably right, but the thought of going back to that castle makes me nervous."

"Where's Finn now?" asked Kate, keeping her voice calm.

"He's running a full-day tour for Dougie's. Up on Skye. He's been putting in a lot of tour hours this summer, says he has to pay for that honeymoon." She laughed. "I hardly get to see him these days; when he's not on a tour he's practicing with his band for the Worlds. She grinned. "He'll be home in time for dinner, though. We're going to the Mustard Seed, where we had our first date.

"That's nice." Kate's voice was vague, as if she hadn't really heard what her friend was saying. "I don't want you to worry, Bree, but I'm glad you two are done with visits to that place for now. I'm sure Duncan Munro is fine; maybe he was just on some new kind of medication or something, He is pretty old."

Aubrey took a deep breath. "You're probably right. Finn always says my imagination scares him." Her laugh was shaky. "I wish now we hadn't been so quick to pick that place for our honeymoon, but Finn paid so much to stay there, and I don't want to spoil it for him."

She shrugged and stood up. "It's a month away, and I'm sure it'll be fine. So let's forget about it—I was just being stupid."

Angus eyed Aubrey. "Ur ye gonnae be aw reit, lass?"

"I am now. You three always make me feel better when my brain runs amok. Thanks." She gave Kate a fond look. "I'm going to work in the book shop until

Finn gets back. He's meeting me here. You two can get back to whatever ... *work* ... you were doing."

She grinned and went off to the shop with Angus, leaving Jack and Kate alone in the workroom again. For a time, neither said anything.

"I don't like it that Finn got involved either, Jack." Kate's voice was low. "And I definitely don't like it that both of them thought there was something wrong with Duncan Munro. Do you think he really could be on some sort of medication, like I said?"

Jack was looking into the distance, a look of intense concentration on his face. He turned to look at her. When he spoke, his words hung in the air between them as if they'd been pinned to the Reign board.

"Or ... drugs?"

Kate stared at him. Then she looked at the crime board. The cards were there, the pathway they had traced from Hugh Ross, murdered piper. Dunebrae Castle, House of Munro Highlanders, Ross, bagpipe drones. She picked up a blank card from the table and wrote a word on it, then tacked it over the question mark Jack had put at the top of the board.

Reign?

She turned to see him staring at the board. "I know it doesn't seem possible. How could drugs be concealed in a set of bagpipes? We know it's the drone pipes themselves that are the key, and they're just hollow tubes. But drugs are the only contraband that can take different forms, right? Pills, liquid, powder? It's the only thing that makes sense!" Her words tumbled over each other. Jack stared at her, green eyes shining with suppressed excitement.

"So," he said, voice almost a whisper, "what if Duncan Munro is smuggling drugs somehow, using his band as the carriers? And what if he's taking his own product? Lots of dealers do."

He sat down heavily. "This is all just guesswork, unless we can get into that workroom at Dunebrae and find some kind of proof." He went to the board and cleared the bottom corner of pictures and yarn strings, leaving their original circle in place. Picking up a marker, he wrote *Facts* on one side, and underlined it. Then he wrote WAG next to it and underlined that as well, finally drawing a vertical line between the two words.

"Let's list what we actually know."

Kate frowned. "What's WAG?" she asked.

"Wild-Ass Guesses," Jack grinned at her. "Well, they are. But some of them might pan out. Stop rolling your eyes." He turned back to the board.

"Okay, let's just go back to some good old-fashioned brainstorming. Throw some stuff out there. Things we know, things we think we might know. Possibilities."

"Hugh Ross was murdered," Kate said, and Jack wrote it under *Facts*. "His bagpipes were stolen." Jack added that under the piper's name.

"Just his drones were kept," he said, erasing *bagpipes* and writing *drone pipes*.

"Duncan Munro's on drugs."

"I think that's got to be a wild-ass guess," said Kate. "Funny eyes? No scientist is going to accept that as evidence."

Jack wrote *Munro on drugs?* under WAG.

"You were shot after being near the House of Munro tent," Kate said.

Jack slanted a glance at her and wrote, *JM horribly injured* on the board, ignoring Kate's snort of derision.

"Ross's drone pipes were made in the Dunebrae workshop," she said, and Jack added it to the facts.

"I'm putting 'drugs in pipes?' under WAG," Jack said. "It might be totally off base, but that's where gut feelings should go, and something's telling me that those damn pipes are the key to all this."

"What about Hector Munro and that stuff about insurance?" Kate asked. "Finn got the idea that Hector was surprised to see him there."

Jack shook his head. "I think that's a pretty normal reaction. Hector doesn't seem to have anything to do with the band or the championships, or even the workshop. He's enough to do being the tour guide for that place. Probably was just surprised to find a stranger on the family side of the castle. Though there might be something in the idea that he seemed worried about his father," he mused. "It would go along with what Finn and Aubrey picked up about Duncan's eyes."

"Well, you know what this means, right?" Kate said. We're going to have to go up there again, but this time I don't think we should let them know we're coming. I'd like to have a look around the outside of that place. I think we'll have to wait another week or so though, till your arm is out of that sling and your *horrible* injury is all better . . . poor baby.

"Wouldn't want your howls of pain to alert Munro to our presence," she added, and ducked as a marker flew by her head.

CHAPTER 20

THE DEVIL TO PAY

"Only two more weeks, and I'll be Mrs. Cameron!" Aubrey executed a little dance around the sitting room, to the delight of Gladys and the despair of Maxine.

"If you fall, you will be married from a wheelchair," she warned darkly.

"Leave her alone, she's happy," clucked Gladys. "It's going to be a beautiful wedding, dear, thank you so much for inviting us."

"Like I could get married without all of you," Aubrey laughed. "I might not even have found Finn if it weren't for your advice, remember?"

When she had first come to Inverness, nearly two years ago now, she had been sunk in despair over Marc Russo's betrayal and determined not to get involved with another man, maybe ever. In short order she'd met not one, but two lovely Scots who had vied for her attention, and for a while it seemed as if she might choose the one not named Fionnlagh Cameron. During a sticking point of confusion and misunderstanding, Gladys had stepped in and told her "Pick the one who makes you sing." And she had. It had always been Finn.

"Just think, Gladys, if I hadn't listened to you, I might have made the worst mistake of my life. I might have ended up with a criminal!"

"Oh, my dear, you should have more faith in yourself. You were never going to choose the wrong one. I just thought you needed a little shove in the right direction, that's all. You did give me a bit of a scare there, but just for a moment. We all knew you had sense."

Aubrey skipped over and hugged the older woman, who blushed and patted her corkscrew curls. Even Ronald was smiling, although he looked somewhat surprised at the unfamiliar feeling. Maxine smiled and swung her elegant foot, keeping time to the music in her head.

"So, where's the groom today?" Gladys asked. "Off somewhere dancing, too, I expect. Never saw a couple so perfect for each other, and you had to cross an ocean to meet. The world is an amazing place, isn't it, dear?"

Aubrey was remembering. From the first time Finn had stepped into the sitting room to wait for Aubrey so they could go out to dinner, the Owls had decided he was the one for her. He had survived, even been amused by the usual grilling that no one escaped in this house and had thereby earned their enduring affection. They had referred to him thereafter as "her lad," refusing to listen to any denials or protestations.

Connor MacConnach had had no such reception. When *he* had picked her up for their first date, he'd rushed her out of the house, his face pale, and declared that they were a load of ghouls. Even Nessie had not trusted Connor, although she was too polite to say so. Aubrey should have known right there and then which way the wind blew.

She pulled herself out of the past to answer Gladys. "He's doing a half-day tour for Dougie's, which is good because I'm picking Fitz up at the airport this afternoon. Kate's going with me. Finn and Jack will meet us back here, and we're all going out to dinner. Take care of them if they get here first, will you?"

Gladys clapped her hands. "Of course. We'll give them some tips on how to keep you girls content." She winked at Aubrey, who groaned and went upstairs to get changed.

Kate met her on the landing wearing her new favorite t-shirt, navy blue with a row of sgian dubhs across the front. Aubrey cocked an eyebrow at it.

"Jack gave it to me," Kate said, pushing past her friend.

"Hmm," said Aubrey. As she walked down the staircase behind Kate, she caught Glady's eye. The Englishwoman winked at her and began humming "My Bonnie Lies Over the Ocean." Maxine smiled, her foot keeping time. Poor Kate, Aubrey thought. The Owls had decided.

As they negotiated the myriad roundabouts that peppered the Scottish motorways, Aubrey slanted a look sideways at her friend.

"What are you going to tell Fitz about Jack?"

"I don't know what you mean. What about Jack?"

"Okay, if that's the way you want to play it, I'll go along," Aubrey said with a snicker.

"There's nothing going on between Jack and me," Kate insisted, her eyes glued on the road ahead.

"Okay."

"Oh, stop it! I'm not ready for a relationship. It's too soon."

"Then why did your voice just go up at the end of that sentence, as if you don't believe what you're saying?"

"It didn't."

"Okay."

"Oh, shut up!" Kate snarled. "Jack and I are just friends. I didn't come to Scotland to find a replacement for Eddie!"

Aubrey's voice was mild. "There is no replacement for Eddie, darling. He'll always occupy a space in your heart. But that doesn't mean you have to join a nunnery. It's been seven months, Kate—no one would fault you for letting yourself live again. Least of all Eddie. And I get the impression that Jack thinks you're a little more than 'just friends.'"

"He's a grouch and a dictator!"

"Then you're perfect for each other," Aubrey laughed. She sneaked a look at Kate's red face and put up a hand in surrender. "All right, I'll stop. But don't think for a minute that Fitz isn't going to worm your dirty little secret out of you!"

"Shut *up!*"

Finn pulled into the car park at Dunebrae Castle, killed the motor, and sat for a minute studying the colossal structure at the top of the bluff. His was the only car in the park, which seemed odd. For some reason he couldn't define, he didn't want to get out of the Audi. He wasn't given to fancy, that was Aubrey's territory, but he'd seen and felt his share of strange things and he couldn't deny that something was niggling at his mind.

They had called as he was checking out at Dougie's and asked him to come up to sign one last document to reserve their spot at the castle for the honeymoon in two weeks. It was something new from the government and couldn't be ignored; they were so sorry, but could he come up right away and take care of it? No, his fiancé didn't need to come with him, it would only take a few minutes.

Dunebrae was only an hour away. Finn knew he could make it easily and be back and changed in plenty of time for dinner, but it was annoying. Sitting here in the empty car park, every nerve ending in his body was telling him to turn the car around and just forget the whole thing. But that was ridiculous—he'd already paid in a lot of money for this honeymoon, and anyway he was here now.

He shrugged off the feeling, pulled out his phone to call Aubrey and let her know about the last-minute change of plans, and saw that the battery was at five percent. Better wait a few minutes and call her on the way home; she wasn't expecting him until five anyway. Maybe they could lend him a charging cord at the castle. He powered off the phone to conserve the little juice that was left, hauled himself out of the car and walked up the narrow, winding lane to the entrance, impatient to get this over with. He raised his hand to the ancient ornate knocker, but before he touched it, the door swung inward and Duncan Munro stood there, smiling.

"Welcome back, Mr. Cameron! Sorry to drag you up here again like this, but it seems we forgot this one last paper that must be signed before you take over the castle for your dream honeymoon. It's new, didn't even know about it myself. For the insurance— just a nuisance, really."

The insurance again! And I couldn't sign it in two weeks when we come to stay? Are they afraid we'll try to wiggle out of the commitment? Besides, it's more than just a nuisance. Finn shook off his irritation and smiled, following Munro into the foyer. Didn't do to be whingeing at his landlord right before the honeymoon. He followed Duncan into the great room. A fire was roaring in the huge fireplace.

"Please, just have a seat. We have no guests this week; we always block out the week before the Worlds to get ready. But of course, you understand."

The Worlds. Of course. That explained the lack of vehicles in the car park. Finn's own band had ramped up practices in the last two weeks to prepare for the World Championships that would begin on Friday next. The simple explanation eased the tension he'd been feeling.

Duncan Munro was moving away. "I'll just go see if my secretary has that paperwork ready. Would you like a whisky while you wait? Or tea?"

"Just tea, thanks. Have to drive home, you know."

Munro chuckled. "Right you are. We forget, living way up here, that others have a drive to get here. It's why the band lives at the castle during the season. Tea it is, then. Our special blend." He moved off into the hallway to the kitchens, leaving Finn alone in the cavernous space.

The chair was beyond comfortable, the fire was warm, and he found himself fighting fatigue as he stared into its depths. The tea arrived moments later, steeping in a gorgeous antique pot with thick gold trim that probably cost more than he made in a year. Munro poured it into a matching china teacup, handed it to Finn, and sat down across from him, crossing one leg over the other. "So, I have to tell you again how excited I am that you've chosen Dunebrae for your honeymoon. It's lovely having the chance to meet a piper like myself."

"Not like you," said Finn, smiling as he sipped the tea. He remembered the brew from his previous visits. Darjeeling? He wasn't sure, but it was wonderful. "I'm not quite in your class."

"Well, House of Munro is the best, I agree, but I may be a bit biased there." Munro smiled. "I'm proud of what we've accomplished. I seldom get to talk bagpiping with another expert, outside of the competitions. He gave Finn that beautiful smile. "I'll probably be guilty of talking your ear off while you're here." He laughed. "Be careful not to let me take up too much of your time, I'm sure you've noticed I can get carried away about my favorite subject. It *is* your honeymoon, after all, so feel free to tell me to go away." Munro grinned. "It can be a lonely life, running a castle, in spite of the guests and my band. We're very isolated here."

"I'm not sure I would want to live so far away from civilization, myself," Finn mused. "But the trade-off is that you are king of your own castle. You're very fortunate to live in such a lovely place, Mr. Munro." He sipped his tea. The man's eyes seemed normal today, and Finn relaxed. Only a trick of the lighting before, probably. He'd be able to reassure Aubrey.

"Duncan, please. If you and your lovely fiancé are to be staying here, we should be on a first-name basis, don't you think? What is her name again?"

"Aubrey. And please call me Finn." Duncan Munro's face seemed to be wavering a little in the light of the fire. *I really am tired!*

"And what do you do when you're not piping, Finn?"

"I'm a professor of Scottish history at the college in Inverness," Finn answered him, wondering how long this conversation was going to go on before he could sign that paper. He'd answered this question on their first visit, after all.

Duncan Munro chuckled. "Scottish history! You probably know more about castles like mine than I do. Are you enjoying the tea?"

"I am. I don't believe I've ever tasted anything like it before." Finn blinked. "I don't mean to be rude, but do you think it will be much longer before I can sign that paper? I have to meet my fiancé and her friends for dinner tonight, and I'd like to get home while it's still light."

"Oh, of course! I understand. I'll just go and check on it now. Wait right here. I tend to forget everything else when I start talking, and I have to remind myself

I have a castle to run." Munro smiled at Finn. "Won't be long now. Enjoy your tea. We have it specially prepared just for Dunebrae; can't get it anywhere else. Except the gift shop, of course." He chuckled and left.

What's with the damn tea? It was wonderful, but he just wanted to get that paper signed and get out of here. He sipped, staring into the fire. His head was beginning to feel muzzy from the heat, and he pushed himself up out of the chair, swaying a little as he regained his feet. *I just need to splash some cold water on my face. I remember there being a toilet off this room—this way I think.*

Finding a doorway that he thought he remembered, Finn made his way into the corridor and turned right. It wasn't the way he had passed before, and within minutes he knew he was lost. *Damn, this is embarrassing!* Turning around to find his way back, he lost his balance and stumbled into the wall. Leaning against the cool surface, he tried to get his bearings. He didn't remember the hallway being so dark before. He continued down the passage, determined to find his way back to the great hall. To hell with the document, he was leaving. He didn't feel well at all. He stopped and bent over, bracing his hands on his knees. *I think I'm going to be sick.*

And then other hands were supporting him, helping him along the darkening passageway. Grateful, he tried to speak. *Call Aubrey.* But the words were only in his head. The hands held him tight—more than one set of hands, he realized. They had him by the elbows and wrists, in an iron grip that kept him upright, and now it didn't feel so much like help. Finn swayed in the firm hold and his head dipped forward. He couldn't seem to hold it up, was having trouble even keeping his eyes open.

As if from a great distance, he thought he heard a voice. Cold, impatient. Familiar.

"He's almost out. The room is ready, the two of you take him up and secure him—wait, I need his car keys and cell phone first."

"Right, boss."

"Nuuhh . . ." Finn's thoughts ran together, then flew apart. He was weightless. Floating, held up only by the arms now locked around his chest. Hands patted him, exploring, and he thought he heard a faint jingle, quickly gone. As the shadows in the hallway closed in, his feet were lifted off the ground and his body hoisted into the air. He grasped for the echo of a thought, but it drifted away like a wraith. His eyes closed and his head fell back. The darkness swept in and claimed him as his body relinquished its hold on consciousness, relaxing into the strong arms that carried him away up the ancient stone staircase.

Murderers are not monsters, they're men.
And that's the most frightening thing about them.

Alice Sebold

SCOTLAND 1644

Her name was Caitriona, and she was the most beautiful woman Gawen had ever seen. Truth be told, he had not seen many, besides his three sisters and his mother, but he was sure that none could match his lady for her innocent beauty or her purity of spirit.

His lady—his love. He dared to call her that in his own mind because he knew she felt the same for him. It was a miracle, their finding each other in a world of war and death driven by the greed of men. In the five months since his garrison had been killed and he had become the Campbell piper, he and Caitriona had spent every moment they could find together, learning each other's hearts and minds, finding love in each other's arms.

It was a dangerous game they played. He knew he was watched and that he would never be allowed to have her for his own. The Campbell had no sons, and his daughter was destined for an alliance that would increase the clan's wealth and prestige in the Highlands. A piper from a minor clan had no place in his plans, but it amused the chieftain to allow his daughter her friendship with the piper, as long as she remained pure. Her mother or one of his men was always near to see to that.

What her mother and her wardens did not know was that they had found ways to be together, and a place that guaranteed secrecy from prying eyes and wagging tongues. No one seeing them walking innocently along the cliff tops, deep in conversation, could guess that they had devised a lover's nest for themselves . . . in a cave.

It was their secret, theirs alone. While practicing his pipes one day on the bluff above the sea, Gawen had fallen into a crevice and been wedged, unable to free himself. Sure that this was the death he had foreseen, he was surprised when the earth beneath him gave way and he tumbled into a huge hole which led ever downward and into a larger cavern before opening out at the edge of the sea. He had told no one of his find, no one but Caitriona, and together they had made a nest for themselves, away from cold and wind and watchers. They had placed branches over the cleft in the bluff, so that no one could stumble onto their secret and betray them.

Caitriona's maid Sorcha was her confidante and ally. A born romantic, she loved her mistress like a sister and relished the danger in her illicit affair. To the maid, the piper was perfect for her lady. She had never seen her mistress so happy, and that was enough to assure her complicity. Many were the days when Sorcha reported that Mistress Campbell's headaches were too severe to allow her out of bed, or that she and Mistress Campbell would be going berry-picking and would be back in time for dinner. For watchers, the maid thought, the wardens were decidedly haphazard at their duty. She herself would never fall for such a transparent lie, but their stupidity was not her problem.

When Gawen and Caitriona lay together, they imagined a life far different from the one fate had decreed for them. They would escape, would melt into the Highlands, and live a simple life, far from the machinations of others. He would put away his pipes and live the life of a farmer, like his father before him. She would give up her fine gowns for homespun and rough wool. They knew it was a dream, that it could never happen, but they clung to its lie because the alternative was unbearable.

In truth, they had no future. She would be sold to the highest bidder, and he—he must watch for his clan and warn them that the enemy awaited them. The six months were nearly up, and the Donald and his army would be returning soon. Gawen knew that they would be walking into a trap unless he did something to stop it. Caitriona also knew, because he kept nothing from her. As they lay in the cave safe in each other's arms, their lovemaking was all the sweeter for its hopelessness.

CHAPTER 21

MISSING PIECES

"I missed this place," Fitz said as she dragged her suitcase up the long pathway to Nessie's house on the hill. "Except for the haggis," she added under her breath. Kate heard her and snorted.

"You and your haggis phobia!" she said. "There are other things to eat in Scotland, you know."

"Never mind that. I can't wait to meet this Jack that you're so interested in *not* talking about." Kate shot her a look but refrained from taking the bait.

"Well," Aubrey said, as she inserted the key into the lock, "your wishes will soon be answered. Although he'll probably be kind of grumpy by now. He and Finn are probably starving. First your plane was late, and then I never thought it would take so long for one airliner to offload luggage. For a while there I thought we were back in Philadelphia!"

They piled into the foyer, Fitz's eager eyes scanning

the area for a sign of the mysterious Jack. The hum of conversation from the sitting room stopped, and Gladys's voice called out, "We're in here, dearies!"

A tall, somewhat fierce-looking man with dark hair and sharp green eyes stood as they entered. He directed a polite smile at Fitz, but then his eyes moved immediately to Kate. The smile broadened, softening that intense face and making him seem suddenly much more handsome. So this is Jack, Fitz thought. *Hmmm. Not like Eddie at all, except for one thing. He's in love with Kate.*

"Welcome back, Colleen," Gladys said. The Owls did not approve of Fitz as a nickname for Aubrey's diminutive friend, and they refused to acknowledge it. Fitz grinned at them all and allowed herself to be absorbed into their world.

"Where's Finn?" said Aubrey.

Gladys blinked. "He's not here, dear. Must be running late."

Aubrey shook her head in confusion. "No, that can't be. He had a morning tour. He should have been back ages ago. He was going to go home and change and then come right here. Excuse me." She stepped out into the foyer and called his number. It went to voicemail.

She left a message, "Where are you? We're hungry. Call me as soon as you get this," and ended the call. She walked back into the sitting room, a frown creasing her brow.

"That's odd," she said. "He's never late. And he wouldn't turn his phone off in the middle of the day."

Jack's eyes darted to Kate's. Her shake of the head was nearly imperceptible, but Aubrey saw.

"There's something wrong, isn't there? You think he's in trouble!" She heard the panic rising in her voice. "What if he's been in an accident?" She groped for the arm of the couch and sat down, suddenly unable to breathe.

"Don't jump to conclusions, Bree," Kate admonished. "Let's take this one step at a time. She took out her phone, brought up the direct employee number that Finn had given her for Dougie's Tours, and placed a call. A moment later she put down the phone.

"He returned the van and clocked out at one o'clock," she said. "Try him again, Aubrey."

The call again went to voicemail.

"That was four hours ago. Something's wrong." The phone slipped out of Aubrey's shaking hands and landed on the floor of the sitting room, unnoticed. This time no one had anything to say.

Jack left the room and went into the kitchen, where Nessie regarded him with solemn eyes. "I heard. Wha' can I do?"

"Whisky," Jack said. Nessie poured a generous dram and gave it to him, and he returned to the sitting room and pressed the glass into Aubrey's hand. "Drink. It'll help." Aubrey took the glass and drank the whisky in one gulp.

"Thanks," she said, without looking at him. "It doesn't help, but thanks anyway." And she burst into tears. Kate knelt on the floor and folded her friend into her arms.

"We'll find him, Bree. I'm sure there's a simple explanation. Maybe he got hooked into another tour, and he left his phone at Dougie's. He's probably kicking himself, and he'll be here any moment so you can yell at him." Aubrey looked at her with bleary eyes. Neither of them believed that. They were the empty words that people said when they had nothing else to give. The truth was, Finn was not careless or inconsiderate. If he had changed his plans or something had happened to his phone, he would have found another way to call.

An hour later found them still crowded together in Nessie's sitting room. Finn had not shown up, and repeated calls to his phone produced no results. For once the Owls had no advice, and this more than anything else told everyone that something was very wrong. Angus had arrived and was sitting in the corner in deep conversation with Old Harry, their dialogue rapid and incomprehensible. Maxine's foot beat in a silent rhythm as she stared with huge liquid eyes at Aubrey, and Gladys—Gladys was quiet.

Jack had called Brown, who promised that he would be there as soon as he could. Kate and Fitz sat on either side of Aubrey, holding her hands and keeping her whisky glass filled. She'd probably be sick at some point, but it was the only way to keep her from running out to look for Finn herself.

Jack appeared in the doorway and beckoned to Kate, who joined him in the dining room.

"You know what we have to do next, don't you?" His voice was grave.

"Yes. You think it's about the investigation, don't you?"

He nodded. "There have been no reports of traffic accidents, and I've checked with Police Scotland.

Your friend Fitz called all the hospitals within a two-hour radius. No one matching Finn's description has been admitted."

"If we only knew the last place he'd been!" Kate said, frustration sharpening her tone. "Why the hell didn't he call Aubrey to tell her where he'd be if he knew he'd be late? It's just not like him at all!"

"No, it isn't," Jack agreed. "Where would he go alone? He knew he was due here for dinner, so it had to be something unplanned."

"Maybe he got a call, someone he didn't expect," Kate said. "And he thought it would be quick and he'd be back in time. But who? Where?"

"I just keep thinking about what Aubrey said, about that weird experience at Dunebrae. Could he have gone up there?"

"They were finished with those visits, weren't they? Paid up, nothing left but the honeymoon." Kate's frustration was mounting. "Could he have remembered something he forgot to do there, and gone back?"

"Or maybe someone there called him and asked him to go back up today," Jack said quietly.

They looked at each other for a long moment, and then Kate said what was on both their minds.

"Lured him there. Because Aubrey was right, and he saw something he shouldn't have."

"And it's all my fault!" a voice came to them from the doorway. It was ragged, filled with pain and self-reproach. Jack and Kate turned to see Aubrey swaying as she held onto the door frame, her eyes clouded with fear and guilt and whisky. "Because I told him to go with that Duncan Munro. I let Finn walk right out of that room with him because I thought he was just a sweet old man. And he isn't, is he? I'll never forgive myself if something has happened!"

Fitz was right behind Aubrey. She grabbed her around the waist and thrust a nearby trash can in front of her as all the whiskey came up, along with everything she'd eaten that day. Nessie joined Fitz and together the two of them wrestled the distraught girl upstairs and into bed. Fitz came back down and into the dining room, plunking herself into a chair.

"I don't know what to do!" she said, her voice bleak. "I'm a nurse, it's my job to know what to do. But this is Bree. She'll never recover from this if something has happened to him, will she?" She ran her hands through her curly red hair. "After everything she's been through, and finally found the perfect guy? It'll kill her!" A lone tear of helpless frustration worked its way out of a bleary blue eye and ran down her pale face.

Kate nodded, on the verge of tears herself. She took a deep breath and pulled herself together. "Well, then, we're just going to have to find him, aren't we?" Her voice was brisk, but inside, her heart ached, and the fear threatened to overwhelm her. In her world, these things seldom turned out well. If she and Jack were right about what might have happened to Finn, the reality was that the chances of his being found alive were fading even as they stood there talking.

These people, if they were the ones to blame for this, had killed one man as if he were a bug to be squashed and had tried to kill Jack in front of thousands at a festival. They would stop at nothing to protect their vile secret. But she could not share that feeling with Fitz. Not yet. It was her cross to bear, hers and Jack's. And besides, they had no proof that Finn's disappearance was connected to Dunebrae—just that awful feeling that hunches can bring.

Brown arrived an hour later, having made the three-hour trip in little over two. It helped to be the chief inspector, Kate thought. He closeted himself with Jack and Kate in Nessie's laundry room and extracted all the details and suppositions from them, saying nothing until they were finished.

"So, Dunebrae Castle is our focus, until we rule it out." Brown's voice was brisk. "Fine. How do you want to proceed?" Kate had always marveled at the chief inspector's ability to let others take the lead when they were possessed of more information than he. It was a rare talent, letting the reins go like that, especially for one in his position. Her admiration for the man rose another notch.

"Kate and I were planning a reconnaissance trip to Dunebrae anyway, now that my arm's well enough." said Jack. "I say we go up to the castle and simply ask if they've seen him, to start." Brown nodded in approval and Jack continued, "It won't do us any good to go storming in, giving away our suspicions. We can't get a search warrant; we have no evidence that anything at all has happened there. And maybe nothing has."

"I agree," said Brown. "You've been there before, so it has to be you two. You're concerned about the disappearance of your friend, and you wonder if he has been by for any last-minute paperwork or details. Don't mention anything about bagpipes, of course. We don't want them to know we've made a connection there."

"And when they tell us they haven't see him?" asked Kate. "Because of course they will. What do we do then?"

"We'll decide that when the time comes," Brown told her. "One step at a time. Watch for their reactions, and then you can come back and put your reconnaissance mission together. But I don't think you should wait any longer to go up there. Every moment Finn is missing is critical, and if he's still alive—"

"He *is* still alive!" Aubrey had come in quietly and was staring at Brown with red-rimmed, bloodshot eyes. "I'd know it if he were dead! I know that sounds like something out of the movies, but it's true. He's alive, and if you two"—she glared at Jack and Kate—"think you're going off to find him without me, think again!" She had her jacket slung over her arm. "So what the hell's keeping you? Let's go!"

None of them spoke during the ride to Dunebrae Castle. Each was thinking about what they might find at the end of their journey, and none of the thoughts were positive. Despite her assurance that Finn was alive someplace, Kate knew that Aubrey's imagination would be working overtime, determined to offer up any number of awful things that could have happened to him.

She scanned the roadside for signs that the Audi had been run off the road. For once her own imagination had kicked into high gear. She pictured Finn lying in a ditch somewhere, calling for help with a weakening voice. Maybe he had gone walking too near the cliffs at Dunebrae and had fallen over the cliffside to lie injured at the bottom, waiting for someone to find him. Kate looked sideways to see tears running silently down Aubrey's face as the car wound around the curves in the darkening Scottish evening. *Oh, Finn! Don't do this to her! Where are you?*

It was after nine o'clock when they pulled into the now well-known car park and Jack killed the engine. Finn's car was not in the park, but none of them had really expected it to be. In fact, Jack realized, there were no cars at all in the park. Where were all the honeymooners? They walked to the huge front door in silence, and Jack pulled back the huge brass ring on the lion door knocker and let it go, twice. Then they waited.

He turned to his companions and fixed them with a gimlet green eye.

"We are here to ask after our friend, and that's all," he said. "He has gone missing, and we have been visiting everywhere that he might have been in the last few days, hoping to have news of him. I will do the talking. Everyone got that?"

"But—" Aubrey began.

"No buts," Jack said. "We keep our eyes open for any twitch, any expression that might tell us that this is not news to them. Watch their eyes. If they are guilty, the eyes will give them away. Again, let me do the talking. Understand?"

They all nodded.

The huge castle door was pulled open, and the

man dressed as a butler looked at them with curious eyes. It was apparent that people did not come to this door without invitation.

"May I help you?" he asked, his voice polite but aloof.

"We need to see Duncan Munro," Jack answered him. "It's important."

"Please wait here. This is highly irregular, but I shall see if he is available," the butler intoned.

Jack glared at him. *You shall indeed see, and he damn well better be available, you pompous ass!* But he swallowed the irritation and let the man lead them to stiff-backed chairs in the huge antechamber. No comfy chairs by the fire today; they were not invited guests. No one sat down. Jack peeked into the great room after the butler had gone, and saw it was empty. Odd, where *were* the guests?

"Mr. MacDonald!" Duncan Munro came into the antechamber, a look of perplexity on his face. "This is a surprise! Is there something I can do for you?"

Jack opened his mouth to speak, but he was thrust aside as a wild figure pushed past him and confronted the old man.

"There's something you can do for *me!*" Aubrey said, her voice shaking with fury. "You can tell me what you've done with my fiancé!"

CHAPTER 22

LEGACY OF VIOLENCE

"They've found a body."

Kate's head jerked up at Jack's words, shock and fear written on her face as all the color drained away.

"Is it—?"

"They don't know. It was a male. He was found in a skip bin in Elgin and taken to the mortuary there. Brown wants us to go up and check it out." His voice was low and raspy, as if his throat hurt to speak. "There's no reason to believe it's him, Kate."

Kate could barely breathe. No, no reason. Except that dead bodies were not found in garbage bins generally, not in the Scottish Highlands. It had been two days since Finn's disappearance, and they were out of clues. She felt glued to the chair, unable to move her limbs. Jack came over and pulled her unresisting body to stand before him and took her into his arms. Kate put her head on his shoulder and began to shake with silent sobs. She felt his hands, warm and capable, and was grateful. After a while she looked up, misty-eyed, and pulled away.

"Thanks. I guess we should go. But how are we going to get past Aubrey? I can hardly look at her as it is, and she'll read me like a book."

"Wait here, I'll go out and talk to Angus. He'll find some way to distract her." He was back in minutes. "That old man is a treasure," he said quietly. "He loves Finn as much as any of us do, but he's determined to hide his own fear and shield Aubrey as long as possible. Let's go."

They walked as quickly as they could out of the workroom and into the bookshop. Angus and Aubrey were nowhere in sight. *Bless you, Angus*, Kate thought.

The thirty-nine-mile drive from Inverness to Elgin would have been beautiful on any other day. The late afternoon sun sparkled off the waters of Beuly Firth. As they passed through Nairn, Kate marveled at the people walking the streets of the ancient seaside town as if they hadn't a care in the world. She supposed she and Jack looked much the same to them. *We just never know what demons another person might be facing, until it's us.*

The mortuary in Elgin was depressing. Single-story, made of a dirty yellow stone, it resembled an old garage more than a medical facility. Kate shuddered at the thought of anyone having to spend time in that place, living or dead.

She forced herself out of the Mini and followed Jack into the unkempt office. Old magazines littered the floor of the waiting area, ash trays overflowed, and there were rents in the faded gray fabric of some of the chairs. The room was empty.

A tired-looking woman with a gray bun that matched the upholstery looked up as they came in. "May I help you?" she asked in a disinterested voice.

Jack presented his credentials. "CI Brown has asked us to look at the body that was brought in yesterday," he told her.

"Just a minute," she said, and disappeared through the door behind her desk. When she returned, she was accompanied by a man in a lab coat that might have been white when he'd started his day but was now a mottled shade of gray and yellow. "Dr. Macrae," he introduced himself. "Medical examiner here. Please follow me."

They followed Macrae down a dark passage that smelled of bacon and cabbage overlaid with an unpleasant scent that neither wanted to think about, past identical doorways to a room at the end of the corridor. As they entered the mortuary room the temperature plummeted, and Kate wrapped her arms around herself, only partly to keep the chill out.

The room had only one occupant, covered by a sheet on a metal table in its center under a large work light that was not lit. Kate felt light-headed with fear. Anxiety had robbed her of breath, and she felt panic building as she struggled to keep from passing out. Jack's hand reached to grip her elbow.

"He was brought in at about half-ten yesterday," the doctor told them. "Stabbed in the back, and his throat was cut. Wasn't killed where they found him, not enough blood. You ready?"

No! Kate was surprised to find that the scream was only in her mind.

"Yes," she managed. Jack's fingers found her own, and they waited for an eternity while the man in the lab coat reached for the top of the sheet and pulled it down.

It wasn't Finn.

Kate staggered and Jack's arm came around to brace her. For a minute, the relief blinded her and leached what little energy she had left. She took a deep breath and forced her attention back to the dismal room and the body on the table.

The man's face was white, nearly the color of the crime board back in Inverness. His pale blue eyes, opaque in death, stared at the ceiling. A huge blood-less gash gaped below his jaw like an obscene smile. The face bore a faint look of surprise—this man had not seen death coming.

"Not who you were expecting?" Dr. Macrae asked them, his sharp eyes watching the color return slowly to Kate's face.

"No," Jack said. "May I see the rest of him?" The doctor pulled the sheet down to the dead man's feet. The torso and long legs were as devoid of color as the face. An athletic body, and one that had seen its share of violence. Several old scars crisscrossed the arms and one thigh. They looked like knife wounds. Macrae rolled the man onto his side and they saw the new wound in his back, low and to the side.

"That one would probably not have been fatal," the doctor gestured to the deceptively small cut. "At least not immediately. He would have been incapacitated, though, likely would have fallen to his knees, allowing his assailant to step up behind him and draw the blade across his throat. Wound that size, he would have bled out in under a minute. Most likely never saw his killer's face."

Jack was curious. "Anything interesting found with the body?"

Macrae checked a file. "Dressed all in black. Black trousers, sweater, black leather jacket. Says here he had a Browning pocket pistol in his jacket pocket, and a dagger in a sheath on his leg. Never had the chance to use either one. Odd the killer didn't take them, though."

"Not an innocent bystander then, or someone in the wrong place at the wrong time," Jack said. His shoulder began to ache where he had been shot . . . by a pocket pistol. Kate met his gaze.

"Where are the gun and dagger now?" Jack asked.

"Elgin Police have them. Is there anything else I can do for you? I want to get back to work on this lad."

"No, thank you. You've been very helpful."

As they emerged from the gloom of the mortuary into the sunshine, Kate let out a shaky breath.

"It's not Finn. Thank God, now I don't have to face Aubrey. Not yet."

"I know. I do wonder about that man, though." Jack's brow was wrinkled in thought. "It's a stretch, I know, but what are the chances that the same man would be carrying both a gun and a dagger? It's obvious that he wasn't on the side of the angels, that one. His body told us that much. We need to get Brown to look into those weapons."

Kate stopped suddenly. "Elgin isn't very far from Forres, is it? Only fifteen miles or so?"

Jack looked at her. "Twelve."

"And how far is it from Dunebrae Castle?"

"Maybe thirty-five."

"And Inverness?"

"About the same. Took us forty minutes. Why?"

"Well, Hugh Ross was killed in Inverness. Knife. You were shot in Forres. And now this man is dumped in Elgin, right in between those two places, carrying a knife *and* a gun. If he is who we think he might be, then he hasn't moved very far in his travels. His base of operations could have been any one of these places. It could have been Dunebrae."

Jack pushed his hair out of his eyes. "It's another wild-ass guess, but things are beginning to line up."

They called Brown and filled him in. Leaving him to deal with the ballistics report on the gun found with the Man in Black, as they were now calling him, they grabbed sandwiches and sat on the edge of the fountain in the High Street, letting the sun warm their faces and chase the residual shadows from their minds.

It could have been Finn, Kate thought. Every time she visualized the body laid out on that metal table in the mortuary, an image of Finn's face appeared in her mind, superimposed on that of the Man in Black. It hadn't been him, but it could have been. And he was still missing.

Jack's phone rang.

"Brown," he said, looking at the display. As he listened, his face went still. He ended the call and looked at Kate.

"It's the same gun," he said, his voice tight. "The Man in Black was the shooter in Forres." They sat in silence, taking it in. Pieces were beginning to knit together, and the image forming in the center of the web, like a huge venomous spider, was a castle on the North Sea only thirty-five miles to the east of where they sat.

"Well," Jack said finally, "I think we have our next step."

They returned to Inverness and met Brown at the bookshop. Angus let them in and told them that Aubrey had gone home for the night and was under Nessie's watchful eye. "Finally gettin' some sleep, poor lass."

As the sun began to sink behind the mist-covered mountains across the River Ness, Jack and Kate climbed back into the little red Mini and began the now familiar journey to Dunebrae Castle. This time they would not be parking in the car park or going to the front door. Precious moments would not be wasted exchanging pleasantries with Duncan Munro.

Kate had sneaked into her room at Nessie's and now wore a black turtleneck sweater and her favorite black leggings. Over this she had put on a heavy hooded black sweatshirt. Jack was dressed in similar dark colors. Kate looked down at herself. Not a fashion combination she would normally wear, but this was not a normal visit.

She stole a glance at Jack to make sure his eyes were on the road, and then eased her pant leg up to admire the sgian dubh resting in the heavy sock just above her boot. He had given it to her before they left, looking embarrassed and unsure. Not a very personal gift for anyone else but Kate, and from him it was better than a diamond necklace. The timing was horrible, but she blushed as she remembered how pleased he'd been with her reaction to the gift. At times of great stress, the simplest gestures took on new meaning.

Would she have the courage to use it? Kate had never been responsible for the death of another human being. As a detective in Harrington, she had rarely faced a real life-or-death situation on the job. She hoped she never would. Without her gun, however, she felt naked and unprotected. The American in her would never understand how Jack could operate without the benefit of a firearm, but police in the UK were seldom armed with anything except a baton. At least he had agreed to bring a small cannister of PAVA spray. Pelargonic acid vaniollyamide, pepper spray in the vernacular.

While Jack navigated the narrow road with practiced ease, Kate thought back to their last visit, on the Saturday night that Finn had failed to return from his tour. Munro's shock at Aubrey's attack had seemed genuine, his distress sincere. Was the man that good an actor? It didn't seem possible, but a man who ran one of the most lethal drug operations in modern history would have covered all the bases. Every one of her senses was telling her that the key to Finn's disappearance would be found at Dunebrae Castle. And this time they were not leaving without an answer.

They drove past the castle entrance and parked behind a stand of trees. There was no traffic on the narrow road at this time of night. In silence they walked back toward the castle, just two more shadows in the growing darkness. Jack reached out and took Kate's hand, giving it a reassuring squeeze. He did not let go, and she was grateful. Despite the chilly sea air that crept around the edges of her sweatshirt, Kate felt warmth spreading through her at his touch.

The castle was almost invisible in the gloom, rising like a ghost on the horizon—a huge hulking shape painted against the black sky. Occasional glimpses of a paper-thin moon cast a dim light on the otherworldly landscape. A feeling of foreboding shook Kate as she looked at the ancient stones. So much death had swirled around this place over the centuries—was it still happening today?

But the ghosts of Dunebrae had nothing to say tonight. No eerie pipes broke the silence of the place, no old ladies in velvet gowns peered out of the gloom. Jack and Kate walked the perimeter of the property toward the coast in silence. They had no plan, but it stood to reason there would be outbuildings; whether they were ruins or still in use remained to be seen. They would start there and rule them out one by one.

After an hour of wandering, they had found several stone structures, all of them abandoned and empty. There was nothing here. Kate turned in frustration to look back at the castle she now hated, and that was when she saw it. A glimmer of light. There was a faint outline almost lost in the trees, perhaps a hundred yards away from the east wall of the ancient keep. A building of some sort.

It was a small barn. Not as old as the stone outbuildings they had just explored, this one was made of wood. It had a narrow driveway leading to a weathered door with a combination padlock. It was the reflection of this shiny modern gadget in the faint moonlight that had caught her eye.

Jack moved to the back of the structure, out of sight of the castle. He was back in seconds, beckoning her with his finger to his lips. He put his lips to her ear and whispered, "There's a window." They moved together to stand under the small square and looked up. Four tiny panes of dirty glass stared back down at them from a height of about eight feet.

"Lift me," Kate whispered, and Jack nodded, intertwining his fingers to form a stirrup. Pulling her cell phone out of her pocket, she stepped into his hands and he lifted her off the ground. Kate found the flashlight on her device and directed the tiny beam through the dirty pane, rotating the light around the space inside. Empty. No, wait—nearly empty. She felt her heart constrict and her hands begin to shake as the beam found a large object shrouded in shadow. It seemed to be the only occupant of the barn, but that was all that was needed to make her blood run cold. Standing in the very center of the space was Finn's gray Audi.

CHAPTER 23

KING OF THE CASTLE

Duncan Munro sat in his workroom and watched as the tools of his trade, the physical manifestation of his passion and pride, were carried out the side door and loaded into the bus. *No one is as blessed as I am. I am truly a king among men.*

His band was set to win another World Championship. They'd won every single competition this year, an unprecedented feat. Last month the Europeans in Forres and at the Scottish Championships, the UK Championships, and the British Championships. This was the year he'd reclaim his crown at Glasgow Green, win the Worlds again and make it a perfect sweep. Would he someday get tired of winning? A twisted smile slid onto Duncan's face. He doubted it.

Sometimes he thought that winning, and the prospect of winning, must be like a drug. It coursed through his body, left him euphoric and yet covetous.

It was never enough. He remembered two years ago, the last time his band had won the Worlds. Every one of the hundred and eighty bands present had come to pay him homage in the March Past, and then had come the epitome, the moment when House of Munro's Highlanders stood and received the ultimate acclamation. The drums had gone silent as thousands of pipers raised blowpipes to their lips and sounded the first note of "Hail the Chief."

Munro frowned. Every win made loss less tolerable. They hadn't won last year. He'd pretended it didn't matter, but the failure still turned his stomach. The prize had gone to his most bitter rival, that upstart band from Northern Ireland, Major Kildare Memorial. The bile rose in his throat, and he forced it down.

There would not be a repeat this year. Sir Harry Magreavy, the captain of Major Kildare, had come to shake his hand and congratulate him on winning the Europeans last month, and Duncan's hand had trembled with his hatred of the man and his band. Now he envisioned that same hand plunging a dagger into the pompous fool's chest, wiping that supercilious smile off his face. *That* was how his forebears had taken care of their rivals. Sometimes he thought he'd been born into the wrong era.

Duncan Munro shook himself back to the present, a cold feeling persisting in his gut. What the hell was wrong with him? He'd always been competitive, hated it when his band lost, but that was a natural reaction if you were at the top. Lately though, he'd sensed himself losing control, alternately flushed with triumph or plunged into despair at the thought of losing his position on the throne. He had a sick feeling that his passion was destroying him, leaching the joy of simple competition out of him and replacing it with something dark and cold.

Duncan sighed. Sometimes he wished he could go back to the early days, when his name was on the rise and the world was new and clean, when he had nothing else to worry about besides his band. He remembered when he'd been like that Cameron fellow. Eager, happy just to be a part of the piping world. Not obsessed. He remembered the simple joy on the young man's face when he'd seen the workroom, the animation when they talked about their craft.

A feeling of dread slithered up his spine as he remembered the look on the fiancé's face as she accused Duncan of having something to do with his disappearance. How had she made that connection? Did she suspect there was something wrong with him?

Fear worked its way through his gut. How could she have known? He didn't think he'd given anything away. He had been losing time lately—well, for a long while now, but he thought he'd kept it under control for the most part. But he *was* different. His natural competitive nature had taken an unpleasant turn. He found himself snapping at his employees and even at his band members. The fear took hold of his heart and squeezed. Had he been *jealous* of the young man and his honest enjoyment of something that had become so much darker for Duncan?

It was a shame, really. Duncan had been looking forward to spending more time with Cameron in a couple of weeks when the couple came up to

Dunebrae for their honeymoon. He had few friends, and none who understood his passion for the pipes. He had thought they had a bond, but it was obvious he'd been wrong.

He knew he had broken his own cardinal rule by taking the young piper on a personal tour of the private enclave of House of Munro, knew what he was risking, but the look on the man's face had been worth it. He had felt better than he had in days, watching Cameron explore the workshop with stars in his eyes—until Hector had come in and spoiled it all.

He frowned. Hector. He loved his son, relied on him for the running of the castle, but what the boy knew about bagpipes would fit into a piper's case. He'd tried to teach his son to play as a young lad, but he was simply not interested. Nor had he inherited the talent. Hector had never shown the slightest interest in his father's passion.

It had worked out for the best in the end. Duncan really didn't want to waste his time seeing to the day-to-day running of his castle's tourist trade, but Hector seemed to love it. His son had turned into a natural innkeeper. He embraced the stories of battles fought centuries before to take and hold Dunebrae, of the violence of those ancient clans. He hated the MacDonalds as if they were still waiting outside to storm his keep.

Most of all, Hector loved his castle's ghosts. The piper who had warned his clan of an ambush and been killed for his loyalty and courage, whose music could still be heard on some evenings as darkness fell. The strange old woman who floated through the hallways as if searching for something. Hector had incorporated his ghosts into his tours, challenging guests to listen for the pipes, watch for the old woman. The literature on Dunebrae's website embraced the spirits and made them unwitting tour guides.

Duncan snorted to himself. Ridiculous, but useful. He found it amusing, and it kept Hector out of his way. At least he knew that when he passed on, he'd be leaving the castle in good hands, and the band? Well, the band was his legacy. It would forever be stamped with the name of Duncan Munro, and that was how it should be.

He frowned. How it *should* be. But lately Duncan had sensed a change. Hector had seemed to be watching him—he seemed uneasy with his own father. Duncan shook his head to clear his thoughts, but the fear persisted. *It's not Hector's fault. Something is wrong with me. Is that why my son seems to be hovering? Is he worried about me? Has he guessed? Maybe I need to be more careful.* He decided to go into his office and have a cup of tea. It always calmed him.

There were no guests the week before the Worlds, no tours scheduled until next Monday. The drums and uniforms were already packed for the trip to Glasgow in four days. All that remained was the loading of the pipes onto the tour bus, and that would be done on Thursday morning.

Duncan always kept the pipers practicing until almost the moment of departure, unwilling to give up even a moment of the time needed to assure perfection. But now his son seemed to be hanging around, checking in on him. He was becoming a nuisance.

Hector had started asking questions, making

suggestions. He'd even shown up at practice. At first Duncan had been amused, thinking he was at last showing an interest in the band, but now it was just annoying. It was far too late to involve Hector in his enterprise. Maybe he'd have to have a few words with his son when they returned from Glasgow. Remind him who was boss.

He made his way up the dim hallway and through the side door into his office, put the kettle on and scooped tea into the diffuser, allowing the familiar ritual to seep into his mind and work its magic. Dunebrae Castle was known for this tea, and the guests were served the delicious brew from the great kitchen in ornate teapots, but Duncan insisted on brewing his own. He was proud of his blend and kept his own canister behind his desk with his kettle and crystal teapot in easy reach.

A stab of annoyance went through him as he noticed a brown residue next to the tea canister. Just a few grains, but still. It didn't do to be careless. The irritation grew. *I'm losing my touch—getting sloppy.* He heard a noise and turned to see Hector in the doorway.

His son was wearing that anxious look on his face again. "Dad? Are you all right?"

Duncan Munro felt a stab of annoyance and then a chill as he looked into his son's concerned eyes. Hector was right to be worried—there was definitely something very wrong with him, and he was going to have to be careful or his son would think he should step in. An errant thought slipped into his mind, and he wondered. *Who's the king of the castle, and who's the dirty rascal?*

CHAPTER 24

HARD TRUTH

He was dead. He knew he was. They had put him in the ground and covered him with wet dirt that pressed in on his body and filled his lungs and throat, black and viscous. The earth softened, became thousands of soft moths, desperate fluttering bodies beating against his mouth and pushing at the insides of his eyes. The moths gave way to a gray fog, flowing in from the north to surround his body and fill his nostrils with the dank smell of the sea. The gray became a wan light, tickling the edges of his eyelids, teasing, urging.

Finn opened his eyes.

He was lying on a narrow camp bed. As his senses began to filter back, he saw that the bed was one of two in a small room with one wooden door and no windows. No, there had to be a window; there was a faint light coming from somewhere. Craning his head, he saw a tiny round window far above and behind him. The gray light of early morning—or was it dusk?—filtered in through the dirty circular pane. He tried to swing his feet to the floor to sit up and found that he could not move his left arm.

His wrist was handcuffed to the metal bar of the bed.

Finn lay back and waited for the dizziness to pass. As his head cleared, he realized he was shivering. The damp stale air of the room seeped under his shirt and circled his bare legs. Bare legs? He struggled onto his right elbow and peered down the length of his body. He was wearing a kilt. *Why am I wearing a kilt?* He lay back and tried to remember.

It was his work kilt, the one he wore to run tours for Dougie's. But he had left Dougie's to go home, hadn't he? Home to Aubrey. He had to call Aubrey. His phone was in his sporran, and someone had removed that and his jacket. His boots were gone, too. He tried to think. His body was beginning to adjust to the chill in the small room and his mind was clearing, but nothing made sense.

Wait. He had received a call from someone at Dunebrae—a paper they had neglected to have him sign last week. They were sorry, but it had to be signed immediately, something about the insurance. He had been met by Duncan Munro. Yes. And then he had felt sick, and looked for the toilets, and he must have passed out. He couldn't remember anything more.

But how had he ended up in this small room, chained to a metal bed? A chill that had nothing to do with the temperature swept through him. Had he been drugged? But that was ridiculous. He thought back and remembered. *The tea!* There must have been something in that tea that Duncan Munro had been so eager to foist on him.

The whirling thoughts in his mind were interrupted by a soft click, and the wooden door opened. A burly man entered, carrying a tray with a pot of tea, a mug, and a plate on which sat a small loaf of bread and a hunk of cheese.

"Where's Duncan?" Finn demanded. "What's going on?"

The man ignored his question. He set the tray on the end of the bed and reached over to unlock the cuff that held Finn's wrist to the rail. He left the cuff dangling. "Eat," he said, went to the door and left, closing it behind him.

Finn rubbed his wrist, massaging the circulation back into his body. He stood up and walked to the door, trying the metal handle and finding that it was locked from the outside. He walked a circle in the small room, taking in the second camp bed across from the one he'd been shackled to. Had that one been meant for Aubrey, if she'd been with him? He was glad now that he'd come alone. At least she was safe. His roving eyes spied something stuffed in a corner, and with a cry of triumph he found his jacket and boots. His sporran had been stuffed into a sleeve of the jacket.

The joy was short-lived. The sporran was empty—they had taken his wallet, phone and keys. Finn threw the sporran onto the bed, put on the jacket and boots, and went back to sit on the bed. He put his head in his hands. He had never had the chance to call Aubrey, she would have no idea where he was.

He could feel his heart quicken with fear and fought a pervasive sense of despair.

His stomach growled, and he looked at the tray. He hadn't eaten since a quick sandwich on the road after the tour—yesterday? He had no idea how long he'd been unconscious. His eyes traveled to the teapot. He was thirsty, his throat felt as if he had swallowed a wad of cotton wool, but there was no damn way he was drinking that tea. *Fool me once!* He'd have to make do with the bread and cheese.

The bread was delicious, as was the cheese. Good Scottish cheddar. He tried to take his time, but hunger took over. As he sat chewing the bread, he wondered at the thinking of his captors. Why would they unchain him so he could eat and then leave him alone? He was going to explore this place as soon as he was finished and find some way of escape. His spirits rose as he looked around the room. Surely there was something here that he could use to pick that lock. Or maybe he could stand the camp bed on its end and reach the window. They'd been foolish to leave him unsecured.

In the dim light he saw something on the floor in another corner, and his heart leapt. Metal? He stood, holding the tray, and felt himself sway as the dizziness returned. He stumbled and the tray fell to the stone floor, scattering tea, bread and cheese onto the dirty stone. Finn stared at the mess in horror as his vision began to tunnel and his eyes lost focus. His heart plummeted and he felt the familiar fading, thoughts scattering as his body folded onto the hard stone floor and the darkness surrounded him once more.

It had been in the food this time. *Fool me twice.*

When he awoke, he was cuffed to the frame as before. The tray and broken teapot had been cleared away, all remnants of the food gone. Finn lay still on the bed, letting the realization spread through him. They had been one step ahead of him the whole time, had known exactly what he would do. He was at their mercy, and for the first time he feared that they had none, that this was going to end badly for him. They were toying with him. Otherwise, why keep him drugged and restrained? At least they'd left him his jacket and boots this time—the bastards had made their point.

The door snicked open again, and Finn turned his head to see a man enter. For a moment they simply stared at each other.

"Well, Mr. Cameron, it seems as if we have come to the end of our acquaintance."

Hector Munro walked over and sat on the empty camp bed across from Finn, studying him in silence. He leaned back against the wall and crossed one leg over the other as if they were sitting in the great hall having a pleasant chat over Dunebrae's fine whisky.

"It was you," Finn whispered through a throat now so parched that he could barely breathe. "Not Duncan. You." He was being strangled by cotton wool from the inside out, and his head pounded.

"No, Mr. Cameron, it was you. You should never have been in that bagpipe room. I'm afraid my father sealed your fate by taking you there, by wanting to show off his pride and joy to another piper." He shook his head in commiseration, but his eyes glinted with malice.

"But there was nothing unusual in that room!" Finn croaked. "It was just a workroom!"

"Come now, you know better than that. You and your detective friend, MacDonald, know the truth about what is going on in that room. He's the one who sent you here, the one who got you to cozy up to my father to get him to take you there so you could snoop." Munro chuckled. The sound was harsh; there was no humor in it. Finn lay silent. There was nothing he could say.

"The amusing thing is, my father knows nothing," Munro went on. "You may have noticed he is not himself. I've been keeping him under control by giving him small doses of my special drug, just enough to keep him docile and malleable." Hector Munro smiled his sweet smile. "He loses great slices of time, which is necessary so that I can complete my work in the bagpipe room without interference."

"You—you drugged your own father?" Finn's voice was barely audible. He stared at the man in horror.

"Oh, don't look so shocked. He has to be the figurehead in the band, doesn't he? I told you I care nothing for the stupidity of pipe bands. Men parading around playing the same boring songs over and over, just to win a championship that most of the world mocks." His lips curled into a sneer. "But House of Munro Highlanders is an institution. No one searches them at airports, they are invited all over the world to perform. The perfect camouflage for my operation. And Duncan Munro is the face of the brand. I need him. It's essential that people think him the chief of this castle. I need *him* to think so. So I pander to his vanity."

He stood and began to pace the small room. It was almost as if he'd forgotten Finn was there.

"You see, bagpipes are good for much more than music. I found that by simply mixing the powder found in my cave with shellac and painting it onto the pipes, I created an impermeable shield for my drug. It is literally a part of the drone pipes, sealed from any observer. It doesn't affect the sound of the bagpipes at all." Hector glanced at Finn as if expecting praise for his cleverness. Seeing only shock, he shrugged and resumed.

"Not all of them are treated, of course. Only a select few trusted associates are given the special pipes, and even they don't know what they carry. They meet with contacts in cities all over Europe and now the Americas, simply exchanging the augmented instruments with ordinary sets of bagpipes. Isn't that brilliant? The drug base goes on to my associates in other cities and other labs, where it is extracted from the pipes and mixed with innocent ingredients." His eyes gleamed. "Eventually the process results in the most wonderful drug ever created, the one that has been given the street name Reign. And all from a beautiful green fungus.

"But the real beauty, the perfection of my operation, is that it is mine! Mine alone. No one else can make the drug, because no one knows where the powder comes from. The cave is hidden from all but my closest acolytes, my inner circle."

Hector stopped and looked into Finn's wide eyes. "But I think you and your associates guessed this, or you were close to doing so. That's why you were down in the workshop, isn't it? Don't deny it—I saw you reaching for one of the metal canisters on the table."

He snorted when Finn shook his head in confusion. "You must really have taken me for a fool. I am not a fool, Mr. Cameron. Is there anything else you would like to know?"

Hector Munro's voice was cultured, polite, but a strain of acid ran beneath the honeyed words. He was enjoying this. Finn said nothing, frozen in astonishment and repugnance. He had known that Jack and Kate were working on the Reign case, and that they had suspected all was not right at Dunebrae, but he'd had no idea of the ramifications. He realized now that they had tried to protect him. Just as he knew that Munro would never believe anything he said. The man's eyes held a glint of madness.

Hector stood, went to the door and signaled to someone outside. He returned with three bottles of water and put them on the floor next to Finn's camp bed.

"Now, here is the part that you might find a bit difficult," he said, sitting back down on the other bed and focusing a sympathetic look on Finn. After a moment he said, "Your friends came here looking for you, you know. Oh, yes, they were right downstairs two nights ago, those detectives and your beautiful fiancé." He laughed. "I watched it all from the hallway. You should have seen my father's face when she accused him of kidnapping you!" Hector sighed at the look of pain on Finn's face. "Ah, yes, so close and yet so far away."

He leaned back against the wall. "You may be wondering why I didn't just have you killed outright." His dry voice sent the clear message that he didn't much care what his unwitting guest might have been wondering, but the dark eyes commanded attention. Finn could not drag his gaze away from the evil reflected there.

"Well, my father likes you, even though he was a bit annoyed that you left without signing that important document I invented for him." Hector's face wore a self-satisfied smirk. "I love my father, you understand. I don't like to upset him." He shrugged. "I was afraid that if you were killed on the property he might try to interfere, and I couldn't allow that." He thrust his hands out in an apologetic gesture. "And there's the problem of what to do with a body, of course."

"So I decided to bring you here and keep you hidden away until the band is ready to leave for the World Championships in Glasgow in three days. As soon as the bus pulls out, you will be leaving." At Finn's look of surprise, he shook his head. "Please don't misunderstand me, you will not be alive when you leave this room. My men have their instructions, and they are very good at what they do. Your body will be placed in the boot of your car and driven to a place far enough down the road from the castle to avoid any connection. They will put you into the driver's seat and send the car over the cliff and into the sea. It's quite possible that you will never be found."

He shrugged. "If you are—well, the road is dangerous at night, and one can hardly be faulted for taking a wrong turn in the dark and losing one's way, with tragic consequences.

"Now, I have to go and help my father with his preparations for the Worlds." He nodded to the bottles of water next to the bed. "I know that your throat must be very dry, but even if you could call out no one would hear you. Of course, it is your choice, but if I were you I would drink that water." He narrowed his eyes at Finn. "You'll feel much better, and it would be easier for all of us if you were to sleep for the remainder of your time as our guest. Don't you agree?"

"Is—is it Reign?" Finn's voice was barely audible, the rasp of dead leaves across pavement.

"Don't be stupid, haven't you been listening? That's not how Reign works. Besides, I wouldn't waste my drug on this little . . . problem. The bottles merely contain a strong sedative, works quickly and lasts for hours. I believe you've enjoyed the effects twice already. There is enough there to see you through the next three days, I assure you. I am not a monster."

He stood. "I believe this is goodbye, Mr. Cameron. I'm afraid you and I will not be seeing each other again." Hector Munro turned and left the room without another word.

Finn lay for a long time staring at the ceiling, letting the truth sink in. This was it. He was never going to see Aubrey again. A sense of despair swept through him at the thought of what she would have to go through, and he gave in and let the tears come. Then he reached down with his free hand, picked up a water bottle, and drank. Munro was right, it would be easier this way. He lay back and closed his eyes, waiting for oblivion.

When he opened them again, the light had dimmed in the room. The empty water bottle was gone, and a woman was seated on the bed across from him, watching.

CHAPTER 25

CAVING IN

Kate swayed and nearly dropped the phone. She stumbled down from Jack's linked fingers and sagged against the wall of the barn, frozen with shock.

"Aubrey was right all along," she said in a low, anguished voice. "Finn's car is in there. Duncan Munro knew where he was all the time. We should never have pulled her off him!" Her voice was bitter. "We have to call Brown, get backup. We've wasted two days, and all the time Munro was laughing at us!" Her voice held the ragged edge of panic, and Jack took her in his arms, his hands warm against her back.

"We'll find him, Kate. If Munro had killed Finn, he wouldn't have kept the car where it could incriminate him. I'm more convinced than I was before that he's alive, and we owe it to both Finn and Aubrey to keep our heads and find him!" He shook her gently.

"Don't go to pieces on me now. Don't you dare!" His voice was fierce.

The rough tone of his voice reached through the terror that gripped Kate, and she felt the panic subside just a little. *He's right. You're a detective, Bianchi. So go detect.* She straightened her spine and stepped back. Brown eyes met green, each drawing strength from the other.

"They have to have him somewhere in that damned castle," she said, looking with loathing at the gray turrets looming over the roofline of the barn. "Somehow we have to get in there without being seen."

"So let's g—" Jack's answer was cut off by the sound of voices, carried to them clearly on the wind.

"Someone's out here, I saw them. At least two, maybe more!"

"Spread out and search, and if you find them, kill them. Boss said no witnesses."

Kate looked at Jack, eyes wide. Too late. They had already been discovered. The voices were coming closer to where they stood at the back of the barn. If they didn't find a place to hide, they'd be caught. "Spread out," the voice had said. It sounded as if the odds were against them. For now, survival meant flight.

Jack grabbed her hand. "Here," he whispered, and pulled her back into the trees behind the barn. "We'll have some cover. Have to get around to the other side, so we can get to the car. We'll back off a way and call Brown, wait for reinforcements."

Trying to remain as silent as possible in the thick bracken that hugged the cliffs, they made their way around the edge of the property. Kate could hear the sea, its waves thundering against the rocks at the bottom of the cliff. At least it helped to drown out the sounds of their flight.

The trees ended suddenly, and they found themselves standing at the very edge of the cliffs at the end of the castle lawn, silhouetted against the horizon in the thin moonlight.

"There, I see them! There's two of them!" The voices were close now, clearly audible over the roar of the angry surf below.

"Run!" Jack hissed, pushing her in front of him and following as they negotiated the worn pathway at the edge of the cliff. The terrain was rougher here, the footing treacherous.

"I see them!" came another voice, from somewhere to the right, not far away. "We've got them trapped! Stop, you!" the voice shouted. "You have nowhere to go but over the cliff. We won't hurt you if you stop now!"

"Sure, and I'm one of the faerye folk," Jack muttered. He grabbed Kate's hand and stepped in front of her, pulling her along the path.

Cursing sounded behind them, but they kept going. Kate could see where the forest on the other side of the open cliffs closed in along the property. If they could just get to those trees—

And then she was yanked off her feet as Jack's hand pulled her to the ground. No, not to the ground, into the ground. The earth had opened up at their feet, and they were falling through brush and leaves, sliding downward toward blackness.

Jack's progress ended abruptly with a sharp jolt that took the wind out of his body as she landed on top of him. She pushed herself up and felt desperately for his face.

"Jack? Are you all right? Jack!"

"You know, you're a lot heavier than you look," his voice wheezed out of the darkness. His hand found her mouth and covered it. "Shut up, woman!"

Faint voices reached them from far above. Looking up, they could see nothing. The bushes must have closed in over the hole.

"Where'd they go?"

"They couldn't have gotten away, we had them hemmed in!"

"Maybe they went over the cliff?" The voice was hopeful.

"Well, we won't be able to see until morning. It's fifty feet onto the rocks. If they're down there, they're dead. But I think they must've made it to the trees. C'mon, let's go."

The voices dwindled and Kate and Jack were left in absolute darkness. Even the sound of the sea was muted here.

"Are you okay? How's your arm?"

"It's fine. It was really more of a slide than a fall. Wonder what we landed in." His voice was curious, not pained, and Kate felt a surge of relief.

"Well, whatever it is, it saved our lives. If there's a way out, that is."

Darkness is rarely complete, and Kate's eyes were beginning to adjust to the gloom. The hole that they'd fallen into was large, with a packed dirt floor and earthen walls from which root endings and rocks protruded. The part that she could see was about ten feet by twelve, the far wall disappearing into darkness.

Jack was rummaging in his sweatshirt pocket. He pulled out his cell phone and flicked it on. "No service," he muttered. "Try yours."

Kate had no better luck with her own phone.

"At least we have power, and the phones have flashlights," she said. "But maybe we should turn one of them off, so we'll be able to call Brown when we get out of here."

"Good idea, that," he said, sounding impressed. "You're not bad for a junior detective." He powered his phone off and stowed it in the zippered pocket of his sweatshirt. "But since we have only the one wee candle there, we'd best get on with exploring our new home."

Kate decided to let the "junior detective" comment go in the interests of finding a way out. Later she could make him pay. She turned on her phone's flashlight and directed its beam around the dismal space. "I'm not sure I want to live here, after all," she said. "Not enough windows."

A chuckle from Jack. "We'll have to stay together, since only one of us has the light."

Kate nodded, even though he couldn't see her in the dark. It was amazing how having another person with you in a harrowing situation like this made it less frightening. Especially when there was trust.

I do trust him. With my life . . . and maybe with more. She took his hand and they started out.

Working around the perimeter of the hole, they found nothing until they came to the farthest wall. There was something piled in the corner here. Directing the light onto the pile, Jack saw what looked like a pattern in the earth. A tartan pattern, shredded and faded, but unmistakably fabric.

"We're not the first to come here," he said, his voice soft. "Someone's been here before us, and by the looks of it, not recently."

"How long does fabric last before it decomposes?" Kate asked him.

"Depends. In a cave like this, out of the elements, probably hundreds of years, if it was undisturbed." He bent down and picked up the edge of fabric between his fingers. It disintegrated at his touch, turning into dust. "And I don't think anyone has been here in a long, long time."

The phone's beam caught the edge of something metal in the corner. Careful not to touch the fabric again, he reached over and picked up the object. It was a goblet, tarnished black but still beautiful in its delicate filigreed design. Another identical goblet lay beside it.

"Jack, we've seen goblets like that!" Kate's voice was hushed. "On our tour of Dunebrae, remember? Hector Munro showed us the old kitchens and said that some of the antiques dated back to the sixteen hundreds, when the Campbells first took over the castle from the MacDonalds! There were goblets just like this one on the shelf!"

But Jack wasn't listening. "Look!" he said. "A jug!" The light showed a finely wrought metal jug that might have been brass, with a narrow neck and bulging body. It was engraved with a circle depicting the head of a boar on a plate of some kind. The words in the circle said *Ne Obliviscaris*.

"*Forget not.*" Jack's words were soft. "The clan motto of the Campbells. But they've been gone from this place for three hundred years!"

"Someone made this cave into a kind of meeting place," said Kate. "Why would they do that?"

"One wine jug, two goblets, a makeshift bed. What do you think?" Jack said.

Kate gaped at him. "A love nest? Surely not! There had to be more comfortable places to meet your lover—even in those days!"

"Not if it was illicit," he said. "Back then marriages were arranged, but not everyone was happy about that." He shrugged. "Women were commodities, and heavily guarded. Looks to me like this couple, whoever they were, found their own little hideaway by the sea. And I say good on them!"

"Very romantic," Kate said. "Aubrey would have a field day with this one." She stopped, remembering where her friend's imagination was probably taking her right now.

"Come on." She stood up and held her hand out to Jack. "Let's get out of here and go find Finn."

An hour later they still had not found a way out of the cave. The wall at the end of the room into which they had fallen was not in fact a wall, but a tunnel of some kind which led ever deeper into the cliff. Spatial awareness had never been Kate's strong suit, and she had no idea whether the cave opened back toward the castle or along the coast. There was no sound from the sea but that meant nothing here. It was a vacuum, an absence of all sensory awareness, and if Jack had not been here, she might have given in to panic and run screaming in the dark until she had no breath left.

The phone screen flickered and went out. For a long second, a mindless fear gripped Kate as she stood in the black nothingness of the cave. She wanted to run, anywhere, to escape the sheer *aloneness* of it all.

But she wasn't alone. Jack was there, his hand reaching, twining his fingers into hers.

"We can't risk using up my phone battery," he whispered into her hair. "We'll have to work our way along the wall until we come to the next opening. Together, okay?"

"Sure. I'm not afraid of the dark, Jack." Kate kept her voice steady. She would not become a burden, she would *not*. She was not a helpless little woman who cowered at the terrors inspired by darkness. She'd killed her share of spiders, oh yes, she had! Her mind latched onto that. *Wonder how big spiders can get in a cave this size? No, scratch that.* Her hand tightened on his, and they worked their way forward.

This was no ordinary darkness, and Kate realized for the first time that real dark, that suffocating blackness that pressed in around her as if seeking a way into her soul, was very different from anything that could be found aboveground. Hell wasn't a place of fire and brimstone, little pointy-tailed demons dancing around the flames with pitchforks. It was a cave, vast and silent, and everything in it was blind.

Time passed as they continued to feel their way down the corridor. How far had they gone? How much time had gone by? Minutes? Hours? Time was an illusion in the all-encompassing darkness.

"Jack," Kate said suddenly. "Is it getting lighter?"

"It is," he said, his voice rising slightly. "Yes! I can see the next turn in the passage!" He grabbed her wrist and pulled her along more quickly now. It had to be an opening in the cliffside. They were free!

As they stumbled out of the passage, they saw that they were standing at the edge of a huge cavern, stone and dirt walls soaring to a ceiling that disappeared into the darkness above. But there was light. It was provided by some kind of fluorescent green plant that grew over the rocks on the cavern floor like a shining moss carpet. Its beauty took Kate's breath away.

"What is it?" she whispered. "It's everywhere!"

"I don't know," Jack said. He moved to the closest plant and bent down. "Some sort of fungus, but it's making its own light. How is that even possible?"

He reached out and touched a leaf of the plant, rubbing it between his fingers. "Soft," he murmured. "Has some sort of bristly things on the underside, though." He broke off the leaf and held it out to Kate. "It's kind of creepy, isn't it?" Kate held the leaf to her nose and sniffed. "Smells moldy." She shivered and dropped the leaf. "Well, whatever it is, it's going to help us find a way out."

Jack took her hand again and moved into the middle of the cavern. "We need to get to the other side. Something is giving this stuff light, and that means there's an opening somewhere." New hope filled his voice.

They continued through the fungal growth until they found the opposite wall. Then they turned to the right and walked along next to the uneven stone, using the glowing green light as their guide.

"Look!" Jack pointed at a small pile of something dark on the floor near the wall. He knelt and picked up one of the objects. "Gloves. Seem to be insulated with something. What would they be doing here? They're not old."

"I don't know. But I don't care. I'm not frightened anymore, Jack. I just know we're going to get out of here!" She grinned at him, feeling a euphoria building inside her. Maybe it was a release of tension due to the discovery of light, or the fascination of the strange plants, or the beauty of the man standing in front of her. She didn't care. The gloves proved that people had been here, and not centuries ago. *Recently.* Everything was going to be all right.

Without thinking, she put her arms around Jack and pressed her lips to his, her need for this man sudden and more powerful than anything she had ever felt before. Forgotten was the danger, the castle, even Finn. All her senses sharpened and centered on the pounding of her heart as it sent a staccato rhythm through her body like a primitive drum.

His response was immediate. In a frenzy of hands and lips they sank to the floor of the cavern, oblivious to everything but the want pulsing between them, a desire older than time itself.

Out of the nothingness of sleep,
The slow dreams of Eternity,
There was a thunder on the deep:
I came, because you called to me.

Rupert Brooke

SCOTLAND 1705

The weather was growing colder. The fierce Highland wind shrieked around the towers and through the chinks in the stones of the old castle, seeking out those who sought warmth from the fire in the great hall of Dunebrae. The damp sea air sank into Caitriona's old bones, and she shivered. She was nearing eighty years old and she knew that her release was at hand. But she had not found Gawen in all those years, and in her heart, she knew that he would not be free to come to her unless she did.

Caitriona had never married. She understood that Gawen had chosen loyalty to his clan over himself, even over his love for her. They had discussed this, and though it broke him she had always known he must. His honor was one of the things she loved most about him. One of so many things. But she had not truly understood how much the loss of him would affect her life. Half of her was gone.

After they had murdered her love in the tower, she had searched for him, wanting to see his body, needing proof that he was truly dead and gone from her. She had raged at her father and hounded his men, but they had been forbidden to tell her the truth of his death. She had kept watch and had not seen him carried out. She had not found a grave on the castle's grounds, and something told her that his body had never left the castle.

In the beginning she had sought to end her life, had stood for hours on the parapet where Gawen had played his pipes for the last time, searching for the courage to jump. And she thought she heard his beloved voice on the wind, telling her that she must live, that she must find him and release his spirit so that someday they could be together again. So she had turned away from death and lived. It was the hardest thing she had ever done. She had begun her search that day, combing the rooms of the castle endlessly to no avail.

When she had faltered, he had come to her in her dreams, as insubstantial as the shadows that huddled in the corners of the old keep, and wrapped his arms around her as she slept. She felt warm for the first time since she had lost him and awakened with tears on her face and the memory of his love in her heart. She rose and began her search again.

Her parents had thought her mind gone, and when she told them she would never marry, that she would kill herself if such a thing were forced upon her, they believed her. She was useless as a pawn in her father's game now, for no one would wed a madwoman. And so she was left alone to wander the halls of Dunebrae, not much more than a ghost herself. She did not care what they thought. She would find him again someday, but *for now she would tell his story to anyone who would listen. She would never stop searching.*

The legend had grown with the years. Visitors to the castle reported hearing strange bagpipe music, though the clan had never taken another piper. Now Caitriona was nearing the end of her life, and still she had not found Gawen. It did not matter. She would never leave the castle without him—not even death could make that decision for her. She would find him, and they would leave together.

Thus she waited, making her way up and down the stairs and corridors of Dunebrae Castle on her painful, crabbed old woman's feet, searching for her love. It did not matter how long it took. She had all the time in the world.

CHAPTER 26

GHOST OF A CHANCE

It was the drugs, of course. The woman seated across from him could not be real. Finn closed his eyes again, willing himself back to that cocoon of black acceptance. His fate was decided, why couldn't he just be allowed to remain in the darkness? Without opening his eyes, he groped with his free hand for one of the two remaining bottles of water.

Do not.

His eyes snapped open. She was still there. A very old woman, gray-skinned but with the shadow of an earlier beauty lingering beneath the wrinkled surface. Her faded lavender dress was from another era, heavily brocaded with a lace shawl and voluminous velvet sleeves. A beaded cap perched on her gray curls. He realized that the dress wasn't faded after all—it was *misty*. Everything about the woman was strangely muted in tone, everything except her eyes, which were a startling blue. As Finn stared at her he felt a chill slither up his spine. He could see the faint outline of the stones in the wall behind her. *Through* her.

The woman was a ghost.

Do not, she said again. *You are needed.*

Her lips didn't move; the voice was in his mind. It was the drugs, he knew that, but he couldn't remember having visions the last two times they'd drugged him. Visions that talked. *That Hector certainly seems to know his way around drugs! Maybe after enough doses of whatever's in those bottles you get brain damage.* Vaguely, he wondered why he was so calm. They were going to kill him. There was nothing he could do about it, and here he was lying handcuffed to a camp bed conversing with a ghost as if it were something he did every day over breakfast.

I need you, the voice in his head repeated, as calm as if it were asking him to pass the sugar.

"What—what can I do for you?" What could he do for anybody in his present predicament? But it couldn't hurt to be polite.

I have found him, but I cannot release him. The specter stared at him with those intense blue eyes.

Finn shook his head. "I don't want to be awake when they come for me," he managed. He groped again for the bottle.

I thought you were a Highlander, the image said, and there was scorn in the voice. *I thought you had courage in you.*

Stung, he pulled his hand back. "Maybe I'll be braver when I'm dead like you," he said with some asperity, surprised that he cared what she thought. "Who are you, anyway?"

She stared at him. *My name is Caitriona, and my clan once owned this castle,* said the voice in his mind.

"Uh-huh. And who is this person you want released?"

The blue eyes lit. *Gawen. I will not move on without him.* The words were flat and final. *I searched for him all my life, but I could not find him while I lived. Now I have found him, but I cannot release him.*

"Why not?" Finn's curiosity was overcoming his shock and fear. He had forgotten that the words and the vision were drug-induced and not real.

The voice was silent, but the woman moved her hand downward until it passed through the edge of the metal bed, and now he saw that her beaded slippers floated just above the floor. Of course, she was incorporeal. Well, there went any thought of her freeing *him.*

"Oh, I see. Well, I wish I could help, but you see what I have to contend with?" Finn rattled the handcuff. He wondered if ghosts retained the ability to sense sarcasm.

Why do you not use that? The woman's head turned toward the corner where he had seen the tiny metal object before. Before the drugs in the food had taken him out again. A day, two days ago? Had it even been real?

But there it was, a faint dark shadow in the gloom, well out of reach. A sliver of hope sliced through him. Working his way into a sitting position, he pushed himself off the bed and stood as straight as he could, swaying with that little bit of effort. He waited for the dizziness to pass and tugged at the metal frame with his free hand, surprised to see that it moved an inch or two. He sat down again, exhausted.

Taking a deep breath, Finn stood again and pulled the bed inch by inch toward the corner where the object lay. Every foot or so he had to sit down, overcome by weakness from the effects of drugs and lack of food. He had no idea how long it took him to finally reach a point where he could bend over and grasp the thing, a rusty piece of iron, with his free hand. Did it even matter? How much time did he have left?

He sat on the edge of the bed and worked the sliver in and out of the handcuff's lock, mind focused on that one task, careful not to let the tiny bit of metal slip out of his trembling fingers. *Looks a hell of a lot easier in the movies.* But he couldn't give up. *I'm a Highlander, damn it!* In and out, in and out.

The handcuff fell open.

Finn sat for a minute simply staring at it. He was free. He struggled to his feet and went to the door. Locked—okay, not quite free. But this was something his captors could not have anticipated. That in itself was a victory.

He stood and stretched his back, working the kinks out, and then looked at the two remaining water bottles. They had checked on him while he was unconscious. Taken the empty away to show him they were in control and watching. Which meant they'd be back to check again, leaving nothing to chance. Finn dragged the camp bed back to its original location, finding the job easier with both hands free. He picked up the two bottles and studied their contents. Taking them to the opposite corner, he unscrewed the lids and poured the water out. He watched as the tainted liquid seeped into the cracks in the ancient stone floor and disappeared. No matter what happened, he was never going back into that morass of despair again.

Good lad, said the voice in his head.

Finn jerked in surprise and turned. The bed across from him was empty. The ghost was gone.

He went back to his own bed and sat down, thinking. His head was clearer now, but the voice and the image remained embedded in his mind. She had wanted him to release someone, had been sure he could do it. Was the person—well, it would have to be another ghost, wouldn't it—somewhere nearby?

He was startled by the sound of a soft moan, seeming to come from the walls themselves. Mournful, low, it began as a woeful monotone and built into a haunting melody. It grew and expanded into a crescendo of music, pulling at the heart and filling the small room. The power and sadness in that tune were almost unbearable. Finn sat up straight, holding his breath. It was the sound of a single set of bagpipes, playing a piece that by now he knew well. "The Piper's Warning to His Master." The song played by the Dunebrae piper, the castle's favorite ghost—suddenly, he knew who Gawen was.

The sound died away, dwindled to nothing. Finn stood and stared at the walls of his prison, looking for a clue. He wished the woman had stayed with him, even in his head. A ghost was at least company. The loneliness pressed in around him, threatening with a return to despair. But now he had no drugged water in which to escape, and there was nothing to do but move on.

The walls of the room were the same unrelieved grey stone all around, blocks about eight inches square and sealed with a grey mortar about a quarter-inch wide. With no idea why, he stood to the right of the door and began to work his way around the room, finding his way by touch more than sight as the only light in the room came from the intermittent moonlight that worked its way through the grimy window high above him. Time crawled.

He had covered one wall and was beginning on the second when he sensed a fading of the darkness in the room. Dawn was brightening his window, sending a soft light to help him. But with the morning came something else, something not so welcome. He heard voices in the hallway outside his prison and approaching footsteps. His guard was back.

Finn crossed to the bed and threw himself down. He slid his wrist through the loosened cuff, praying they wouldn't look too closely at it or hear his heart pounding. He closed his eyes and made his face go slack. The door snicked open.

"Ugh, he's like that every time we check. Definitely takin' the easy way out," said a voice. "Boss said he would. Weird, how he's just layin' there like he's dead already." The voice sounded strained. "Creeps me out."

Footsteps approached the bed.

"Hey," said a second voice, "he drank both bottles this time." A harsh chuckle. "Think he's trying to kill himself and save us the trouble?"

A snort, very close by. "Very accommodating, our lad."

Finn lay still, eyes closed, willing his breathing to

remain slow and even. A hand pushed at his shoulder, lifted his arm and let it fall. He forced himself to remain limp.

"He's really under. Maybe he won't wake up at all." The hand patted his cheek. "Better for him if he doesn't."

The first voice, moving farther away, "Better for us, too. Two more days and this'll be over. We don't need to come back till then, do we? It's not like he's goin' anywhere. C,mon, I hate this room."

The footsteps receded, the door closed, and silence descended on the room again. Finn lay still for several more minutes and then opened his eyes the tiniest fraction, looking under his lashes at the door. He was alone. The empty water bottles had been replaced with two full ones.

Two more days. Hector had said they were leaving for Glasgow on Thursday, so this must be Tuesday. He'd been in this room for three days! Shaking off the clutching fear and gnawing hunger, he emptied the bottles into the corner and began to probe the stone walls of his prison once more. Working through the day and into the night, his hands probed as far up as he could reach, and down to the floor.

The room was much larger than he'd realized from his position on the camp bed, and he began to despair as time passed in a monotonous blur. Still he kept on, probing every inch of the walls, afraid to miss anything. The light from the dirty window waxed and waned as the hours passed, too quickly. He slept, aware that his body was shutting down, and forced himself to get up and start once more.

He reached the last wall. This one was farthest from the pitiful source of light, and almost invisible in the gloom. Still, he could tell that light was growing in the room behind him. A new day—his last—was beginning, and he had found nothing. A knot of panic curled in his stomach. One more day. Time was moving too fast, and he didn't even know what he was searching for. He was going on the word of a ghost!

Finn sensed his movements slowing as his body weakened and his throat cried out for water. At some point he took off his jacket and threw it onto the bed, hoping that the insidious cold brought on by dehydration would help to keep him awake. He kept pushing and prodding, searching for anything to keep his attention on the mindless task.

The thoughts of Aubrey that he had pushed to the back of his mind seeped back into his consciousness. Her warm hazel eyes, her brilliant smile. For some reason, thinking of her no longer sent him into despair. No matter what happened in the next hours, he was glad she was here with him. He began to talk to her in his mind as he studied, poked, prodded.

"Well, darling, I can tell you one thing," he said to her as his fingers moved over one square gray block and onto the next. "Our house is going to be made of wood. I never want to see another stone block again!

"No wonder castles were so cold," he told her. "These people didn't know shite about insulation. I can feel the wind right through this mortar. Terrible workmanship. And look, here there's no mortar at all!"

He stopped. *No mortar at all. That was curious.* He backed up a few feet and studied the wall from a distance. He was right, an entire section of the wall had nothing between the blocks. They were jammed up tight against each other, wedged firmly together with no space between as with the mortared blocks. Odd.

Finn began to push on the blocks. Tight, seamless, they didn't budge. They weren't as evenly placed as the mortared stones, though, almost as if the builders had been in a hurry to finish. He kept pushing.

A block moved. In the dim light he felt the tiniest shift under his fingers and pushed it harder. It moved inward on the wall a fraction of an inch. He began to jiggle it back and forth against the blocks beside it and was rewarded by more progress. The block was definitely moving inward! Excited now, Finn pushed with his little remaining strength, and suddenly the block slid back and tumbled into a hole behind the wall.

An odd, stale odor emanated from the opening, air that had been trapped perhaps for centuries emerging for the first time into the larger space. Finn took a deep breath. But why was there a space behind the wall in the first place? These keeps were built simply, with a single layer of stone forming the barrier between rooms, or between a room and the outside. This was unusual. There must have been an alcove behind the wall at one time. He felt his pulse begin to race. Could there be a secret passage back there, or a door? A way out? With renewed energy he attacked the block next to the hole, and it fell in behind the wall to join its fellow.

Reaching an arm into the enlarged space, Finn began to pull the un-mortared stones toward him, out into the room. It took precious minutes with his diminishing strength and he could feel himself losing the battle, but he stacked each block against the wall and went back to his task, excitement mounting. The daylight from the tiny window had faded, and he could not see more than a few inches into the opening. Hunger and thirst were winning; he had to stop after every stone and bend over to catch his breath and clear his head. The shivering was intensifying as his body shut down. But he kept going.

He stopped and looked into the hole he had made, roughly three feet square now. He could see the shadow of another wall about three feet behind this one. Renewing his efforts, he continued to pull out stones until he had cleared a narrow hole from chest height almost to the floor. He leaned over to catch his breath one more time, hands on his knees, and then knelt and pulled out the bottom stone.

A heap of rotting fabric—leather?—sat on the floor inside the hole. On top of the fabric rested three carved wooden sticks. No, not sticks—they were hollow, like pipes. A new chill crawled down Finn's spine as he realized he was looking at the remnants of an ancient set of Great Highland Bagpipes.

A larger heap of sticks littered the floor next to the bag, and with a gasp of horror he saw what was perched on top. Staring back at him from empty sockets, a human skull lay on top of the pile of sticks. Only they weren't sticks.

They were bones.

CHAPTER 27

HIGHLANDER

Kate's head was pounding. She pushed herself to a sitting position, wondering how she'd wound up on the floor. No, not the floor. She was lying half on rough stone, half on—she flinched as reality flooded back—she was lying wrapped in the arms of Jack MacDonald. And she was shivering. *Oh God, I'm half naked! What the hell?*

Clarity forced its way into her mind as she struggled to make some space between them. Jack pulled her back, mumbling something in a low voice, and then stiffened and pushed her roughly away. Kate stared into green eyes round with shock, and then both dove for their clothing, racing each other to get dressed.

Kate watched Jack warily from her cocoon of mortification, waiting for him to say something—anything. She had never seen the perfectly controlled detective MacDonald so rattled before. His hair straggled over his forehead; his breath came in gasps. Despite her embarrassment she was amused at his discomfiture—until the memory of what they had been doing moments earlier began to filter back into her consciousness. She covered her flaming face with both hands.

"What the hell?" He rasped, and then clutched his head with both hands. "What just happened?"

A surge of anger unlike anything Kate had ever felt before coursed through her. Her hands snapped down and became fists, white-knuckled and trembling.

"What do you mean, you bastard?" She hissed at him. "How *could* you? I trusted you! What in hell did you give me?" She was surprised to feel tears rolling down her face. She would have given herself to him willingly, but this? This was a betrayal of everything she was coming to feel for this man.

"I don't know what you're talking about!" Jack's face was beet-red, and his breath rasped like the bellows of a steam engine. "How the hell would I slip you anything? And *why* in God's name would I?"

Kate stared into furious green eyes, eyes in which the pupils were strangely dilated, and slowly it began to sink in. He wouldn't. Of course he wouldn't. She did trust Jack MacDonald, and with returning sanity came the realization that she wasn't the only one who was floundering here. She pushed herself back against the rough stone wall and tried to focus, shame coursing through her body and taking the anger with it.

"I'm s-sorry. Really, Jack, I didn't mean that. We've been drugged. Both of us. But how?"

Dragging his gaze away from her, Jack looked around the huge cavern. Innocent green plants stared placidly back at him, their weird phosphorescent light reflecting off the stone walls, illuminating the passageway and the pile of gloves.

Gloves. He walked to the pile and knelt to pick up a glove. It was black, made of some sort of thick rubber, maybe silicone, and at least 20 inches in length. Next to the gloves was a large box of heavy-duty trash bags.

Jack studied the glove. "PVC maybe," he murmured. "The kind they use in HazMat work or with chemicals. Why would they need these here?"

His eyes met Kate's. Together they looked from the gloves to the only other thing of substance in the cavern.

"It's the plants." Kate's voice was almost a whisper, as if she feared the green fungi could hear her. "We touched the plants."

Jack picked up three more gloves and came over to hand her a pair. "We're getting out of here—now," he said. He put on his gloves, walked over to the bank of fungi and carefully pulled a plant up by its shallow roots. His voice was shaking as he returned to her. "If these plants are what I think they are, we've discovered the answer to everything. I want to take one of these things with us to show Brown. Kate!" He stared into her astonished eyes. "I think we've discovered the source of Reign!"

"There's just one problem," Kate told him. She looked at the beautiful plant and shuddered. "We can't carry that . . . *thing* around with us when we get out. We have to find Finn."

"We will find him." Jack's eyes were shining. "But you're right." He dropped the plant but kept the gloves on. We'll find Finn first, come back and pick up the fungus there, and get it to Brown. Now we know what they were hiding! We're almost there, Kate!"

Kate looked around. "So all we have to do is find a way out, avoid getting captured by Munro's goons, sneak into the castle and find Finn, rescue him, come back and grab our nasty green friend there, and too-dle on down the road to Inverness without letting the thing drug us again. Easy-peasy."

Jack glared at her. "You're not helping."

"I'm sorry," she said, her voice almost steady. "I tend to get sarcastic when I'm scared."

"I noticed," Jack assured her. "So, first step—get-ting out. There has to be something easier than the way we got in, right?" He looked around the dark cavern, lit by the eerie glow of the plants. "The key is the gloves," he decided. "We know how many people come in and out of this cavern, because there were three sets of gloves in that pile. They must put the gloves on there and return them to the pile after they bag the plants."

"And," Kate walked over to the pile, "the entrance must be somewhere near here, because they wouldn't risk walking too far into the cave without protection." She began to run her hands along the wall at the point where the light of the plants tapered into darkness.

Jack joined her, and together they inched their way further away from the plants. Fifteen minutes later they stood in the darkness, having found nothing. Kate could feel herself near tears with frustration.

Come.

"What?" Kate said to Jack.

"I didn't say anything," he began, and then stopped.

You must come.

They'd both heard it this time. Turning slowly, Kate grabbed and held Jack's gloved hand as a woman came out of the darkness. She was a very old woman. Her voluminous velvet gown cascaded to the floor from a bodice that had been beautifully brocaded in beadwork that would have cost a fortune, had it been made recently. But Kate knew it had not been made in Edinburgh or London, or in any modern city. She knew it because she recognized the woman. She had seen her once before, gliding across the hall in Dunebrae Castle in those beaded slippers that didn't quite touch the floor.

Up close, Kate could see that the woman's coloring was a pale grey that owed none of its pallor to her advanced years. Everything about her was muted, nearly colorless—everything except her eyes, which were a radiant blue. Those eyes were lit with a joy that called to Kate in the deepest recesses of her heart. They were the eyes of a woman in love. A ghost in love, Kate corrected herself, for that was what she was.

He is free.

The voice trembled with excitement, and Kate turned to see that Jack had heard it too, although the old woman's lips had not moved.

The Highlander has released him.

"R-released?" Kate felt as if her tongue was glued to the roof of her mouth. "Who is free?"

Come. The Highlander needs your help. You must hurry.

The ghost turned and floated away into the darkness, and after a look at each other Kate and Jack followed.

She led them through a narrow crevice in the rock wall and down a passageway. Before they had gone fifty feet, they could hear the surf crashing onto the rocky beach below Dunebrae Castle, and a moment later they emerged into the grey light of a North Highlands morning. The ghost was nowhere to be seen.

With great care they took off the gloves and stuffed them under a rock. Jack fished his phone out of his sweatshirt pocket and powered it on. After so long in darkness, the light on the display seemed out of place, alien, but oh, so welcome.

"It's half-seven," Jack said, and then gasped. "Half-seven on *Thursday!*" Kate gaped at him. They'd been in the cave for two days. It could have been two weeks, or two months, it didn't matter. Time had lost all meaning in the darkness.

She looked at the cliff face in front of them, and saw the opening to a narrow path which seemed to disappear into the cliff itself. As they drew closer, they could see that although it was overgrown with bushes, the path wound along the face of the cliff and gradually led upward toward the top, one hundred feet above the rocky beach.

"Ready?" Jack asked her, striding ahead with confidant steps.

She nodded but didn't move.

He turned back. "What?"

"Jack . . . I just want you to know, in case—I don't regret what we did . . . in the cave. I'm glad it happened." Her steady gaze held his.

Jack covered the distance between them in two steps and crushed her to his chest, covering her lips with his own.

"Oh, Kate," he murmured. "I feel as if I've waited a lifetime to hear you say that." He stepped back, eyes sparkling. "But next time, let's try it without the drugs, aye?"

He took her hand and pulled her along toward the cliff face. Despite the danger, and the ghost, despite the crushing fear for Finn, Kate couldn't help the grin that spread across her face as she followed in his wake.

As they made their way up the steep twisting path toward the top, it became obvious that this was an access route, probably used by the drug harvesters. It had been carefully tended to be serviceable but invisible. Gorse bushes and heather had been cleverly planted to appear random and wild, but close up it was obvious that each bush and plant had its purpose in disguising the pathway from casual observers. As they passed, the plants closed in behind them over the path.

Jack stopped near the top and squeezed Kate's hand. Nothing could be heard except the endless roar of the surf behind them, but they were taking no chances. Munro seemed to have a great number of men in his employ, and they might still be on the lookout for the trespassers they'd chased two nights ago.

Jack poked his head above the cliff edge at the top of the path. Nothing. Motioning Kate to follow, he crept on hands and knees through the tall grass until he reached the trees at the edge of the property. There they stood up and surveyed their surroundings, expecting any minute to hear a shout of alarm that would signal their discovery. Still nothing.

Keeping to the tree line, the two worked their way toward the castle. Now they could hear shouts ahead, and it became clear why no one seemed to be searching for them. Men called to each other as they passed in and out of a door at the back of the castle and emerged carrying drums and bagpipe cases. The equipment was being loaded into the luggage hold of a huge tour bus emblazoned with the name *The House of Munro.*

"They're packing up for the Worlds!" Jack said in a low voice. They watched as two men carried a huge trunk and carefully stowed it under the bus.

"What if they're taking Finn with them?" whispered Kate. "What if he's in one of those trunks? What if he's—" she stopped, unable to articulate the thought.

"Shhh," he said into her hair, and put his arm around her shoulder. "We can't think that! I doubt they'd risk being caught carrying a kidnap victim on their tour bus," he murmured. "I think he's somewhere in the castle. But it's time to call Brown. I'm going to tell him to intercept that bus before it gets to Glasgow, just to be sure." He pulled out his phone and made the call, keeping his report to the bare minimum and requesting backup immediately. He hung up, and for a while they watched the men going in and out of the castle, unsure how to get into the great keep without being discovered.

Come.

Kate heard the voice before she saw the ghost. She pointed to a space where the trees nearly butted up to the castle. A flash of faded lavender velvet disappeared around the corner away from the activity surrounding the bus. Kate and Jack followed.

On this side of the castle the grass had been left to grow wild, and the forest had encroached nearly to the walls. At first glance there were no doors there, just impenetrable gray stone.

Hurry.

An amorphous shape flickered against the stones, and in the next second was gone. Kate and Jack crept up to the blank wall and were shocked to see that a section of it was in reality a door built right into the foundation and nearly invisible. It had probably been constructed centuries ago as an escape route from the castle in case of attack. Unless one was right next to the wall it was impossible to see. And now it was their way in.

The door pushed inward soundlessly, and they found themselves in a dark passageway. *Not really so dark*, Kate thought. After spending nearly two days in a cave, she had a new appreciation for the nuances of light and dark. *Pooh, this is nothing!* She squeezed Jack's hand and they moved forward.

The ghost led them onward. The spectre was more like a sensation than an actual presence, but there was no doubt that she was showing them the way. But to what? Who had been released? Was it Finn? And who was the person who had released him? One of Munro's men? The ghost had called him "the

Highlander," but that wasn't very helpful. Everyone in the north of Scotland was a Highlander. For a moment Kate wondered if they were going insane, wasting time following a ghost around the halls of an ancient castle.

We're on a wild ghost chase, she thought to herself, and wondered when she'd become so accustomed to the idea of ghosts that she could joke about them.

When I saw the look on her face. That's when I really began to believe. Their journey through passageways and up staircases seemed achingly slow, but it gave Kate the opportunity to examine the reality of her ghost. The woman had been real, a human being with joys and sorrows. She had lived, and she had loved.

The sheer ecstasy on the old woman's face was something that Kate would remember for the rest of her life because she knew that feeling. It was how she had felt about Eddie. It was how she suspected she was beginning to feel about Jack. She tightened her hand in his and smiled in the darkness.

Another hallway, another staircase. It seemed to be taking forever, but they had to proceed with painful caution to avoid discovery. They had heard no one during their journey, but surely everyone couldn't be outside loading the bus. And where was Duncan Munro?

A man stepped out into the corridor ahead of them, and they froze in place. If he turned to look behind him there was no way he wouldn't see them standing there. He continued on, however, and a moment later disappeared down a side corridor.

A flash of lavender ahead, another stone staircase.

This had to be the topmost floor of the castle, and it was obvious that few used these passageways or rooms. Dust bunnies chased each other in the corners of the hall, and ancient wooden doors stood open to empty rooms that smelled of age and decay. All except one—the last door in the hallway was closed.

"Look!" Kate tugged Jack's hand as they approached. The dust had been disturbed in front of this door; there was the faint outline of footprints leading to and away from it down another hallway. Jack put his finger to his lips and reached forward, slowly placing his hand on the iron door handle. He pushed it down, but the door didn't open. Locked.

They froze in place as they heard a sound in the room. Faint, like a whisper of movement. Mice?

In the next instant Jack's vision narrowed to a pinpoint of red agony as a blinding pain exploded in his head. Rough hands wrenched him away from the door and threw him against the wall, and through a curtain of pain he saw a muscular arm slide around Kate's neck.

CHAPTER 28

REIGN FALL

Hector Munro sat alone in his great room and watched through the massive mullioned windows as the big tour bus pulled around from the back, heading for the car park and the road to Glasgow. With his father safely on his way to the Worlds and another ridiculous championship, it was time to clean up the last of the loose ends. *All's well that ends well, for those who deserve it.*

He rested his head against the back of the luxurious upholstery and closed his eyes as he mentally ticked off the challenges he had faced and overcome. The traitor Hugh Ross, his favorite assassin, his father. All taken care of, no longer a threat. It seemed that his worries had been too soon; his empire was safe after all. There would be no need to wrap up the operation or cease production. Only one or two problems left, and those were well in hand.

He opened his eyes and cast them up to the ornate carved molding on the ceiling of the great room. His men had gone up to the tower room an hour ago to take care of one of those last niggling problems. With Cameron gone, all that would remain were the two persistent detectives, that MacDonald policeman and his American partner, and plans were in place for them as well.

Two nights ago, some of his guards had reported intruders near the cliff edge of the property. The men had thought their quarry trapped, but somehow they'd escaped. Probably gone back to Inverness, frustrated that their snooping had gone for nothing. He was sure he knew who they were, and if he was right, they'd be back. He'd have to double the guards.

Hector was not foolish enough to think that Cameron's death would put an end to their meddling. On the contrary, grief and anger might spur them on to increase their investigation of the castle and its connection to Reign. They would be able to prove nothing, but they would continue to bite at his ankles like rabid dogs until they were put down. A cold smile spread across his handsome features. He was looking forward to that.

He would like nothing better than to see them slither back into his home in their guise as potential honeymooners. Like the spider and the fly, he envisioned throwing wide his doors and inviting them to walk into his parlor, never to emerge. But that he could not do. He might be able to avoid any connection to Cameron's accident, but he would never be able to explain the disappearance of two police detectives. They had colleagues and bosses, and he was certain that they had not been working alone.

No, he was going to have to settle for something altogether less satisfying. His investigators had told him that the American girl was almost at the end of her visitor's visa. She'd been here since April, which meant that by this time next month she would be on a plane back to her own country. Once she was gone, he could bide his time and take care of MacDonald at his leisure—another unfortunate accident of some kind, far away from Dunebrae.

He hated the need to wait, despised the man for much more than his meddling. Wasn't it ironic that MacDonald's ancestors had once held this castle for a brief time, before the Campbells had taken back their property from the interlopers? The Campbells and the Munros had been allies since the eighteenth century, and Hector felt it nothing more than his duty to rid the world of another MacDonald bastard.

He despised all MacDonalds with every fiber of his being, felt the old enmity course through his veins every time he heard the name. He'd tried to explain his bloodlust to his father, but the old man cared little for history, unless it was the history of bagpipes. He knew his father laughed at him for his passion; he'd never been able to hide his amusement.

His father. Sending him to the Worlds this year had been a risk, because the drug was beginning to take its toll on the old man's health and mental state. Hector worried that others were starting to notice Duncan's lapses in concentration and his instability.

Hector had been dosing his father with Reign

in his beloved tea for nearly two years now and, though judiciously moderated, it had begun to take over Duncan's personality. The euphoria was being replaced with flashes of anger totally unlike his normal aura of bonhomie, and people who knew him well would soon notice.

But it was necessary. Duncan had to be kept away from the operation, and that meant the workroom, when the pipes were being prepared for delivery. His blackout periods assured his ignorance and compliance and kept him occupied. And there was another reason—perhaps the most important, although Hector didn't like to admit it because it hinted at a weakness he preferred not to acknowledge even to himself.

The old man had become close to Cameron in just those few short visits. Hector knew that in the young piper his father saw the son that Hector had never been, the one who shared his vision and his passion. It hurt to see the two of them deep in conversation about things he had never understood and cared even less about. When he had found his father showing Cameron the bagpipe workroom—*his* workroom now—he had found his excuse to exorcise his jealousy and remove a threat to the operation at the same time. Perfect.

But then he'd gotten careless. He'd neglected to place the old man's precious tea back in place exactly as Duncan left it—the special brew that contained just the tiniest dose of Reign. Maybe his subconscious had done it on purpose. He knew that the time was nearing when his father would have to be taken out of the picture, and it broke his heart.

Hector had not lied when he'd told Cameron he loved his father. Even though he couldn't be the son Duncan Munro deserved, he had tried. He had taken the running of the castle off the older Munro's hands, left him to his passion while he, Hector, did all the work to keep it from disappearing into the mists of time like so many other old keeps. And Duncan was grateful, he knew that much was true. They shared a deep affection for each other despite their differences. It was going to be difficult to say goodbye.

That was why he'd decided to do it himself. Maybe it was a good thing that Duncan's behavior had become so erratic lately. Hector was glad he'd sent his father on this last trip to the Worlds. One more triumph, one more day in the sun. His fellow captains, those who knew him best, would discuss his sad decline and wonder what would happen to the world's top pipe band when he was gone. They would shake their heads in understanding when later he was found to have died in his sleep. But they could never know how hard it would be for Hector. He felt a tear slide down his cheek and wiped it away.

He sat up. His men should be well down the road with Cameron by now. They had been told to carry the piper's body out through the utility door near the bagpipe room and from there to the barn where his car was hidden. A sudden morbid curiosity had Hector hurrying through the door to the hallway that had been swarming with band members such a short time ago. He had to see for himself. He stopped before a bookshelf next to the doorway and extracted a small handgun from a secret compartment before entering the darkened corridor. He hadn't come this far by rushing into things, and it never hurt to be prepared.

Everything was quiet now, the door to the bag-pipe workshop shut and locked as it should be, the newly treated pipes safely stowed and on their way to Glasgow Green. Hector made his way out to where the barn stood nearly hidden by the trees. The door was closed and locked, the padlock winking in the weak morning sunlight. He rifled in his pocket for his keys and removed the one he wanted, heart pound-ing in anticipation as he inserted it into the lock and pulled back the double doors.

The Audi stood silent in the gloom of the dark garage.

Hector stared in disbelief at the vehicle and felt something cold and clammy slip up his spine. Something was wrong; his men and their burden should have been long gone by now. He turned to run back to the castle but froze in the shadows of the trees that hid the barn. Before his disbelieving eyes cars poured up the driveway, past the car park and onto the vast manicured lawn. The distinctive blue and yellow stripes of Police Scotland registered in Hector's mind seconds before the cars ground to a halt and officers leapt out of the vehicles, spreading out to surround his home.

It couldn't be! Had his own men betrayed him?

Hector shook himself out of his shock and began to run through the trees to the edge of his property. He had one chance now: the cave. No one knew its secret—he could hide there until the police gave up searching and went away. Then he would take one of his cars and join Duncan in Glasgow. He would enjoy a weekend at the World Pipe Band Championships, just as his father had always wanted. The police would have no reason to question him. They might have thought they had traced the drug to Dunebrae, but they could prove nothing. There were no drugs on the property. They could search all they wanted, but they would never find anything.

He stumbled as a shaft of bitter realization reached through the shock and hit his mind like a bludgeon. Hector's vision narrowed to a dot of anguish and he fell to his hands and knees, shaking.

They would find Cameron.

Cameron, drugged and shackled to a cot in the tower room. Cameron, to whom he'd poured out every detail of the operation called Reign in his unwavering conviction that he was talking to a dead man. Hector struggled to his feet and grabbed at a branch. He held on, swaying, as the truth swept through him with the force of a North Sea storm. An odd, acrid taste filled his mouth. He had never experienced it before, but he knew it for what it was—the bitter taste of failure.

It was over.

CHAPTER 29

CAITRIONA'S GIFT

As if in a dream, Kate watched Jack's forehead snap sideways as a fist ploughed into the side of his head. In the next second she felt an arm snake around her own neck and a hand push her head forward.

There was a second of sheer panic and then her training kicked in. She heard Rob Morelli's voice as if he were right beside her, coaching her through the department's self-defense classes. *In a rear naked choke hold*, he said, *size doesn't matter. Speed and practice are the key. You must get the upper hand before your attacker can get his arm into place around your throat—if you don't, you will be unconscious in five seconds and dead within minutes.*

Kate had always imagined that this type of attack would happen at the speed of light, but instead everything seemed to stop for a long second. Then the world went into slow-motion, and she gave herself up to memory and let her training take over.

Bury your chin in the crook of his elbow, Morelli's voice said. *Protect your throat.*

It was a lethal dance. Kate lowered her chin so that the muscular arm squeezed against the hard bone of her jaw. It hurt like hell, but that meant she was still conscious, still fighting. She put both hands on the elbow locked around her neck and pulled it in toward her chest.

Twist in the direction of your attacker's arm, Morelli's calm voice came to her out of the shadows in the dim hallway.

Kate spun to her right, and at the same time swung her left leg and pivoted in the same direction. The man's arm became a gate, his elbow the hinge, and that gate swung wide open. She was free. She whirled and hammered her fist into her assailant's kidney, gratified to hear a gasp of pain.

Run, if you can, Morelli's voice told her, but that was not an option. She was not leaving Jack, no matter what happened. And she remembered what her partner had said over and over about the realities of self-defense training. *In a world with no rules, strike first, and don't stop until the battle is over.* She punched again and again at anything she could reach.

Her attacker was faster than she thought possible for his size. Everything went black, then red, as he punched her in the face with a meaty fist. The pain was excruciating, and she fought not to pass out. She tasted blood and smelled the metallic tang of copper, knew her nose was probably broken. Forcing the pain away she ducked under the burly arm, came up in front of him and jabbed the fingers of both hands into his eyes, at the same time forcing her knee between his legs and wrenching it sideways. A howl of pain escaped the man's mouth as he fell over onto the floor, but Kate wasn't finished. She felt a blood-lust building inside her, and knew she wanted to kill this piece of garbage, for Jack, for Finn, for herself.

"This is how women fight!" she snarled at him and kicked him in the groin with all her strength. He crumpled into a heap and curled into the fetal position, whimpering. Kate saw herself as if from a distance, saw her warrior-self bring a booted foot down on his temple with everything she had left in her battered body. He went still.

I did it! Morelli, I did it! For a few seconds Kate forgot where she was in the sheer glory of victory, and then she turned to see Jack locked in a struggle with another huge opponent. *Were all Duncan Munro's employees giants?* Her left eye was swelling, and blood streamed from her nose, but she didn't notice. Somehow Jack was still on his feet, trading punches with his massive adversary. The man outweighed him by at least fifty pounds, and none of that bulk was fat. Jack's lighter build might have given him the advantage of speed and agility, but the attacker had utilized the element of surprise and she could see Jack wince as his left arm was wrenched behind him and his head slammed again into the wall.

Half-blind and choking on her own blood, Kate began to punch their adversary with all she had left. He hardly moved, simply reached behind and swept her aside. Her interference gave Jack the time to twist out of his grasp, however, and he regained his footing with a grimace and planted his good arm into the man's solar plexus. It was like a fly buzzing in a horse's face. With a small *oof*, the attacker shrugged off the blow, put his hands around Jack's neck, and squeezed.

Kate felt as if she were moving through a vat of molasses. *Too slow, I can't stop him and Jack can't reach the PAVA!* Despair flooded her mind, nearly stopping her breath, and then her pain-soaked brain remembered the sgian dubh still strapped to her ankle. Her souvenir of Scotland, gift from Jack. Without allowing herself to think, she bent and pulled it from its leather sheath.

Jack's face was turning purple. His eyes bulged and his one good arm flapped helplessly in the air. Still the murderous hands squeezed, closing off the air from his victim's lungs. Jack's legs buckled as the oxygen to his brain was shut off and his limbs turned to rubber. He began to slide down the wall toward the floor.

Intent on his task, the killer had forgotten the nuisance that was Kate Bianchi. With a force born of desperation, she called on the last bit of strength left in her body, reaching up to thrust the short blade into his neck, watching as blood splattered the wall of the hallway.

Not enough blood; she hadn't hit anything vital. Still, the small dagger had done its job and the man's hands left Jack's throat and went to his own, scrabbling to find the source of the searing pain. It was enough.

Jack sucked in a huge breath of air and lunged forward. He grasped the sgian dubh with his right hand and planted it in his attacker's chest, thrusting upward between the ribs with the last of his strength. As the knife slid in sideways to the hilt, the man's eyes went wide with surprise and his meaty hands pawed at his chest. Kate and Jack were forgotten as his mouth opened and closed and he stood swaying. Then, almost gracefully, he folded to the floor and lay still, blank eyes staring at the ceiling. An eerie silence returned to the hallway.

Jack leaned back against the wall and slowly slid to the floor. Kate limped over and sank down beside him, put her throbbing head against his shoulder, and stared at the bodies of the men who would have killed them. She didn't know if the first man was dead or only unconscious, and she didn't care. Jack was alive. The good guys had won this round.

They sat still for a long time, holding each other as the adrenaline drained out of their bodies. Minutes that could have been hours inched by, and neither had the will to rise. Kate felt her nose with tentative fingers and was gratified to find that it had stopped bleeding, although it pounded like a drum and the pain made her want to vomit. Jack took short breaths to ease the pain in his constricted throat. None of it mattered. They were alive.

Another noise, a sort of soft scraping sound, came through the locked wooden door, reminding them that they still had a job to do. Something was in that room, and it wasn't a mouse. Jack struggled to his feet and pulled Kate up with his good arm, wincing. They stared at the door, clutching each other for support.

"See if one of these guys has a key," Jack rasped. "I don't think they were up here because of us."

Unwilling to touch the dead man, Kate went through the pockets of the one she had incapacitated. Grinning in triumph she held up a ring of keys, and Jack met her grim smile with one of his own as he rose from the other body holding a cell phone and a set of car keys with the distinctive Audi logo emblazoned on its fob.

Kate handed Jack the key ring and he turned to the door and inserted one. Nothing. He tried keys until there was a snicking noise and the lock disengaged. The door swung inward an inch and stopped as it came in contact with something just inside the room, blocking their access. Jack took a deep breath, pushed—and fell over a camp bed that had been placed in front of the door.

"Jesus! Shite! What the hell!" he yelled, as he landed on his injured arm on the stone floor. Kate shoved the bed out of the doorway and took a stand in front of him as he struggled to his feet. She swung her one-eyed gaze around the room, taking in the details quickly.

The room was dim, lit only by a tiny round window far above them on the wall to their left. Nothing but stone straight ahead. Near the corner of the wall to their right was a gaping hole, and nearly lost in the gloom another camp bed, empty. In front of it stood Finn Cameron, dull-eyed and grim, clutching a large block of stone in shaking hands as he swayed back and forth like a drunk.

The man was filthy. Dirt streaked his pale, sunken face and covered his kilt and a shirt that might have been white in another lifetime. His blue eyes were dull and red-rimmed, and his skin was the pasty gray of prolonged dehydration. They stared at each other in shock as Jack clambered to a standing position, holding his arm. For a long moment it seemed as if Finn didn't recognize them. Then the stone block slipped from his hands and thudded to the floor.

"K-Kate?" he whispered through cracked lips. "Jack?" Finn's eyes rolled up into his head and he pitched forward into Kate's arms, taking them both into the bed in the middle of the room. Holding his unconscious body in her arms, Kate looked up at Jack, her face tight with fury.

"They've starved him," she said, feeling the heat begin to build. "The bastards!"

Finn's eyes opened and he took a long, raspy breath. "W-water?" he whispered.

"We'll get you out of here and find you some water. Hang on."

Jack looked at the metal bed, and at the hand-cuff dangling from one rail. Understanding dawned as he looked from the cuff to the bruises around Finn's wrist. His face tightened and his eyes blazed. Without a word he left the room, and a moment later returned dragging the unconscious body of the henchman who had attacked Kate.

"Do you mind lending me your handcuff?" Jack said, his voice a thin snarl.

Finn stared in confusion. Kate eased herself out from under him and helped him to stand braced against the wall. She crossed to help her partner heft the body of the attacker onto the cot and snap the cuff around the man's wrist.

Jack straightened with a glare. "I can't think of a better use for it, can you?"

Kate limped back to the handcuff's former owner. "Can you walk, Finn?" She assessed his condition through her working eye. "We need you to move on your own, if you can. We'll get you water, but first we have to get you out of here."

Finn struggled to stand erect. "I can w-walk," he told her in a voice that sounded like a rusty gate. "But wait." He stopped to get a fresh breath and put a hand out to brace himself against the wall. "You need to meet s-someone."

"What?" Jack sputtered. "Are you serious?" We have to go! Now!"

"I know." Finn swayed for a moment, and then focused on his friend's face with determination. He lurched forward and nearly fell again, and Jack reached out with his good arm to steady him. Finn clutched at the arm and pulled Jack over to the other bed. With a shaking finger, he pointed at something lying on it. Kate followed, wondering if the experience had broken their friend's sanity. Then she saw where he was pointing, and all other thoughts fled her mind.

They were looking at a skeleton. Its bones had been carefully laid out on the narrow bed as if in repose, but whoever this had once been he had been sleeping for a very long time. The bones were brown and cracked and most of the joints were missing. The skull had been placed at the top of the cot and the hands folded over each other below the ribs, finger bones aligned like puzzle pieces. Jack and Kate stared at the remains, speechless.

"I sh-shouldn't have moved him, but I had to. He—
he deserved better than where they put him." Finn
indicated the large hole in the wall and cleared a
throat that had not spoken to another human being in
three days. "I'd . . . like to introduce you to Gawen"—he
took a shuddering breath—"the Piper of Dunebrae."

Kate stared at the skeleton, hearing the ghost's
words in her head.

The Highlander has released him.

"Finn," she said softly, pulling her eyes away from
the bones, "how do you know his name?"

Finn looked startled, and then met her one clear
brown eye with his own bleary blue ones. He forced
the words out of parched lips. "Um—y-you're not
going to . . . believe me."

"Try me," she urged, reaching out to support him
as he swayed before her next to the camp bed. Her
voice shook, but the grip she had on his arm was
firm. "I might." She met Jack's eyes across the room.

"Caitriona told me." Finn sighed, his words barely
audible. "I was about to give up, and she t-told me to
keep trying. She told me to find him. Gawen." He held
her gaze as if afraid to go on.

"Caitriona is an old woman, isn't she?" Kate asked
him carefully. "In a lavender gown. And she told you
to release him."

Finn nodded, eyes wide. "H-how did you know?"
he whispered.

"You're the Highlander, aren't you?" She stared at
him.

Finn looked confused for a minute, then he met
her steady gaze. He hesitated and then nodded again,

unable even to whisper any longer.

"Gawen was her lover," Kate said, remembering the look on the old woman's face. "She's the one who saved you, Finn. You released him from his prison, and she guided us to you. She saved your life." She stopped. "And she's a ghost."

Finn stared at her, relief flooding his ravaged face. His knees gave out and he sagged to the floor, sobbing. The sound was heartbreaking, harsh and dry, his body having long since lost the ability to manufacture tears.

They gave him time, waiting until the torturous sounds subsided and then, without a word, Kate and Jack pulled him back to his feet. They grabbed his sporran, helped him into his jacket, and placed his arms around their shoulders, supporting his weight between them. Without a backward look at the tower room the three battered figures stumbled out of Finn's cell, leaving it to the unconscious human prisoner and the ghost who was free at last.

CHAPTER 30

THE PIPER'S RECKONING

hief Inspector Brown turned to meet the three bedraggled figures as they staggered into the great room of Dunebrae Castle.

"Get him some water!" Jack said, his voice terse. Brown signaled a policeman, who rushed over with a bottle from his own pack. They all watched as Finn chugged the first untainted liquid he'd had in five days, spilling much of it down his chin in the process. He looked up, gratitude written across his drawn features.

"Go back to the kitchen and see if you can find him some food," Brown told the policeman, but Finn held up a hand in protest.

"No!" he rasped. "I'm not eating anything from this damned castle!"

Another constable came over with a small package of shortbread. "I brought this with me," he said. Finn eyed the biscuits with suspicion, then nodded and nibbled at one in small, tentative bites, swallowing with difficulty. The constable helped him over to an ornate sofa and eased him down onto its luxurious brocaded surface. Another officer found a blanket and placed it over him.

"Please, call Aubrey," Finn murmured. He lay back and closed his eyes in exhaustion.

Kate found her phone and made one of the most satisfying calls of her life. Grinning, she took the phone over to Finn and left them to their reunion.

"Well," Brown said, eyeing his two detectives. "You look as if you've had a time of it."

"We had a little altercation with two of Duncan's men," Jack told him. "One's dead, and the other one is probably still unconscious. "We handcuffed him to a cot in the room they had Finn in," he added with pleasure. "Door's locked, here's the key." He handed it to Brown, who sent two of his men up to check on the erstwhile attackers.

"Where's Duncan Munro?" Kate asked suddenly.

"Duncan is on his way to the Worlds with his band," Brown told her. "The castle is still being searched, but it seems to be empty." He lowered his voice, glancing at the sofa.

"Those two upstairs must have been left behind to deal with Finn," he said. His eyes narrowed and his face tightened in a departure from his normally calm demeanor. "Don't worry, Duncan won't be arriving at Glasgow Green."

"Not Duncan," a harsh voice grated from the sofa. Finn's feverish blue eyes were fixed on Brown's. "Hector. It was all Hector."

Eight hours later there was still no sign of Hector. The bus had been stopped en route to Glasgow, but the younger Munro was not on board. No cars were missing from the carriage house. The castle had been searched from top to bottom several times, although an ancient keep that size had any number of places that could be used to hide, and Hector would know them all. He could have gone to ground anywhere, but if he were in the castle they'd find him. More police had arrived to aid in the search. They weren't leaving until Munro was in custody.

He was not in the cave. Speleologists from Edinburgh had determined that the huge cavern which housed the deceptive green plant was the extent of the cave system under the Dunebrae cliffs. Officers from the National Crime Agency's drug force had arrived two hours ago and were now bagging and labeling samples of the beautiful fungus that had tried to rule the world. No other signs of life, human or otherwise, had been detected.

The dead man and Kate's attacker had been removed by ambulance, the latter handcuffed to a trolley and moaning. An earlier ambulance had taken Finn to Raighmore Hospital in Inverness, where Aubrey was waiting. She had called in the afternoon to say he was responding well and would be fine, and Angus told Jack in a rough voice that he would be standing him to free whisky for the rest of his life. Knowing Angus, Jack had his doubts about that, but the gesture and the ferocity with which it was delivered were touching.

A forensic anthropologist was on his way from the University of Dundee to take charge of the skeleton in the tower room. After almost four centuries locked in the walls of Dunebrae Castle, Gawen MacPherson was going to college.

The House of Munro Highlanders would not be participating in the World Pipe Band Championships this year. Their instruments had been confiscated and sent to Edinburgh. The band members were being held until it could be determined which of them were involved in the drug operation. Duncan Munro was now closeted with CI Brown, who had commandeered his office, listening to the sordid details of his son's betrayal and depravity. With a voice teetering on the edge of hysteria, he had offered up the combination to the bagpipes room and his knowledge of anywhere that Hector could possibly be hiding inside the castle.

"I feel sorry for him. He looks as if he's being held together by a piece of thread," Kate murmured to Jack, after they were called in to offer their own evidence. "Poor man, to find out your own son was drugging you and running a cartel out of your home. I don't think he'll ever recover from this."

Jack shrugged. "Hmph. It's a bit hard for me to understand how he could have been so clueless, even if he was impaired."

Kate noted that Jack was back to his grumpy self, and she grinned. The medics had done as much as they could for both of them, since they refused to go to the hospital. Jack's arm was once again in a sling and his throat sported a necklace of bruises. Kate had a lovely shiner to go with the splint across her broken nose, but she knew they'd been lucky. The outcome could so easily have been very different. They would heal.

Both had been adamant. It was their case, and they felt they deserved to be in at the endgame.

"I want to be here when they find Hector," Kate told Brown, her brows lowered over stubborn brown eyes. "Besides, I don't want Aubrey to see what I look like—she might kick me out of the bridesmaid business." Her tone was hopeful, and Brown shook his head laughing.

"All right, but you two stay out of the way. You won't be bringing anybody down in your condition."

As the evening wore on, boredom joined the pain, and by six o'clock Kate was beginning to rethink her decision to hang around. They sat on the sofa in the great room watching the action and feeling useless. Hector was still missing. The pain in Kate's nose felt like an incessant hammer to her brain, and Jack's irritation was increasing as his medication wore off and nothing interesting happened.

Suddenly he sat up straight.

"Let's go for a walk."

She nodded. They checked to make sure Brown was nowhere in sight, then walked casually into the corridor that led to the private part of the castle.

The door to the bagpipe workshop stood open. A few policemen were there, bagging and tagging evidence. No one paid any attention to Jack and Kate as they stood in the doorway of the room that had been Duncan's pride and joy and Hector's dark obsession. Still wearing the dark clothing they'd been in for nearly three days now, they attracted no notice as they slipped out onto the great lawn of Dunebrae Castle and into the darkness of early evening.

The sun would not set for another half hour, but the mist was rolling in from the sea, creating a pea soup fog over the yard.

"He has to be hiding out here somewhere," Kate said, frustration in her voice. "There's nowhere else he could go!"

They walked to the edge of the cliff where the path from the cave opened onto the lawn, careful to stay back several feet. Unseen in the fog, the sea crashed angrily against the rocks far below. Darkness was encroaching.

"He's down there somewhere," Jack muttered. "Probably somewhere deeper in the cave. He knew every crack and hole in that place; it wouldn't be too difficult to hide. But he has to come out sometime, and then we'll have him!"

"We can't get down that path in the dark, Jack!" Kate kept her voice low, knowing that sound carried in the misty air.

"We're not going down. We're going to wait for him to come up. If I'm right, he'll wait for full dark and head for the carriage house and his cars, and we can call Brown to intercept him."

They found a place behind the cover of some low bushes a few yards from the path and lay down in the long grass. Damp soaked into their clothing and Kate began to shiver. The roar of the sea drowned out all other sound and the mist and invading darkness erased any sense of time. They waited for what seemed like hours, listening to the roar of the wind and the crash of surf against the rocks far below.

The wind died for a moment. Kate moved her body to warm herself—and froze. She had registered a sound that didn't belong with the pounding surf or the incessant wind. A sound she knew only too well as an American cop.

It was the click of a handgun being cocked.

"*Don't* move," came a soft voice behind them. "Now, stand up slowly—one at a time." The voice was laced with venom. "Back up—toward the castle—stop there!"

Nearly rigid with shock, they obeyed.

The silhouette of a man stood a few feet away at the edge of the cliff, outlined against the darkening horizon.

"Did you think I would have only one way up and down the cliff?" Hector Munro asked. "This is *my* land, *my* castle! I know every inch of it. I won't let it be taken by a *MacDonald!*" He spat out the name. "You thought you were so clever." His words were a hiss. "Pretending, sneaking around." The voice rose, shrill and furious. "You've ruined everything! You should have been dead two months ago, but my man couldn't get the job done. And I think I'm glad he failed because now I get to do it."

He had forgotten about her, Kate realized, all his hatred focused on Jack. If she could get close enough . . .

Hector's eyes found her. "Don't even think about it, you bitch. Come over here."

Jack said, his voice steady. "You know it's over, Hector. Let her go, I'm the one you want."

"Shut up!" Hector pulled his eyes away from Kate and began to pace back and forth at the cliff's edge. "It's not over! You've failed again, MacDonald! This is Munro land—*your* clan will never hold this castle!" The voice had risen to an inhuman shriek. The hand holding the gun came up.

Kate felt her heart stop at the insanity in those words, and a roaring began in her head. *He's going to shoot, and I can't stop him!* Panic gripped her like a vise, and despair flooded her senses. She felt her muscles tense as she prepared to leap at Hector, knowing she'd never make it. She held Jack's gaze with her own, pouring everything she felt into that last look. *I love you.*

The shot never came. Hector's arm jerked suddenly, and he froze, staring at something behind them. Startled, she turned her head, following his dazed eyes.

The roaring was no longer in Kate's head. It was coming from the fog, and now it began to change. A new sound rose on the night air, a single long drone that chilled her blood. Somewhere between a moan and a shriek, it began to take form as a melody. The notes reached into her soul and filled her heart, and she forgot the danger, the gun, forgot everything but the majesty and terrifying power of that music. She searched the mist and darkness for its source but saw nothing.

A moan snapped her gaze back to Hector. He seemed to have forgotten both of them now as he stood helpless, frozen in place. The gun dropped from his hand, and he put his arms up in a warding gesture, a look of stunned horror on his face.

Kate turned back and stifled a scream. Out of the darkness came a figure straight from another time. A Highlander in full regalia, seeming almost at one with the mist and fog. He carried a set of bagpipes and marched in time to the mournful music flowing from his instrument, filling the world with its call to battle. It was the most heartbreaking sound she had ever heard. She would have followed it anywhere.

And now Kate saw that he *was* part of the mist swirling above the cliff and the sea. His tartan was subdued, almost gray in tone, the colors blending into the air around him—through him. Because she realized that she could see the faint outline of the castle through his body and his instrument.

Gawen MacPherson, piper to Clan MacDonald, bore down on the enemy who threatened his clansman. A low, inhuman squeal began in Hector's throat, rising into a scream of terror so shrill it could be heard over the pipes. In panicked desperation he backed away from the approaching spectre, but there was nowhere to go. Time slowed as his foot slipped on the wet grass at the cliff's edge. His arms cartwheeled helplessly, and they watched, numb with shock, as he fell backward over the edge and was lost to sight, his trailing scream cut off as his body hit the rocks below.

The music died away. Jack and Kate stood for a moment in silence as their brains struggled to process what had just happened, and then relief and need drove them together, arms entwining as naturally as if they had spent a lifetime in each other's embrace.

Together they turned to look at their rescuer. The piper smiled. His face bore a look of such joy that Kate felt she was looking into Heaven...and maybe she was. She had seen that look once before in her life, on the face of another spirit, and she knew it for the gift it was.

How young he is, she thought. *He barely had a chance to live, and yet he found more happiness than most people will ever know.*

Gawen nodded as if he understood what she was thinking, and then slowly his form began to dissipate, tendrils of fog melting into the mist above the North Sea until there was nothing left but the echo of the Great Highland Pipes.

Jack cupped Kate's chin in his hand and bent to touch her lips with his. She felt something well up and burst free inside her and allowed the sensation to pour out and into the kiss, feeling that her heart might just break from the beauty of this moment.

The Owls told the story of the wedding of Aubrey Cumming and Fionnlagh Cameron over and over, to each other and to anyone else who came within their reach.

"She was the most beautiful bride I've ever seen," chirped Gladys. "And her lad was so handsome in his jacket and kilt! And to think it almost didn't happen, after all the work we did." She shuddered. "I never want to go through anything like that again, I'll tell you. That horrible man in that awful castle."

"I did tell them that it was a bad place," said Maxine. "No one listened to me. No one ever does."

"We always listen to you, dear," Gladys patted her friend's arm. A snort came from behind the newspaper in the corner.

Gladys ignored Old Harry. "And it all worked out for the best, didn't it, Ronnie?" Ronald blinked, surprised as always to find that he was included in the conversation, and Gladys rushed on.

"So now our Aubrey is taken care of. I think we're about finished with darling Kathleen, too; she might not understand what she wants yet, but she will, and Jack is perfect for her. Did you see them at the wedding? They couldn't take their eyes off each other, bruises and all. Weren't they a picture?" Gladys sighed. "I'll admit I had my doubts. I thought for a minute I was losing my touch, but Aubrey says that nice Inspector Brown wants to offer our Kathleen a job working for the police in Edinburgh. Where Jack works," she added in triumph. "Need I say more?"

"Ye nivver need tae say mair, ye auld minny, but that doesna stop ye," came a fond voice from behind the newspaper.

"So now we have to get busy with that Colleen, and she's going to be trouble. Hasn't the sense about men that God gave her, does she? Which means she needs us maybe most of all." Gladys looked around the sitting room and beamed.

"Isn't Scotland the most romantic place in the world?"

SCOTLAND, PRESENT DAY

O n a cool, windy day in October, Gawen MacPherson was laid to rest in the kirkyard at Dunebrae Castle next to the grave of Caitriona Campbell. Those who saw him on his journey included a MacDonald clansman, a fellow piper, and two travelers from a distant shore—unlikely comrades for a humble bagpiper, but these few owed him everything and were honored to see him home.

Inside the castle an old man sat alone, grieving for the loss of his son and his honor. His time in the sun was over—never again would The House of Munro rise to challenge the world. His pipers had scattered to other cities, other bands, some to prisons where they would likely spend their days wondering what had gone wrong with a world that had held so much promise.

The castle was in decay. It was not obvious yet, but the incipient signs were already there. No one came to service its needs anymore, to admire its wondrous furnishings, touch its lavish woodwork or sample the best of its kitchens. Weeds were beginning to invade the formal gardens. Dust gathered in dark corners and waited to be noticed, but there was no one to notice. The old man had never cared much for the castle, only for his pipers, and they were gone.

He would have to sell. Soon someone would come and take his castle from him, as invaders had done so many times over the centuries. He wondered if the conquered clans of ages past had sat waiting for the end as he was waiting. He wondered if any of them had lost the castle through the betrayal of a clansman, as he had. Probably so. It was part of the cycle of the Highlands. Murder, betrayal, conspiracy. A few moments of glory, and then violence and death. Duncan Munro bowed his head and wept.

Out in the kirkyard there was no weeping. A sense of joy and purpose surrounded the little group gathered around the gravesite. The man they were burying had known pain and anguish, to be sure, but he had also known love and honor and steadfastness. A priest had spoken the ancient words of the Scottish Rite, and a bell had been rung as it would have been in the piper's day. It was time.

Two men picked up the handles of the simple wooden casket and prepared to lower it into the ground, and another piper stepped forward. As his wife watched with pride, Finn Cameron shouldered his pipes and put the blowpipe to his lips. The mournful melody poured out into the crisp air as it had almost four hundred years ago when Gawen MacPherson had played it to warn his clan. "Piobaireachd-dhum-Naomhaid"— "The Piper's Warning to His Master."

Kate Bianchi stood next to Jack MacDonald with her eyes on the gravesite, but her thoughts were elsewhere. She was thinking about the man she had come to love so deeply that parting from him would be like tearing herself in two. Never had she imagined that in this lifetime she would find two men who filled her heart so completely, but the world was an astonishing place where love and sorrow twined to form a new thread of life. All she needed was the courage to take hold of that thread.

She would have to go home, at least for a while. Her visa was expiring. Her time as a visitor in Scotland was over, but she knew that if he asked, she would be back. CI Brown had offered her a job; she had a future here if she wanted it.

Gawen MacPherson and Caitriona Campbell had shown her that hope was eternal, that a true heart could not be conquered by time. Nothing was really that simple, she knew, but with love anything was possible.

She turned to see that love blazing from glorious green eyes.

"Don't," he said softly. She looked at him in question.

"Don't go back," he said. "Stay here. Marry me."

"Yes," she said. It was that simple, after all.

Two others watched the burial from the ramparts of the ancient castle. The Piper of Dunebrae looked on in wonder as his remains were lowered into the ground and the pipes were played—this time for him. He turned to the woman at his side and saw that the love of his life was watching him with those brilliant blue eyes that had always held his soul in thrall.

Others had seen her as an old woman, but to him she looked the same as the last time they had lain together and shared their bodies and their souls. These forms were not real, after all, merely vessels to hold their spirits while on this plane. Life did not end with death. There was so much more, and now they could go. She had waited for him, had found the way to free him from his prison. There was no greater gift.

Gawen bent to kiss his Caitriona, and together they faded away into their future.

AUTHOR'S NOTE

The legend of the piper of Dunebrae is real. There was a piper named MacPherson who was given to clan MacDonald in 1644 as a gift. He participated in a battle that saw the MacDonalds take over a castle and was spared when the Campbells took it back. He did indeed play "The Piper's Warning to his Master." In doing so, he saved his adopted clan, and his punishment was death.

History, however, gives the legend to Castle Duntrune, a lovely old keep in Argyll owned by the Malcolm family since the 1700s. You can visit it here: http://www.duntrunecastle.com. Better yet, go to Scotland.

I renamed the piper Gawen and gave him a romance and a fictional castle on the edge of the North Sea, in which he was walled up and subsequently released. He is a lovely young man, and he was very grateful.

BOOKS IN THE HIGHLAND SPIRITS SERIES

The Comyn's Curse
The Piper's Warning

The Healer's Legacy (available in 2020)

CPSIA information can be obtained
at www.ICGtesting.com
Printed in the USA
FSHW021608241019
63358FS